MW01147741

KEEP MY SECRETS

STEPHANIE JULIAN

A seductive affair twisted by secrets...

To the outside world, Dane Connelly is the playboy heir of a media mogul, his life a series of one-night stands with no commitments. Only in the Salon does he satisfy his darker urges with willing partners. Life was perfect...until his best friend fell in love. Now Dane knows exactly what he's been missing—and exactly who he wants.

Talia Driscoll enjoys creating perfection. She loves bright, glittery parties and fairy tale weddings. But she knows the illusion is short-lived. Nothing lasts forever and everyone lies to get what they want. After all, she lies about her true identity every day.

After an explosive night at the Salon, Dane is determined to sway the reluctant Talia to be his completely. But the secrets that keep them apart are at odds with the erotic passion that draws them together...

A Salon Games novel

AUTHOR'S NOTE

Welcome to the Salon at Haven Hotel, where sensual fantasies become reality and happily-ever-after is guaranteed.

Want to know more? Please join Stephanie Julian's Reader Salon on Facebook. And sign up for exclusive news and info at http://bit.ly/SJNewsletter.

ONE

"Jesus, Dane. Are you going to tell me what the hell's wrong or do I have to beat it out of you?"

Dane Connelly didn't bother to answer. He let the middle finger on his right hand do the talking as he continued to eat breakfast in Jared Golden's apartment at Haven Hotel in Philadephia.

Of course, that wouldn't stop Jed from continuing to hound him. His best friend since high school, Jed had known Dane long enough to realize something was up.

And there was. It just wasn't anything Dane could discuss with Jed, considering Dane was obsessed with Jed's fiancée.

Across the table, Jed leaned back in his chair, arms crossed over his chest. "Okay, so now you're going to make me play 'What the Fuck Is Wrong with Dane?' Fine. Where should I start?"

Dane looked up from the files he'd been scanning on his tablet. He and Jared were having their weekly breakfast meeting, during which, before Annabelle, the talk had centered around Jed's hotel, Dane's magazine, and what trouble they could get into at the Salon that weekend.

"Is it work?" Jed tipped his blond head to the side, sharp blue eyes narrowed.

They didn't talk much about the Salon anymore because Jed and Annabelle hadn't had much time for it lately.

Dane, on the other hand, had been spending a hell of a lot of time there, when he wasn't spending it in bed with Annabelle and Jed.

Which hadn't happened in weeks. For a variety of reasons.

Dane raised one eyebrow before he dropped his gaze back to his tablet and continued to eat. As always, the food at Haven was delicious. Too bad he really wasn't hungry. But if he didn't eat, Jed would be relentless.

"Work's fine." Dane shrugged. "I've had to juggle some stuff at the magazine around. One of the hotels we were going to feature was hit by a tropical storm, so we had to scramble to find something to fill a hole. And I got a new case."

Jed's eyes narrowed. "You didn't tell me you had a new case."

Dane refused to rise to Jed's bait and continued to eat. "I'm telling you now. You've been a little preoccupied lately."

Jed grimaced, but it quickly morphed into a grin. "Lot of work involved in a wedding."

"I thought you hired a wedding planner? Isn't she supposed to handle everything?"

"She does, but we still have to make decisions about colors and food and guest lists and the rehearsal dinner and grooms-men's gifts—"

"Wait." Dane's brow furrowed. "What the fuck are grooms-men's gifts?"

Jed huffed. "I don't have the first damn clue. That's why we have the damn wedding planner, but apparently I'm supposed to pick out gifts for you and Ty. So what the hell do you want?"

Shaking his head, Dane put down his tablet. "Why do you need to give me a gift when you're the one getting married?"

"Fuck if I know."

"Well, good luck with that, buddy." Dane laughed at the finger Jed stuck up at him. "Sounds like you've got a lot on your plate, and there's nothing wrong with me, so you can stop asking. So, you wanna hear about this new case or not?"

Dane wasn't sure Jed was going to let him off the hook so easily but, after a sigh, Jed nodded.

"Sure. What've you got?"

What Dane had was a serious case of misplaced desire that he refused to allow to devolve into a friendship-ending problem.

Leaning back in his chair, Dane ran through the salient points in Janet Freeman's child abduction case. The father had taken the child with him to visit family in Honduras and was refusing to return with her to the States. Janet didn't have the money to make the trip herself, and the government was unwilling to help due to some technicality in the custody agreement.

Dane had received the request for help not from Janet but from her brother, whose skills Dane occasionally used when he needed muscle. In other words, her brother was former military, now private security. And very good at what he did.

"So when's your next trip?"

"Are you going somewhere, Dane?"

Shit.

Annabelle walked out of the bedroom, buttoning a cream silk blouse tight enough to showcase her full breasts. She'd tucked the shirt into a slim plaid skirt that delineated every beautiful curve of her ass and hips.

Her auburn hair bounced and curled around her shoulders and her full mouth curved in a happy smile. She'd used that mouth on his body many times and he'd enjoyed the hell out of it. Just like he enjoyed the hell out of Annabelle.

But she wasn't his.

Yes, he loved her. But he wasn't in love with her. Not like Jed. Jed adored her.

Dane did, too. It just wasn't the same.

Annabelle moved to Jed and bent for a kiss, which Jed returned with a smile and a hand on her ass. Annabelle lingered, her hand lifting to caress Jed's jaw.

In the next second, Jed caught her around the waist and tumbled her onto his lap, kissing her, long and deep.

When Jared finally let her up for air, Annabelle laughed.

Dane found himself grinning and, when Annabelle turned toward him again, she wrinkled her nose at him.

"So I have a favor to ask," she said. "I know you're a busy guy, but are you going to be around today? Kate just called and said something came up, so she won't be here and I need some male input when I meet with Talia."

"Talia?" The name sounded familiar, but he wasn't coming up with a face and, for him, that was a total lapse in his skills.

"The wedding planner," Belle prompted.

"Ah, the one who wants Jed to buy the groomsmen gifts." Dane mock-shuddered. "Yeah, I think I'll pass."

"Hey!" Annabelle tried for outrage but she was too damn happy to make it work. "Don't diss Talia. She's been amazing. I couldn't do this without her."

"Then I'm glad she's working out for you. But I've got—"

"She's going to be here in a few minutes." Annabelle batted big green eyes at him. "Please? Jared has a meeting he says he can't miss and I'd really like a guy's opinion."

Her smile turned pleading. Dane's gaze narrowed at Jed. "Wait, why doesn't he have to go?"

"Because he has a meeting with the mayor about... something." She waved a hand in front of her. "I have no idea what. But Jared said he absolutely couldn't be there. I don't want this wedding to be over-the-top girly, and you know Jared better than anyone. You'll be able to tell me if he won't like something."

When she stared at him like that, he knew exactly why Jed had bent over backward to find her and keep her. And when she smiled at Jed, Dane understood why Jed never worried about losing her to Dane, even though Dane occasionally shared Annabelle.

And when he said "share," he meant have sex with. Sex he enjoyed very much.

Which was why spending time with her alone was dangerous.

"Uh... I'm not sure..."

"Please."

Annabelle turned her smile on him now. *Shit.*

He bit back a sigh. "I've got a few hours this morning. What time's the meeting?"

"In..."—she glanced at the clock—"ten minutes."

Well, at least he wouldn't have long to sit and think about it.

"Fine. Let's go see a woman about a wedding."

————

TALIA CHECKED her hair one last time in the mirror in the restroom in Haven Hotel's restaurant.

Not a blond strand out of place in the chignon it'd taken nearly an hour to create. She smoothed a hand down the skirt of her winter-white suit, making sure she hadn't spilled anything on herself and failed to notice.

Which was ridiculous. She hadn't even taken a sip of water since getting dressed.

She made a face at her reflection and huffed. "You're being ridiculous."

Which she totally was.

Annabelle was a friend. A good friend. She shouldn't be this nervous.

Then again, she'd never planned a wedding for someone of Jared's social standing.

Which was also ridiculous. She gave every event she planned one hundred percent of her attention. It didn't matter if the groom was a multimillionaire entrepreneur or the bride worked at the local supermarket.

They all deserved her best. And she had every faith in herself to make it happen. It was just...

What?

For one thing, if everything went as planned, she'd make one hell of a name for herself and her business. Expand and grow.

Of course, if that happened... Well, she'd deal with that if and when the time came.

Right now, she didn't have time to spend mulling over problems that hadn't happened. She had last-minute details to go over with Annabelle and Jared, important pieces of the overall puzzle that would create the perfect event.

Annabelle trusted Talia to deliver the wedding of her dreams. And that's exactly what she was going to do.

Straightening her back, Talia took a deep breath and headed for the lobby, where she was supposed to meet Annabelle in a few minutes.

Talia always showed up at least five minutes early for any meeting, whether she sat in her car or headed for a bathroom to make sure she looked the part.

Successful, perfectly put together, and totally confident.

A woman who had the ability to give the bride the wedding of her dreams.

No matter what.

With her Coach tote hanging from one arm, Talia smiled at the woman behind the desk when she looked up from her computer screen. "Hey, Sabrina. How are you?"

"Talia!"

With a huge grin, Sabrina Rodriguez scurried around the counter to wrap her arms around Talia for a bear hug. Talia returned the embrace just as tightly.

"Damn, girl, you look amazing." Sabrina gave Talia a thumbs-up before heading back behind the reception desk. "Are you here to meet Annabelle?"

"Yes, we've got some last-minute details to figure out. How are you? I haven't seen you for ages."

Sabrina's sunny smile got even brighter. "Busy, busy, busy. Seems like there's never a dull moment."

"How's Greg?"

Sabrina's mouth curved in an adorable smile. "He has more battery power than the Energizer Bunny. He survives on three hours of sleep a night, I swear. If he's not editing his movie, he's taking meetings with contractors and politicians and government people, and I swear, I have no idea what the hell he's up to most of the time."

Talia caught a hint of nervous apprehension in Sabrina's voice and took a closer look at her friend.

Sabrina was twenty-three and one of the sweetest people Talia knew. Which made Talia suspicious of Sabrina's forced-looking smile.

She wondered if her friend had finally realized that having a relationship with Greg Hicks, one of the most powerful producer-directors in Hollywood, was more work than she'd realized it would be.

And she hoped like hell that Greg, who'd forsaken the rat race of the left coast film industry to start a new production company based in Philadelphia, treated Sabrina the way she deserved.

Talia had met Greg a few times and been nearly blown away by his personality. He was like a steamroller, with a smile that could make women's panties drop at a hundred paces.

Sure, he seemed completely in love with Sabrina, but the man was used to getting what he wanted and, right now, he wanted Sabrina.

"This meeting with Annabelle shouldn't be more than an hour. Can you take a break around ten or so? Maybe we can grab coffee before I have to drive back to Wyomissing?"

Talia had recently moved her office to a shiny new space in a beautifully renovated building in a small suburb of Reading and out of her former apartment in her hometown of Adamstown, which is where she'd met Annabelle, Sabrina, and Kate Song, Annabelle's best friend and maid of honor. Kate was supposed to be here for this meeting as well but had called off at the last minute.

"Ooh, that sounds great." Sabrina's true smile was back and Talia was determined to make sure Sabrina was okay before she left. "Stop back when you're done. It'll be nice to talk girl stuff, even if it's only for a few minutes."

Yes, there was definitely something up with Sabrina. Guilt tweaked at Talia's conscience and made her more determined than before to spend a little time with Sabrina before she left.

It'd been a while since the four of them had gotten together for dinner and drinks because they'd all been so busy. Annabelle with her antiques business and the wedding. Kate with her new lingerie business and the boutique here in Haven. Talia with her burgeoning wedding-planning business.

Sabrina seemed to have gotten a little lost in the shuffle.

Not today.

"Hey, you're early. I knew you would be. You're too damn efficient for your own good."

Talia turned at the sound of Annabelle's voice and felt her friend's smile infect her. Annabelle had that glow a woman got when she was happy with the world.

And who wouldn't be in her position? She was marrying one of Philadelphia's most eligible bachelors who treated her like a queen and gave her anything she wanted, usually before she wanted it.

According to Annabelle, Jared was perfect.

Too damn perfect, if you asked Talia. But no one had, and she'd been told more than once that she had a skewed outlook on men.

Considering her history, who could blame her? Then again, not many people knew her history, so most men wrote her off as a cold bitch. Usually she was okay with that.

Annabelle gave her a huge hug, threw a smile and a wave at Sabrina, then started pulling Talia toward the atrium.

"I had Tyler set up a table for us in the atrium. It's beautiful out there right now and since we're having the wedding in there, you won't have to visualize what we're talking about."

"I just have a few details we need to finalize and—"

"Hold that thought," Annabelle said as she waved toward the elevator. "Dane, come meet Talia."

Talia turned in the direction Annabelle was looking and saw a man walking toward them. She blinked as her brain tried to process how utterly, distractingly handsome he was.

She noticed his hair first. A black so dark, hints of blue flashed under the bright lights of the lobby. He wore it longer than convention dictated, so perfectly straight that she wondered if he actually used a flatiron, and long enough that he had it tucked behind one ear to keep it out of his face.

And damn, what a face. Sharp, dark eyes above cheekbones so

straight she wanted to run her finger along them. Then there was his mouth... Full lips that could probably kiss a woman into a coma.

Damn, the man is too freaking pretty for his own good.

Of course, *pretty* probably wasn't a word he'd appreciate. Then again, he was probably used to women wanting to pet him.

"Talia, this is Dane Connelly, Jared's best man. I can't believe you two haven't met yet."

Dane met her eyes, gave her a brief once-over, then nodded. "Nice to meet you."

He held out his hand, and Talia took it out of habit. She told herself the shiver that ran through her had nothing to do with his touch and everything to do with a breeze blowing through the lobby from the opening of the front door.

Total bullshit, but still.

Of course, while she'd been knocked off balance, he seemed to be completely immune to her.

Which was a little disconcerting. She was tall and blond and men typically took a second look. She'd gotten good at deflecting attention and had had loads of practice from the time she was a teenager.

"Nice to meet you, Talia."

And wow, the voice fit that face. Low and a little husky. And totally disinterested in her.

Well, that'll teach you. She laughed silently to herself and released his hand. "Nice to meet you, too."

Turning her attention back to Annabelle, Talia caught a glimpse of something in Annabelle's expression. As if she'd been expecting a response she hadn't gotten.

Then it passed, and Annabelle was leading her and Dane toward the atrium.

For the next hour, she and Annabelle went over the checklist Talia had compiled. There were quite a few items on the list, but not because Talia had forgotten anything in the weeks leading up to the big event.

No, she'd simply learned that there were things that only needed to be discussed at certain times and, through a great deal of trial and error, Talia had learned how and when to approach them.

However, she usually dealt with the bride and groom for this meeting, so Dane's presence was throwing her off her game a little.

One of the things she typically discussed with the grooms at this meeting was the groomsmen's gifts. But since this *was* a groomsman...

"Uh-oh, you have that look on your face, Tal." Annabelle frowned at her. "What's up?"

They'd gone over every other item on her list and she really hated not to cross off everything.

"It's just..." She glanced at Dane, who'd been silent throughout much of the meeting.

Oh, he'd spoken when Annabelle had asked for his opinion, which she'd done several times. And he'd given remarkably thoughtful answers, including one about whether or not they should include the formerly estranged mother of Annabelle's deceased second father in the family pictures.

Talia could honestly say she'd never come up against this problem in all the years she'd been planning weddings, but Dane had had the perfect response.

"Does she seem like family to you, Belle?" he'd asked.

Annabelle had turned to Dane with a wryly amused laugh then reached out to poke him in the side with her finger. As if she knew exactly where he was ticklish.

"How do you always know the right question to ask?"

He shrugged and raised his eyebrows at her, his expression slightly haughty, but even Talia could see the affection beneath.

"Because I'm just that good. You should know that by now."

Annabelle shook her head then turned back to Talia. "Then yes, Grammy Aurelia makes the cut."

"So you've met her?" Talia closed the pad on her tablet and stowed it back in her tote. "Last time we talked you hadn't."

"Yes, Dane checked her out for me and discovered a very lonely old woman living alone in a rent-controlled, midtown Manhattan apartment with her two little dogs. I couldn't believe she responded to the invitation. I never thought she would. I wasn't even sure she was still alive. Granddad never really talked about her, and I'd almost forgotten she existed until we started talking about the guest list. After Dane, uh, investigated her, I found out she'd made me the beneficiary of her will years ago, even though she wasn't sure she'd ever see me again."

Talia shook her head, still amazed at the life Annabelle had led. Sure, Talia's teenage years had been pretty damn shitty, but Annabelle's younger life had been downright tragic.

There was a part of Talia that wanted to make Annabelle's wedding the fairy tale every girl dreamed of. Because Annabelle was such a sweetheart and she deserved it.

Then there was the practical realization that this was the most important wedding she'd done up until this point.

Because even though she'd pulled off a state senator's daughter's wedding for three hundred, this wedding could move her business to the next level, open doors that would probably take her years to attain otherwise.

"So I should include her in all family activities? Photos, rehearsal dinner, seating arrangements?"

She retrieved her tablet and started tapping away as Annabelle continued to talk.

When she looked up after revising her lists, she realized

Dane was staring at her with narrowed eyes. Disconcerting, to say the least.

"Oh, I almost forgot." Annabelle practically bounced in her seat. "We're having people over for dinner Saturday night. We want you to come. And totally *not* as our wedding planner. As a friend. We'll put you up here for the night."

Since she'd been contemplating a Saturday night alone on her couch in her pajamas with a bottle of merlot, a bowl of popcorn, and a binge session of *Orange Is the New Black*, she stopped to think before she gave her answer.

Then realized how much of an idiot she was being.

"Sure, I'd love to." She smiled, hoping like hell it looked natural. "Thanks. Can I bring anything?"

"Just your lovely self." Annabelle shot a look at the clock on the wall. "Oh, wow. I'm late. I've got to get back to the shop. Have a client meeting I can't miss. I'm so sorry I have to run."

Annabelle stood and so did Talia and Dane. "No problem, I'm meeting Sabrina for coffee before I leave."

"Okay, then, I'll leave you in Dane's capable hands."

And off she ran. Leaving her alone with a man who'd barely acknowledged her presence throughout the entire hour-long meeting.

But now she had his full attention.

He turned that dark gaze on her and she had to admit, he set all her feminine receptors to extremely receptive. She definitely wouldn't kick the man out of her bed if she ever happened to find him there.

However, his marked lack of interest in her probably meant that would never happen. Because she didn't pursue. She didn't have the time to fall for someone who made her chase him down and beg him to go out with her.

And she certainly wasn't going to waste energy on a man who so clearly didn't find her pursuable in return.

"It was nice to meet you, Dane." She held out her hand. "I'll see you at the wedding."

He took her hand but didn't release her right away. "Could I have a couple more minutes of your time? I had a few questions of my own."

"Of course." She sat again, noting that he didn't retake his seat until she had. The man had ingrained manners, and now she had a second to realize his name sounded familiar. Especially his last name.

But she'd have to worry about that later.

"As a groomsman, I realize I have certain duties to perform. I wanted to ask if there was anything else I needed to know."

She smiled, her estimation of this man rising. Not that he'd done anything to make her think he was a jerk before, but he seemed genuinely interested in her response.

"Besides pictures and making sure your bridesmaid doesn't trip down the aisle and fall on her face, I think anything you can do to make it easier on Jared and Annabelle the day of the wedding is the best gift you could give them."

He nodded and she figured they were finished. But he continued to stare at her as if formulating another question.

"So why aren't you in the wedding party? You're one of Annabelle's best friends. She talks about you a lot. I'm kind of surprised we haven't met before."

His question surprised her. "I didn't feel I could give her wedding the attention it needed if I was also in the wedding party. I wanted to be able to slip behind the scenes if anything needed to be taken care of."

"So your business comes first?"

She bristled at the thought. "No, Annabelle comes first. This is her wedding, *her* day, and I want it to be perfect. If something happens, I don't want to be running around in a bridesmaid dress trying to fix things."

That gorgeous mouth curved in a smile and, oh, wow, was this man handsome.

"Okay, I guess I can see that. So, how long have you known Annabelle?"

She couldn't decide if he was giving her the third degree, and if so, why. "We went to high school together. We grew closer when she returned to run her granddad's shop after college."

"You had a lot more in common then. Young women running your own businesses."

Perceptive guy. And getting a little too interested in her for comfort. "Yes. It's nice to have friends with similar problems. Makes the bitch sessions more enjoyable."

He laughed and the sound echoed through the atrium, currently housing a whole jungle of orchids.

Jared's brother, Tyler, had designed the atrium and dictated the placement of every flower, bush, tree, and statue. And she had to give the guy credit. He had a masterful eye for detail. If he weren't so in love with Kate, one of her best friends and collaborators, Talia had to admit she would've definitely tried to get him into bed because, oh, my, he was just as nice to look at as Jared.

Of course, Dane was certainly nothing to sneeze at. "Yummy" described him fairly well.

And you have way too much to do to even think about a diversion right now, even one as yummy as this.

Too true.

"So you'll be at the party Saturday?" he asked.

Was that merely polite curiosity or did she hear actual interest in his voice?

Which shouldn't really matter one way or the other.

"Yes. I assume I'll see you there, as well. Do you have any other questions? I promised my friend we'd get coffee, and I need to be back in my office for a phone consult this afternoon."

Which wasn't total bullshit because she did have a phone consult, but it wasn't until four p.m.

But the longer she sat there, the more her brain tried to imagine Dane naked. Not that that was a bad thing, but an infatuation with a man who didn't seem interested in her in that way was probably not a good thing for her productivity right now. She needed to keep her eye on the prize. And that was building her business.

"Yes, you will. Have a nice time with Sabrina."

Okay, that was strange. "How did you know—"

His lips curved. "I saw you talking to her at the desk. I know she's a good friend of Kate and Belle's. Not a difficult line to draw."

Shaking her head, she smiled as she stood, holding out her hand. "Well, it was nice to meet you, Dane. I'll see you this weekend."

He rose before he took her hand and she had to tilt her head back to look at him. She was tall for a woman, close to five-ten, but he had several inches on her, even though she was wearing heels.

She liked that.

"I look forward to it."

This time when she looked into his eyes, their gazes caught and held.

And for a very brief second, she definitely felt a spark fly between them.

Maybe the party Saturday night would be a lot more fun than she'd first anticipated.

Then he turned toward the exit and waved a hand at her to precede him. She took a quick peek at his ass before she headed for the door.

Nice ass. Really nice ass.

DAMN FINE ASS.

Damn beautiful woman.

Dane tried not to be obvious as he watched Talia walk across the lobby to the reception area where Sabrina waited with a smile.

Obviously, he must have been staring, because he didn't realize Tyler stood next to him.

"Jesus, Ty. Where the hell did you come from? And why the hell are you sneaking around?"

"I don't sneak. And it's my hotel. I can sneak if I damn well please." Ty raised his eyebrows at Dane. "The more interesting question is, what are you doing?"

A quick glance at Tyler told Dane that question was mainly rhetorical. Ty had an amused look in his eyes and a small smile on his lips.

Shit.

"I'm heading out now. I met with Annabelle and the wedding planner to go over last-minute details because your brother bailed."

"My brother is meeting with the mayor to talk about zoning concessions for expanding the club. He didn't exactly bail. And it looks like you might have gotten something out of the meeting other than the color of the napkins and which dishes we're using."

"I don't give a shit which dishes you use. And I don't know what the hell you're talking about."

Tyler actually laughed at him, which just set Dane's back even straighter.

He fucking hated that his friends could read him so easily. Then again, *only* his friends could read him so easily.

"Anything you want to know about her?"

Dane heard no snark in Tyler's tone. "Why would you think that?"

"Maybe just the way you were undressing her with your eyes." Tyler paused. "You okay?"

Shit. "I'm fine. Got a new case that's going to require some out-of-the-box maneuvering."

"And you are king of out-of-the-box."

Usually, yes, he was. Years of honing his skills had made him very, very good at what he did. And he'd managed to maintain his many secrets.

"High praise from you." Dane glanced at Tyler again and found the man still staring at him. "What? Do I have something on my face?"

Tyler clapped him on the back and Dane gave himself credit for sticking his feet to the floor. The guy had some serious muscle beneath that conservative black suit.

"Nope, not a thing. Have a good one."

Yeah, he could only hope.

"SO WHAT DO you think of Dane?"

The amused smile on Sabrina's face made Talia want to roll her eyes, but she contained the urge. No use giving her friend any ammunition.

"Rich playboy. Nice looking, yes, but totally self-involved."

"Oh, that's not true." Sabrina leaped to Dane's defense, which made Talia cover a sigh. "Yes, he's rich, and yeah, he gets around... Well, according to the scuttlebutt around the hotel, he *used* to get around a lot more. And by get around, I mean he used to be a huge manwhore. Lately, though... Not so much."

"And why should I care?"

"Oh, please. I saw the way you looked at him. And he was totally checking you out, too."

Talia shrugged as she sipped her coffee, trying not to let that give her any ideas.

"So I looked. Who wouldn't? But he knows exactly what he looks like and I'm sure he's used to getting whatever he wants. I just don't have time for him." Of course, she certainly wouldn't mind one night.

"Oh, you so want him." Sabrina sat back in her chair in the corner of the hotel's club, grinning even wider now. "And you should take what you can get. You look stressed. I mean, you look great but I can tell you're tired. You need to get an assistant."

"And I keep asking you and you keep turning me down."

Sabrina wrinkled her nose. "And you know I'd take you up on the offer if I didn't love my job here so much. But seriously, Tal, you need to loosen the reins a little and get a minion."

"As soon as I have time to break someone in, I will. But for right now, I've got everything under control."

"What you mean is you've got all of your energy focused on your job and no time for you."

"And don't I recall a certain person telling me just a few months ago that all she wanted was to focus on her career?"

Sabrina waved a hand in front of her face. "Yeah, yeah. I said that, but I did finally realize the error of my ways. Honey, you need to get laid. Seriously."

"And you think Dane is the right person for that?"

Sabrina's nose scrunched again and her gaze dropped. "Well, maybe not Dane exactly, but there are going to be loads of single men at the wedding. Live a little. Pick one off the buffet line and have a feast for a night."

Talia had to laugh. "You've certainly changed your tune. So how goes it with Greg?"

Sabrina's smile was instantaneous, which was good, but it had a hint of melancholy, as well. "Fine when we're together. Which hasn't been a lot lately. He's busy and I get that. I mean, I really do understand. He works all hours of the day, but when it's just the two of us, uninterrupted, well, it's pretty damn good."

"And when it's not just the two of you?"

Sabrina shrugged. "It can be tough. But no relationship is happiness and flowers all the time. You've got to work at it. And it's not worth much if you give up when it gets hard."

Hallelujah, sister. Talia wanted to raise her hand to testify. "Which is why I'm not in the market for a relationship right now. I don't have the time and I'm not willing to give what little free time I do have to a man. Most of them aren't worth the hassle."

Grimacing, Sabrina nodded. "True, but when you find the right one, he's worth *all* the trouble."

Unless, of course, he was the cause of all the trouble.

As Talia drove back to her office later, still chewing over that last thought, she made a call.

"Hey, Mom. How goes it?"

"Hi, honey. I'm fine. What's wrong?"

Talia sighed. That was always her mom's first response when Talia called unexpectedly. Not that she blamed her mom for being suspicious. Amelia Driscoll had had good reason to fear unexpected phone calls for so many years.

"Nothing's wrong. Just checking in. I haven't talked to you for a little while."

"Oh, well, nothing new to report here. Although... Sammy's going to graduate cum laude. Did he tell you?"

No, her younger brother hadn't told her, but then she hadn't spoken to him in the past week. A fifth-year senior at Penn State in the mechanical engineering department, Sammy would graduate in May. And with honors, apparently. "Good for him. I'll text him later. I never know what a good time is to call him."

"Apparently that's never. He's always up to something." Her mom sighed. "Both of you are always so busy. I worry about you."

It went unspoken, but Talia knew why her mom worried. "We're fine, Mom. I'm thinking about hiring some help finally."

For the rest of the ride home, Talia let the easy conversation with her mom level out her mood, which had remained jittery after her talk with Sabrina.

Oh, hell, at least be honest with yourself. It's because of Dane.

Yes, it was, a fact she really wasn't happy with.

And after she hung up with her mom when she reached her office, Talia seriously considered calling Annabelle and canceling on her for Saturday night's party.

Then she thought about the look Dane had given her before they'd parted.

Sabrina was right. Talia needed to get laid. Considering she couldn't remember the last time she'd had sex, and the fact that simply looking at Dane had made her hot, maybe Saturday night out was just what she needed.

No strings, hot sex, and out the door the next morning.

Sounded like a plan. And Talia loved plans.

TWO

"I'm so glad you could make it. Come in. You're the last to arrive."

Talia bent to kiss Annabelle on the cheek. "I'm really sorry. Traffic was horrendous on the Schuylkill."

"I think the Flyers and the 'Sixers are playing tonight so that makes things miserable, I know. But you're here now and you don't have to go anywhere until tomorrow. Time for you to have a drink in your hand. Dane, get this woman a Seven and Seven."

Talia's gaze immediately sought out the owner of that name and found him across the living room at the built-in bar beneath the window that looked out over the city.

Her heart actually skipped a beat at the sight of him. In a suit, he'd looked spectacular. In broken-in jeans and a maroon cotton Henley that clung to a broad chest, Dane looked like any girl's wet dream.

Seriously, the man made her panties damp.

Jesus, she hoped he was as good in bed as his looks promised. Because any man who looked like that had to have a lot of practice.

And everyone knew that practice makes perfect.

"Go ahead and get your drink." Annabelle waved her toward Dane. "I'll be right back."

Making her way across the room, Talia said hello to Kate and Tyler, speaking to a couple they introduced as Mel and Geoff Black. A little farther along, she got a hug from Sabrina and another from Greg, who looked like he should be in bed asleep instead of here. But the smile he gave Sabrina made it clear why he wasn't. They were talking to Sebastian, the rock guitarist who was scoring Greg's latest movie. When Sebastian reached for her hand, the tattoos covering his arms showed below the rolled-up sleeves of his button-down shirt.

She'd never heard of his band but she wasn't really into music. And he barely spared more than a glance at her. Immediately after shaking her hand, he excused himself and continued his conversation with the woman he was sitting next to on the couch.

Talia had briefly met Trudeau, Greg's assistant, at the hotel, one day. She was a bright woman whom Talia would've hired in a heartbeat. And whom Greg would never allow to be stolen away. She was apparently worth her weight in gold.

By the time she got to the bar, Dane had a glass in his hand that he held out to her when she was within reach.

"Hello again." She smiled at him as she lifted the glass to her lips and took a sip. "And thank you for this. The drive down was hellacious."

His return smile was welcoming enough to reassure her about her decision. Yes, sleeping with friends of friends could be problematic, but Dane didn't look like a man who was looking for a long-term relationship. He looked like a man who would be just fine with a one-night stand.

Or a string of them, if the sex was that good. And, damn, she really hoped the sex was that good.

"Nice to see you again, Talia. I hope you don't mind having

me foisted on you for the night, but we seem to be the only two people here without dates."

Was he digging for information? No problem, she wouldn't mind a few answers herself. She didn't know all that much about him, and she found herself curious.

"I don't mind at all. And there's no one in my life who'd take offense."

He nodded, his smile growing. "Then I'll confess to the same circumstances. So how long have you been planning weddings?"

"For about five years. I started with a larger company right out of college, but the market tanked and I found myself out of a job. I started working for a local caterer, who helped me find my first brides, and it's been a slow build since then. What about you, Dane? What do you do?"

"I work for the family business. My father's Victor Connelly. He owns Connelly Media."

She tried not to look shocked. Probably failed. But she hoped she managed to cover the fact that his news made her feel like she'd gotten slammed in the gut with a baseball bat.

Of course she knew about Connelly Media. They were one of the largest media firms on the East Coast. Several newspapers in different states, magazines ranging from celebrity gossip to political news, and one small but growing twenty-four-hour news network that could eventually give CNN a run for its money.

"Talia, are you okay?"

She smiled, hoping like hell that Dane couldn't see through it. "Yes. What do you do at the company?"

"I'm the managing editor of *Exotic Escapes* magazine."

She shook her head. "I'm sorry. I've never heard of that one."

"No problem." His smile turned up a notch. "It's a specialty magazine targeted at a very specific group of readers."

"And who are those readers?"

"People with obscene amounts of money who want to know about the private islands or exclusive resorts that are going to be all the rage next year so they can book now and tell all their friends they already had their trips planned when word filters out to the two-percenters."

"Do you write for the magazine? Get to visit those places?"

He moved out from behind the bar and guided her toward a couch a few feet away. He waited until she sat before joining her, and she mentally shook her head at his manners. Her mother would be so impressed.

"I travel a lot, yes. Partly for the job. Partly because I enjoy it."

And he had the money to indulge his hobby. Talia had spent the first thirteen years of her life living as if money was no object. Men like Dane had been her friends.

Until it had all come crashing down around her and her life had fallen apart and those friends had wanted nothing more to do with her.

Old prejudices made her want to say something scathing about how it must be nice to live without a care for where the money for the electric bill or gas for the car was going to come from.

But she didn't get the sense that Dane was anything like those boys who'd turned on her at a time in her life when she'd been so vulnerable.

Besides, Annabelle considered him a good friend. Talia knew he had to be a decent guy to gain Annabelle's trust.

So Talia nodded. "Sounds like a wonderful job."

"Most days it is. I'm not gonna lie. It's pretty damn awesome to get paid to spend a few days on a beach in the Pacific Ocean on a private island with a butler and a chef and a personal masseuse."

"And what about the days it's not awesome?"

She caught a glimpse of something passing through his gaze but it was gone before she could tell what she'd seen. A hint of something dark, which totally didn't fit with this man's image.

"Then your flight's delayed because of a monsoon or the boat that's supposed to take you across the fjord has mechanical problems and the only other boat available is a fishing trawler."

That explanation coming from another man with his background might've sounded elitist or smug. Dane gave it just the right amount of knowing self-deprecation.

She liked that. She really liked him.

But would she be able to get beyond the fact that he was Victor Connelly's son? What if he'd inherited his father's nose for news?

Then again, why would he have cause to want to snoop around in her past? She wanted to sleep with the man, not move in with him.

"So tell me about the most exotic place you've ever been."

———

DANE WAS PRETTY sure Talia's opinion of him had changed since he'd seen her last as he told her about some of the places he'd been.

After their meeting Monday with Annabelle, he'd almost had himself convinced that Talia didn't like him. Not that it made any difference one way or the other to him.

Yes, she was beautiful and, yeah, he definitely appreciated those cool blue eyes, the blond hair, and the regal face. Grace Kelly came to mind. That haughty, almost untouchable air that came from being blessed in the genetics department.

And yes, she had a body any woman would kill for... long legs, nice tits, and that killer ass.

She'd looked amazing in that suit earlier in the week.

Tonight she looked downright hot in jeans that clung to every curve of her hips and ass and a blouse the perfect shade of pink that made her pale skin glow.

Yeah, he wanted her, but any single guy with a hetero bone in his body would want her.

However, he'd been fairly certain there was no way they were going to hook up.

And frankly, it was probably a bad idea.

He was pretty sure Talia had no idea he occasionally shared Annabelle with Jed.

Annabelle had never mentioned inviting Talia to the Salon, so he'd assumed Annabelle didn't want Talia to know. Since there were only a little more than twenty people who actually attended the Salon games and usually no more than ten at a time, it was easy to keep their adult playground secret.

He wondered what Talia would think if she knew that half of this floor was dedicated to some of the most sensual pleasures in the entire city.

Would she be as interested as Annabelle had been?

Annabelle had taken to the freedom offered at the Salon like a true sensualist. She'd allowed Dane into her bed along with Jed. And while he knew Annabelle loved Jed, he also knew she had real affection for him.

Some people might consider their relationship twisted. For the first time, Dane wondered what Talia would think if she ever found out.

Why would she?

Dane wanted to fuck her. He didn't plan on marrying her.

Hell, he didn't plan on marrying anyone. He wasn't sure he

had it in him to be that kind of man. To tie himself to one woman for the rest of his life.

He was still months from turning thirty and considered that way too young to settle down. He wasn't sure he ever would.

Of course, Jed had been the same until he'd met Annabelle.

Unconsciously, his gaze sought her out. Sitting next to Jed on a couch across the room, staring up at her fiancé like he hung the moon. So damn pretty, he had to smile.

"They make a beautiful couple."

Damn. He'd let his gaze linger a little longer than he should have. He directed a wry smile at Talia as he turned his full attention back to her, but she continued to stare at Jed and Annabelle.

"They're going to make beautiful babies."

Dane laughed at a mental image of Jared trying to change a diaper. "More power to them. I sincerely hope they don't expect me to babysit. Ever."

Talia glanced back at him, and he saw no condemnation in her eyes. "Me either. They're cute... but not that cute."

They shared a laugh over that and now he noticed how she lit up when she laughed. That cool beauty infused with a warmth that showed him a glimpse of what she'd be like in bed.

Arousal twisted his guts with a sharp grip.

Out of the corner of his eye, he caught Jed glancing their way, which caused Annabelle to do the same.

And he knew if he slept with Talia, he'd never be back in bed with Annabelle and Jed.

Annabelle's glance turned into a smile. A smile he didn't know how to interpret. Then Annabelle stood and announced dinner, waving people to the table.

The number was even despite the fact that there were only four true couples out of the fourteen people here.

Annabelle and Jed, Ty and Kate, Greg and Sabrina, and

Mel and Geoff Black, the only married couple. He and Jed had known Geoff since college, and Mel and Geoff had been members of the Salon since Jed and Ty had opened the hotel.

Sebastian and Trudeau were new to the group, colleagues of Greg's who'd fit well into their circle. Dane liked Baz, even though the guy was a little rough around the edges. He hadn't really gotten to know Tru, but she had a sharp wit and a brain to go with it, so he was sure he'd like her just fine.

Liane Ryder and Cory Shirk were also members of the Salon, both attorneys. Liane an ADA for the city and Cory a defense attorney for a major firm.

Dane had learned to take a step back and watch the fireworks when those two started in on each other, but whenever they were together in the Salon, the sparks they created were amazing. And since they were both exhibitionists, everyone got a great show.

Not that anyone would even mention the Salon tonight, not with Baz, Tru, and Talia here.

Anyone who entered the Salon signed a strict nondisclosure, and no one dared break it. No one wanted to be banished. And everyone who got an invitation was thoroughly vetted by Dane before they got to sign the nondisclosure.

Everyone except Annabelle, Kate, and Sabrina.

Fortunately, that hadn't come back to bite anyone. Yet.

Call him cynical, but Dane had been around his father and the media business long enough to realize that, just because you were cynical, it didn't mean you weren't right and all hell wouldn't break loose eventually.

But not now.

All through dinner, he continued his conversation with Talia. He found himself trying to get her to laugh, wanting to see that warmth again. Letting it stoke his arousal.

He cared for Annabelle, but he realized it was time to move on. Past time, actually.

He'd fallen into a rut and the way out was smiling at him across the table.

He couldn't wait to strip Talia down and climb out of that rut and into bliss.

TALIA KNEW the exact moment Dane made the decision to pursue her.

She wouldn't have been able to explain it to anyone else. She only knew because she'd been watching him so closely all night and, at that moment, when he looked at her, she went up in flames.

Her skin went tight and her muscles clenched, particularly her thigh muscles. And her pussy.

Wow. If the man could do that with just a look, she couldn't wait to get him in a bed and let him have at her until they were both too tired to move.

"So, Talia, do you do events other than weddings?"

Talia dragged her gaze away from Dane to look at Greg's assistant, Tru, who had asked the question low enough that Talia had to think about what she'd actually said. Getting her arousal-addled brain to cooperate took a second but she finally did manage to answer.

"Yes, I do all sorts of events. Birthday parties, bar mitzvahs, retirement, anniversary, corporate functions. I worked for a major corporate event planner for a few years before the business went under, unfortunately. I decided to diversify and I actually love doing weddings. But I enjoy keeping my fingers in the corporate world when I can. Keeps me on my toes."

"Then I'd like to set up a time to talk—"

"Jesus, Trudy, can't you ever just give it a rest? I swear to god you don't know the meaning of the term *night off*. Greg, you seriously need to find the off button for her."

With a roll of her eyes and an almost comical look of disgust, Tru turned to face Baz, sitting on the other side of her. "The only off button anyone needs to find is the one for your mouth."

Across the table, Greg snorted, Sabrina laughed before covering her mouth with her hand, and Dane grinned outright.

Talia didn't quite see the humor in the situation, but apparently no one else was worried about the zingers these two were throwing at each other.

In fact, Greg actually raised an eyebrow at Baz, as if daring him to respond to Tru's dig.

And Baz didn't disappoint. "Oh, honey, there's one way I know for sure to shut me up. Why don't you let me show you?"

Instead of being pissed off at Baz's blatant sexual innuendo, Tru gave him a cool once-over and declared, "I wouldn't want to get in the way of your self-gratification. But don't wear yourself out, big boy. We still need you to finish the score."

Greg threw back his head and laughed along with Sabrina, who had to wipe her streaming eyes with her napkin.

Baz didn't look at all offended. In fact, his gaze narrowed, as if he had the perfect response but didn't want to say it aloud.

Instead, he leaned forward until his lips were only millimeters away from Tru's ear and whispered something. Tru was good. No reaction showed on her face, but when Baz pulled away looking satisfied, she turned back to Talia with a smile.

"I'll call you. We'll talk. Unless Baz's bad behavior manages to chase you away before then."

"I've got a thick skin." Talia shrugged, knowing Dane had redirected his attention back to her. "A little male bravado isn't going to chase me away."

"Glad to hear it."

Tru smiled then, her pretty face transforming into something quite spectacular now. Out of the corner of her eye, Talia saw Baz's gaze narrow again as he continued to stare at Greg's assistant. But as soon as she turned to say something to Greg, Baz looked the other way.

And Talia got caught once again in Dane's gaze.

She honestly didn't know what to say at that moment, but she figured asking him to come back to her room with her after dinner was probably not the right way to start a conversation.

Still, the smile she gave him was probably blatant enough.

And the one he gave her in return...

She never thought she'd say this, but dessert be damned. She wished the night was over.

THREE

"Can I walk with you to the elevator?"

Talia smiled up at Dane as Annabelle closed the door of the apartment behind them. They'd been among the first to leave. Talia had pled exhaustion and it hadn't been an excuse. She'd had a full day, several phone meetings, and a site consult, and she'd begun to lag about half an hour ago.

"Sure. Dinner was wonderful. Of course, it's hard not to be when a chef makes it."

Dane nodded. "True. Annabelle's a good cook but she's been busy lately. Between her shop and the wedding, she's burning the candle at both ends. The honeymoon will be good for her."

Dane sounded truly concerned and he went up another notch in Talia's estimation. "She's always been like this, though. Always busy. I think she likes it that way."

"Sounds like you're pretty busy yourself."

"Only way to be. It means you're doing something right."

The elevator arrived with a muted ding. Talia pressed the button for her floor as Dane leaned back against the mirrored wall.

He didn't respond, simply continued to watch her with those dark eyes.

Her breath caught, her chest tightened, and it became harder to draw in air.

Talia decided it was time to lay their cards on the table.

"Would you like to come to my room for a drink? I'm not quite ready to turn in yet."

He paused, and she had a second or two to wonder if she'd made a mistake before his lips curved. "I'd like that. Thanks."

The elevator stopped and the doors opened, and Talia wanted to fan her hand in front of her face.

God, her skin felt tight and hot all over. And she wanted to shake her hands out because she felt like she'd been clenching them all night.

"Annabelle was kind enough to stock the bar with my favorite whiskey, but I hate to drink alone."

Opening the door to her suite, Talia walked through the door, hyperaware of Dane following close behind.

Dropping her purse on the chair by the door, she moved toward the small bar on the side wall.

"Rocks or neat?"

"Neat, please. Where'd you get your taste for whiskey?"

The question threw her for a second, because her immediate response was her dad. But there was no way she wanted to open that line of questioning.

"High school. I've never liked the taste of beer, and I had boyfriend whose father owned a whiskey company."

She didn't tell him that the company had one of the most famous names in the American whiskey industry. Too many questions.

"And where does the accent come from?"

She didn't fumble the bottle as she poured his drink but he'd caught her off guard with that one. She'd done her best to lose her accent when she and her mom and brother had moved north. Most people never noticed.

She was beginning to realize Dane noticed everything.

"I was born in Kentucky. We moved to Adamstown when I was a teenager."

Handing him the glass, she moved to sit on the couch by the windows. She expected him to sit next to her and was surprised when he took the seat across from her.

He sprawled in the leather chair, looking completely relaxed. She almost felt like the subject of an interrogation, as if he'd shined a spotlight on her. But being this turned on definitely did not feel like interrogation tactics.

Any other man who'd tried to dig into her past had been shut down and shut out. She should be doing the same to Dane.

Only... she didn't want to. She wanted him to kiss her. To put his hands on her. To strip her down and lay his naked body on top of hers. Or maybe spread out underneath hers.

Oh, hell. Why not wish for the entire *Kama Sutra* in one night? She'd be tired and sore, but those yoga classes she'd been taking had to be worth something, right?

As she watched, Dane's mouth slowly curved in a smile, as if he could read her mind.

"I'd love to know what just went through your mind," he said.

"I was led to believe you could read minds." She took another sip of whiskey and let the warmth relax her.

This was just sex. They both knew it.

"And who told you that?"

"Annabelle talks about three men. Jared, Tyler, and you. The way she talks about Jared, you can see how much in love she is with him. Tyler amuses her. You..."

His gaze narrowed as she paused. "Me?"

"She likes you. And if Annabelle likes you, that's high

praise. You also get high marks from Kate, and she's an even tougher judge of character."

Talia had learned from the best how to lead a conversation away from dangerous subjects, away from anything that could lead to her own past. A past she refused to discuss for fear it would affect her life now.

"Nice to know I'm so highly regarded."

"You sound disappointed."

He shook his head. "Not at all. I like Kate. She tells it like it is and I admire that in people. Jed loves Annabelle and it's clear why. She's one of the sweetest people I've ever met."

Did she hear a hint of jealousy in his tone? Not a trace of it showed in his expression but Talia definitely heard something in his voice.

"Are you worried about your friendship with Jared changing after the wedding? Some people have a difficult time when their friends get married. I've seen friendships implode through a wedding. But then, most of those weren't true friendships to begin with."

"I guess you see a lot of drama in your profession."

Laughing, Talia shook her head. "You can't even imagine. The word *bridezilla* didn't come into being on a whim. But those really are few and far between. You can certainly draw correlations between the cost of the wedding and the creation of a bridezilla, though."

"So what got you into event planning?"

"I love a good party." She laughed at Dane's raised eyebrows. "I know that sounds childish but I do. I love the atmosphere you can create at a party. Since I do more than weddings, I get to create all sorts of different events. I love themed birthday parties, especially for children. There's nothing like putting a smile on the face of a ten-year-old who wants to be a princess for a day, even though she's afraid she's too old to be a princess.

"And the weddings are that ten-year-old's dream come true. Even if the marriage might not last a year, I want to make damn sure that wedding is everything she's ever dreamed of wrapped with a bow and a cherry on top, if that's what she really wants."

"So you sell fantasy?"

"Absolutely. But I also do corporate events. And I love doing adoption ceremonies. Those are actually my most favorite, even above the weddings. I think they're the most pure."

"I've never heard of those."

"They're fairly new. I've only done a couple but they were the most rewarding experiences. There's a sense of joy you don't get from other events."

"Guess there's not a lot of joy at corporate events."

She shrugged. "Depends on the event. Give them enough liquor and even the most boring businessman gets a little joyful. Of course, they usually get a little grabby, too."

Dane laughed. "You strike me as someone who knows how to take care of herself."

Coming from this man, that sounded like high praise. And she enjoyed it a little too much. "I'm amazingly self-sufficient. My mother worked a lot when I was younger and my brother is five years younger, so I had to take care of him sometimes. He was a total pain in the ass. He's lucky I love him. What about you? Brothers and sisters?"

"One of each. I'm the youngest."

"Ah."

He smiled, as if he knew what she was going to say but asked the questions anyway. "'Ah' what?"

"You were spoiled rotten, weren't you?"

He didn't look at all offended. On the contrary, he was amused. "Yes, I was. My parents are crazy in love with each other, which surprises a lot of people. Some people think that because we have a lot of money, we don't have much heart. If you ever meet my parents, you'll know that's not true."

Her parents had been in love, too. That hadn't worked out well for either of them. "Sounds like you had a happy childhood."

"Charmed, some people would say."

"And would they be right?"

"For the most part, yes, they would."

"So how did you and Jared meet?"

"In high school. We went to the same private school. Attended the same college. Got into a hell of a lot of trouble together and stayed friends. I love him like a brother. Probably because he isn't."

Talia smiled at the undisguised affection in Dane's voice. She liked that he wasn't afraid to show his feelings for his best friend. A lot of guys she met weren't confident enough to admit something like that. "Don't you get along with your brother?"

"Yes, but he's eight years older than me. And even more perfect."

Laughing, Talia shook her head. "You sound jealous."

"He's a great guy." Dane's lips curved in a totally devastating smile as he raised a hand as if testifying. "Honestly. And my sister is a sweetheart, but she's ten years older and provided the first grandchildren, so she's even more perfect than my brother and me combined."

"So you have nephews? Nieces?"

"Two nieces. Four and two. My mom is in heaven, my dad's thrilled, and I get to play the doting uncle, and they love me because I give them presents and candy."

"I can see the appeal."

"And then they go back home with their mom at the end of

the day. Don't get me wrong, I love them, but my eardrums need the break after an extended visit."

The conversation stalled out as they both sipped their drinks, but it wasn't an awkward silence. No, it was filled with a building sense of anticipation.

And finally, she'd had enough idle conversation.

"So, Dane. Are we going to sit here all night and talk? Or have I completely misread your intentions?"

Dane's smile widened immediately and she breathed a silent sigh of relief. "I think you're too good at reading people to mistake my intentions."

More high praise from him. Praise that made her tingly all over. She wanted him to follow that up with action but he remained seated across from her, staring. Waiting.

For her to make the first move? She thought she had.

"Are you going to continue sitting so far away?" she asked.

"Would you like me to come closer? Because I want to. I just don't want there to be any misunderstandings."

She raised her brows. "Have there been misunderstandings in your past?"

"Occasionally, yes."

Interesting. "And what did those misunderstandings entail? Just so I don't make the same mistake, of course."

"The woman's mistake was in believing I was looking for a relationship."

"Then you and I will get along just fine because I'm simply looking for sex."

Dane's laughter surprised her. Deep and a little rough and definitely sexy.

She hoped the sex matched because, damn, she was turned on.

"I like you, Ms. Driscoll." Dane set his empty glass on the table next to him then leaned forward, elbows on his knees, dark eyes fixed on hers. "Now, tell me what kind of sex you're looking for. Fast and dirty? Or slow and controlled? Both have their advantages. Or we can do a combination. Trust me, I'm up for all of it."

Her heart had started to pound as soon as he'd begun to speak, but by the time he'd finished, her panties were wetter than they'd been before and she had to force herself to unclench her thighs.

"I guess we could start fast and dirty because, honestly, I'm not sure I have the patience to wait for slow right now."

Dane stood so fast, she sucked in a small gasp. She was startled, not frightened, and luckily he realized the difference.

She had just enough time to place her glass on the coffee table before Dane reached for her hand and pulled her out of the chair.

She stood, teetering forward but not falling. He was too close for that. But she did get plastered against his body.

Her hands gripped his broad shoulders, her breasts crushed tight against his hard chest. She'd only need to take a tiny step forward and she could press her pelvis against his.

So she did and found him erect and thick.

She had to tilt her head back a little to look into his eyes, which brought her lips within range of his.

Lifting one big hand, he cupped her cheek, brushing his thumb across her lower lip and sending tingles through her nervous system, straight to her clit.

The sensation made her gasp, though she tried to contain it. Self-preservation was a hard habit to kick.

For so long she'd pushed away any man who threatened her self-control. Just easier that way.

Even though she'd made the decision to sleep with Dane, that didn't mean she couldn't still maintain control.

But wasn't that the point? Losing control.

Lifting onto her toes, she cut off that line of thought by kissing him. Hard.

And he let her. Let her work her lips against his, let her slip her tongue into his mouth to flick against his.

And damn, he tasted good. Hot, erotic, and she wanted more.

Her hands came up to cup his head, turning it so she could kiss him deeper.

Beneath hers, his lips curved. A warning. As was the hand he pressed against her lower back, making sure she was completely aligned with him.

With his erection digging into her lower stomach, her sex clenched and an ache she hadn't had to deal with in months roared to life.

God, why hadn't she realized how horny she'd been? Or was it simply him?

Moaning into his mouth, she shivered and buried those thoughts deep, chalking her reaction up to the fact that the man could kiss.

He'd taken over now, and she was more than happy to let him because, holy crap, the man had magic lips.

He kissed her with such indulgence and single-minded determination, as if he wanted to make her come simply with his mouth on hers, his tongue playing along hers.

Talia felt her reins slipping. Part of her wanted to grab them tighter and take back control.

Then there was the part that wanted to submit. That part gained a little bit of ground every time he clutched her closer and shifted his mouth to kiss her at a different angle.

When he released her mouth, she gasped at the sudden shock of it but moaned as he laid a straight line of kisses along her jaw to her earlobe. Which he bit.

Pleasure radiated through her body. Her nipples peaked

into tight points and she wanted him to put his mouth on her breasts and bite her there. Then lick her as his hands moved farther south.

She'd beg if she had to.

"I'm going to take your shirt off, sweetheart. I promise I won't let you get cold."

She had no doubt he'd live up to his word. But she wasn't ready to surrender completely. It simply wasn't in her nature.

"Then I get to take yours off, too."

Staring up at him, she saw his gorgeous mouth curved in a grin and her heart actually skipped a beat.

His dark eyes practically glittered in the room's low light, mesmerizing her. She'd never looked at another man like this and felt an overwhelming need to *have* him. Now.

"Go right ahead." He bent and kissed her again, quick and hard. "I can't wait to feel your skin against mine."

Her panties would be soaked through if he kept talking. And she *so* wanted him to keep talking. She'd never had another man's voice affect her like his did.

Drifting her hands from his shoulders down his back to his waistband, she tugged on the tucked-in tails of his shirt until they came free.

She wanted to stick her hands up the shirt to reach bare skin but restrained herself. Barely.

Despite her claim earlier, she didn't want this to be over too soon. She wanted to explore every inch of his beautiful body.

And right now, she wanted to see his chest.

Leaning away from him far enough to unbutton his shirt made her lower body fit even more tightly against his. His cock throbbed, which she felt through his jeans and hers, and she had the almost overwhelming urge to rub against it.

Patience.

Her gaze, which she'd lowered to watch as she lifted his shirt, shot back to his.

"Don't stop now. We're just getting to the good part."

The drawl in his tone made her smile and his answering grin was a revelation. The man was just too damn sexy for her sanity. Every time he smiled, she wanted him to kiss her and show her exactly how he planned to make her lose control.

That should scare the hell out of her.

The fact that it didn't, well... Something to think about later, because right now, she wanted to strip him naked and run her hands all over him.

Her fingers made quick work of the shirt, pushing it up until he took over and pulled it over his head. He wasn't wearing an undershirt and dark hair furred his broad chest.

Smiling, she ran her fingertips over that hair. Broad, firm chest. Defined abs. Muscular but not overly. So very biteable.

Hell, even his nipples were perfect. Small and round and hard.

She brushed her fingers over those tiny nubs and heard him suck in a quick breath. And when she leaned forward and flicked her tongue over them, she wanted to pump her fists in triumph as he shoved his fingers in her hair and held her there.

"So pretty." She ran her tongue around the nipple then blew on it, leaning back to watch it harden even more.

"Hell, Tally. You can call me whatever you damn well please. Just keep using your mouth on me."

So she did, running her tongue around the areola and feeling his shoulders tense beneath her hands. His chest rose and fell at an ever-increasing rate, which her own body matched with every breath.

When she put her lips around his nipple and sucked on him, he groaned.

God, yes. She loved that sound. Loved the feeling that she could bring this strong man under her control.

Kissing her way up his chest to his jaw, she used her teeth to nip at his stubble-laden chin then rubbed her cheek against it, loving the feeling. Wanting to feel it on other parts of her body...

Dane gripped her hips, grinding his cock against her for a few seconds before releasing her and grabbing her shirt.

"Lift."

She knew what he wanted and she pulled away just slightly, but she didn't give in right away and lift her arms. Instead, she raised her eyebrows and let her lips curl in a slight grin.

He returned the look with one she totally understood. He was going to make her pay. In the best possible way.

Finally, after several long seconds, she raised her arms to allow him to pull her shirt over her head. The tight cotton material clung as he worked it up her body, but Dane obviously had more than enough experience at this.

When he finally had it over her head, he dropped it on the couch behind him, never looking away from her now mostly nude upper body.

Only the barely there cream lace bra, one of Kate's creations, made any kind of attempt at modesty. And it was a pretty weak one at that.

The see-through lace left nothing to the imagination. Her hard nipples poked against the delicate fabric, already strained with the weight of her breasts.

Kate's lingerie never failed to amaze her. It looked so delicate, like it couldn't possibly hold up, giving even Talia's average-sized breasts the illusion of weight and substance.

And apparently Dane found them to his liking because his hands immediately cupped her, molding her breasts into his palms and squeezing. Not hard enough to hurt. No, just hard enough to make her moan with pleasure.

"I'm going to kiss every inch of you, starting with your breasts. Then I'm going to work my way down your body until I've got my mouth between your legs. Then I'm going to make you scream."

She tried to bite back a moan but wasn't entirely successful as he pinched her already overstimulated nipples between his thumbs and forefingers.

"But first, I want you to take off the rest of your clothes for me."

If any other man had said that same thing with that same tone of command in his voice, Talia would've been thrown out of the mood.

She had no desire to think about why she wasn't now. She only wanted to give him what he wanted so he'd continue to please her.

But she had enough self-preservation remaining to respond with "You, too."

His mouth, which he was using to suck at the juncture of her neck and shoulders, curved into a grin she felt against her skin. Then he tweaked her nipples, hard enough to make her gasp.

God, this man had the power to bring her to her knees. And that was dangerous.

"Whatever you want."

She didn't get her wish immediately, however. He bent to put his mouth on the swell of her breasts, kissing one and biting the other. When he released her, her knees actually felt weak.

Her hands fell to the button on her jeans but she stilled as he whipped his belt out of the loops and tossed it toward the sofa. Then he reached for his button.

And left her hanging.

She glanced up and found him staring down at her.

"You first," he said.

He was playing with her. When was the last time she'd had playful sex?

She couldn't remember. Maybe not ever.

Without looking away, she popped the button on her jeans and lowered her zipper. Then cocked an eyebrow at him.

In her peripheral vision, she saw him do the same. She wanted to look but he held her gaze steady. Until he shoved his jeans down, taking his boxers with them, and she couldn't resist. She had to look.

And, oh, wow, she was glad she hadn't resisted.

"Not fair," he murmured.

Well, he'd gotten that right. It definitely wasn't fair to cover his body. Guys sometimes looked funny standing there naked, their erect cocks standing out from their body like a piece of a puzzle that didn't quite fit.

Not Dane. Holy mother of—

He should be starring in porn films made for women because oh, my god, he was perfect.

"Tally, honey. My turn."

Yes, please.

Trying not to rush, or fall flat on her face in an attempt to get her tight jeans off, she wriggled the denim down her legs, kicking off her short boots before bending to get the jeans around her ankles and then stepping out of them.

Amazingly, when she looked up again, he stared at her like he wanted to devour her.

"You are fucking beautiful."

She felt laughter bubble in her chest but couldn't muster up the air because he'd stolen all of it. She could barely breathe, his gaze so hot, she swore it burned her skin everywhere it touched.

And it touched everywhere.

Starting at her head, Dane checked out every inch of her. By the time his gaze reached her toes and he started back up again, she wanted to clench her legs together because she was afraid he'd see the proof of her desire slicking the inside of her thighs.

She'd left her underwear on deliberately, because she thought Dane would appreciate the matched set. She was pretty sure she'd guessed right.

"You're not going to hold it against me if the first time is really fucking fast, are you? I promise I'll make it up to you later."

"Absolutely not. Go fast. But I'm holding you to a second time."

Eyes dark as ink as he smiled. "A girl after my own heart."

Reaching for her, he wrapped his hands around her hips and pulled her flush against him. His cock flattened against her stomach, iron hard and so hot. His lips were cool, though, when he lowered his head to kiss her again.

But his calm was starting to fracture a little. His fingers bit into her skin a little more deeply. She really liked the feel of them against her flesh. She wanted him to lose even more control.

Reaching behind him, she put her hand on his ass and squeezed. Jesus, the guy had a great ass, tight and sleek. Then she ran her hands up his back, feeling the play of muscle beneath the skin as his arms tightened around her and he flattened his hands on her ass. His fingers slid beneath her panties, teasing between her cheeks.

She shuddered, arching against him, trying to ease some of that delicious ache between her legs. Knowing it would only ease when he made her come. Which she hoped would be soon. At least this first time. Next time, he could draw it out all he wanted.

Maybe he needed a little incentive.

Scoring her nails down his back made him groan, a sound that had her swallowing hard. Drawing her hand around to his front and wrapping her fingers around his cock got her a bite on the shoulder.

She'd probably have a mark there and she couldn't care less. What was hot sex without a few reminders?

Pumping her fist along his cock from root to tip, she felt the shaft throb in her grip. The man had a gorgeous cock to go with his amazing body. Long and thick and perfectly straight.

She wondered for a brief second if there was anything wrong with him, because right now she couldn't find a thing.

Which was totally insane. Of course there was something wrong with him. It just wouldn't matter because there wouldn't be a repeat of this night. Which was a damn shame.

So make sure it's memorable.

That definitely wasn't going to be a problem. Not with this man.

Dane chose that moment to shove her panties down her legs, his palms a little rough against her thighs, sending flashes of heat to her pussy.

While she kicked off the scrap of lace and cotton, he lifted her off the floor and took the few steps to the couch where he'd conveniently tossed his jeans.

"You still carry condoms in your wallet?"

His mouth curved in a grin. "I was never a Boy Scout, but they had the right idea about always being prepared. If a guy tells you he doesn't keep one in his wallet, he's either lying or stupid. And definitely not a Boy Scout."

Sitting on the couch, he settled her with her knees on either side of his thighs.

Reaching for his wallet, he dug out the condom then held it out to her.

"Only one?" She raised her brows at him, grinning. "Good thing I actually *was* a Girl Scout."

"Glad to hear it. Otherwise I was going to have to call room service."

His grin made her sex clench. "If you're as good as you think you are, that might still be an option. Less talk now."

Bending forward, she plucked the condom from his fingers and leaned closer to kiss him.

Their lips met in a hard, searing kiss. She didn't hold back anything and heard him groan, low and deep.

Her now-frantic need made her tear open the foil wrapper blindly as their lips meshed. Dane's hands molded to her breasts, kneading the mounds with a firm grip, sending waves of pleasure through her body.

The condom slipped in her fingers and she made a conscious effort not to accidentally rip it.

"Let me put this on before I have to find another one."

He pulled back only far enough to see her eyes. "And why would you need to do that?"

"Because if you keep touching me like that, I'm going to rip this."

His mouth curved slightly. "And we definitely don't want that. I have a feeling we're going to need every damn condom in the room before the end of the night."

Burning-hot desire exploded in her veins, making her skin feel electrified. She had to fight to draw in a breath, and Dane's expression tightened with even more desire.

"Keep looking at me like that and this is going to get dirty."

Talia blinked at the raw tone of his voice. Her lips parted but nothing emerged. She couldn't speak immediately.

"Tal—"

"Promise?"

His smile had disappeared, but she saw the heat in his gaze smolder lava-hot. "Anything you want. I'm up for it."

Anything, huh? She wondered—

No, she had no time for wondering.

She had reality in front of her right now.

Holding his gaze, she let her free hand drop to his lap and wrap around his cock.

She stroked him several times, watching his eyes narrow down to slits and feeling his cock thicken between her fingers.

She didn't go fast or tight at first. She wanted to tease. And he let her.

His cock fascinated her, so straight and thick and *hot*. She teased the hell out of herself thinking about riding him. Every second she denied herself the pleasure of sinking onto that silky column and fucking him, of her body riding him until the pleasure was just too much, was one second closer to heaven.

Then she'd want to do it again. And again.

"Talia." His tone held a harsh note. "If you keep that up, I'm not going to be responsible for the consequences."

She smiled at him. "Oh, I think you have much more control than that."

"I'm not talking about coming too fast. I'm talking about throwing you over the arm of the couch and fucking you fast and hard."

The images he put in her head made her eyes glaze over and her lips part to draw in air. She caught a quick glimpse of Dane's eyes narrowing before he stood, lifting her as easily as if she weighed nothing.

She barely had time to register the fact that she was moving before she found herself draped over the rolled arm of the couch, ass in the air.

The cushioned arm cradled her pelvis and a second later, he had his cock wedged in the crack of her ass.

"Give it to me."

She knew what he wanted, but instead of handing over the condom, she shook her head, biting her lip against a smile.

"Then I guess I'll have to punish you for that."

Yes, please.

She managed not to say the words aloud, but she was pretty sure he could read her excitement in the slight wiggle of her ass against his pelvis.

She was expecting the smack on her ass. She knew she'd like it. She just didn't know she'd like it so much.

Shuddering as his palm made contact, she felt that sting echo through her entire body, a wave of heat so intense, she nearly cried out.

The sharp crack of his flesh connecting with hers had her biting her tongue against making a sound. All part of the play. And she liked to play.

It'd been hard to find a match for her particular form of kink. Most guys she'd met hadn't picked up on her cues. And if they had, they'd been particularly unskilled.

One had actually been too terrified of hurting her to continue. She'd ended that night alone with her vibrator after he'd thrown on his clothing and hightailed it out the door.

She couldn't imagine Dane leaving her high and dry. Because the next slap made her thighs slick with her desire.

This time she did make a sound, sort of a muffled squeak. And when she did, she felt Dane's hand smooth over her hot flesh.

"Now give me the condom, sweetheart. And I'll make it so much better."

As he spoke, he rubbed his cock between her cheeks and gripped her hips with both hands to hold her still.

Lifting her hand behind her, she held out the slippery disc to him.

Bending closer, he pressed a kiss to her back as he took the condom. Which forced her pelvis harder into the couch arm and made her clit throb in response.

She moaned, unable to help herself.

"I fucking love hearing you make that sound." His voice had lowered to a growl.

"Keep making me feel like this and I'll give you what you want."

"Anything I want?"

She paused, feeling his hand slip around her thigh and his fingertips brush her clit, making her buck back against him.

When she caught her breath, she said, "I guess that depends on how good you are."

His laughter was a barely audible huff that she felt brush across her shoulder blades.

"Guess I better be pretty damn good, then."

He stepped away from her and cooler air rushed against her now-exposed thighs and ass. The temperature change provided another sensation that made her shiver. Then she felt him put one hand on her back, tilting her forward the tiniest bit more. Her toes barely touched the floor now and she felt off balance and out of breath.

And so horny, she wanted to scream.

When he finally slid his cock between her thighs, she felt an almost immediate relief that quickly turned back into a burning desire that made her even more slick and achy. His shaft slipped along her sex lips, branding the delicate tissue with heat.

She wanted to rub against him but her position didn't allow for much movement. She had to plant her hands on the cushion to keep from tipping too far forward and ending up with her face buried.

But if he didn't hurry—

The tip of his cock pressed against her opening, building pressure but not fully penetrating.

A slight wriggle of her hips and he pressed a little farther.

That earned her a quick, sharp slap on her ass, which made it even more difficult to breathe.

"I'm going to go as slow as I possibly can," Dane said, "because otherwise, I'll come as soon as I'm inside your tight pussy."

Words had always worked for her, and now was no different. The sound of his voice triggered a contraction lower in her body that made her desperate for him to fuck her.

"Dane. I want you. Do me. Now."

One hand smoothed up her back, the other gently pulling one thigh to the side as he made small thrusts, coating his cock in her wetness.

"So eager. Jesus, you're absolutely beautiful."

"Glad to hear it. Now, please."

She heard the smile in his words. "Impatient and demanding. Definitely a woman after my own heart."

He angled his cock and sank a little deeper, spreading her clenching channel so slowly, she wanted to scream. Every millimeter he pressed forward threw fuel on the fiery ache building low in her body.

She wanted him to hurry but wanted this feeling to last forever because she knew the eventual explosion would be that much better.

Still, the impatient part of her wanted him to thrust hard and sink deep. And then keep going at her until she couldn't feel her bones anymore.

It'd been so long since she'd indulged in sex and now she wanted to gorge. But on her terms.

And Dane seemed like just the man to give her what she wanted.

"Fuck me, Dane. Now."

The hand he had on her hip tightened almost to the point of

pain and, damn, she really liked that. She liked it even better when he pulled back and gave her exactly what she wanted.

She must have cried out when he slammed his pelvis against her ass, because he froze with his cock lodged deep inside her.

"Talia. Are you—"

"Yes! I'm fine. Just move."

She was stretched so tight around him, she'd probably be walking funny tomorrow. But, oh, god, it would so be worth it.

"Then hold on, baby. I'm taking you at your word."

She felt his fingers wind through her hair, tugging her head back as he began to move. She resisted, and the slight burn on her scalp made her shudder with pleasure.

"Jesus, Tally."

Those were the last words she heard him speak, because he began to fuck her exactly how she wanted.

So hard and fast, she had to brace herself and lock her elbows so she didn't fall forward.

Every time he thrust inside, his cock hitting every nerve ending in her sheath, it sent ripples of pleasure through her body.

She wanted to move with him but the position didn't allow for it. Frustration bled into the building pleasure, creating a frantic need. She needed him to go faster, harder, deeper. Most men treated her like a porcelain doll, afraid she'd break.

This man seemed to know exactly what to do to both give her what she wanted and make her want even more.

And she wanted so much more.

Letting her head hang just a little lower, she absorbed the sting, a delicious counterpoint to the soothing massage of his hand on her ass and the friction of his cock against her vaginal walls.

With her eyes closed, she concentrated on the myriad sensations ripping through her. Pleasure and pain and frustration continued to build. Her body tensed for an orgasm...

And he stopped.

She wanted to screech in denial but the only sound that emerged was a breathy huff. Because he felt so damn good even when he wasn't moving.

"Dane."

His cock twitched but he continued to hold steady.

"Move, damn you."

He released her hip and ran his hand up her spine in a rough caress. When he reached her shoulders, he curled his fingers around one and thrust just the tiniest bit deeper.

Moaning, she tried to move and found she couldn't. He had her pinned in a way that she had no leeway.

Oh, god. Perfect.

Bending forward, he put his lips next to her ear, the damp warmth of his body pressed against her back.

"Now, I'm going to give you what you want."

Dane fucked her like a man who had only enough control left not to hurt her.

And the next few minutes were the most erotic of her life.

FOUR

Dane hoped to hell he'd read Talia right.

He'd never treated another woman he'd just met with the same level of force he'd used on her.

And even though what they'd done was a far cry from true domination, he didn't know her well enough to be certain he hadn't crossed any lines.

Of course, Talia hadn't made any complaints during sex or now, as he picked her up off the arm of the couch and carried her to bed. She lay curled against his chest, arms around his shoulders, head tucked under his chin. Warm and boneless and still breathing heavily, the soft huff of her breath across his skin making his body believe he could go again in just a few minutes.

She felt content. And hopefully as sated as he was.

It'd been a damn long time since he'd fucked a woman on his own who'd aroused him as much as Talia had. He liked it. A lot.

He couldn't wait to get her in a bed and start all over, this time slower. With more thoroughness. Lay her out and kiss his way down her body from her head to her toes. And every place in between.

His cock began to thicken and his gait picked up.

"You seem to be in a hurry to get somewhere." Talia's smoky tone held a faint trace of a question.

"I'm going to get you in a bed. Then I plan to start all over."

He made sure his tone held no hint of a question. She'd taken well to his authority before, so he'd continue and see where it led them. He was nothing if not flexible, especially when he wanted something.

And he wanted Talia at least once more tonight.

"Confident, aren't you?"

They'd reached the dark bedroom but he didn't turn on a light. A slight glow from the open bathroom door gave enough light for him to see the bed. He headed straight for it, using one hand to pull down the covers before laying her out on the pristine white sheets and straightening to stare down at her.

"I know what I want."

With a slight smile on her beautiful lips, Talia stretched, arms above her head, hips twisting one way, her torso the other. Long, lean muscles lengthened and flexed as he watched, his mouth actually watering at the sight.

He let himself look, even after she stopped, arms above her head, as she stared up at him.

"Are you going to make good on your promise now? Or are you going to stand there and just look at me?"

"Who says I can't do both?"

She raised a pale brow at him. "Does that mean I can't touch you?"

Lifting herself onto one elbow, she lifted her other hand toward him.

His breath caught in his throat as he waited for her touch. Her hand started low, as if she were going to reach for his cock, then lifted, pressing one fingertip in the middle of his chest.

"You're so warm. You give off heat like a furnace."

"Too hot for you?"

He smiled at her to let her know he was teasing. He knew he wasn't tough to look at. He kept in shape and took care of himself. Genetics had blessed him with decent looks and he'd never had a problem seducing any woman he put his mind to.

Her mouth curved in an answering smile. "I like to burn."

And that probably answered his unspoken question. Still, he'd rather hear her say it straight out than leave anything unsaid.

"Did I cross any lines earlier?"

She didn't say anything but she drew her finger down his chest to circle one nipple. "Why would you think that? Did I give you any indication I didn't like what we did?"

"No. But I don't like to leave things unsaid. Causes less problems farther down the line."

Her gaze had dropped to watch her finger as it drew a line across his chest to his other nipple. He didn't think she was avoiding his gaze, but he really didn't know this woman well enough to know better.

That said, just the touch of her finger on his skin made his cock begin to pulse. He'd have a full erection again in only minutes.

"I realize we haven't known each other that long but, trust me, if I didn't like something, I would've told you."

She punctuated her statement by pinching his nipple between her thumb and forefinger.

The tiny but sharp pain shot a bolt of lightning straight to his balls. But as much as he wanted to spread her legs and pump into her, he held himself still and let her continue to caress him.

"So you like it a little rough?"

Her gaze flicked up to his as her finger began to trail down his chest.

"Sometimes. Sometimes I don't. Depends on my mood."

Her finger stopped just above his belly button. "Depends on the man."

Irrational jealousy bit at him as she mentioned another man. Stupid, yes. But still...

"What about you, Dane? Do you like to be the dominant?"

"Would you like me to show you how dominant I can get?"

His voice had dropped, an unconscious response to their conversation. And when her gaze narrowed and her lips parted, he knew she'd been turned on by it.

Good. Because every single thing about her turned him on.

Without answering, she let her finger continue its downward slide. His cock had stiffened to the point that it was almost fully erect, but she deliberately skirted her finger to the left and scraped her nail across his hip bone.

"I think first I'd like to make you beg."

He felt her words like a jab in the gut. He managed to contain almost all outward reaction, but he was fairly certain she saw his cock throb. Couldn't control that. Of course, now her gaze was fastened on his shaft.

"You can certainly try."

"Ah, a challenge." Her smile widened. "I love a good challenge."

He didn't think it would be that much of a challenge. He was close to groaning out her name already. But he'd let her play and make her work for it, because that's what she wanted. And he prided himself on being a fairly perceptive guy.

Her finger slid even farther, barely brushing the short, dark hair surrounding his genitals.

"So do I," he said. "So when you're done making me beg, I'm going to make you scream."

Her gaze snapped back to his. "I'm not a screamer."

Her hand slipped between his thighs, turning to cup his

balls. He hissed in a breath, not because she'd hurt him but because it felt so damn good.

He bit back a grunt as she rolled his balls in her palm, gently, slowly. As if she knew he was still sensitive from coming shortly before.

"You will be."

"So sure of yourself." Her voice lowered to a bare murmur, her hand finally wrapping around his cock. He wanted her to stroke him but he didn't ask for it, just let her go at her own pace. "I like that in a guy."

He wanted to growl at her not to remind him that there'd been other men in her life. Then stopped short when he realized how crazy that would sound. "I've never had any complaints before."

"I'm sure you haven't."

Did he hear a note of pique in her tone?

Her hand tightened on the base of his cock and his eyes closed for a brief second at the pleasure.

"Stroke me harder," he demanded.

"I think I've got something better in mind."

Releasing him, she rose to her knees, hand still on his cock. Then she leaned forward and took him between her lips.

His hands went to her head, sliding through her hair as she took him into the wet warmth of her mouth.

So damn good. So hot. So wet.

He grunted, containing the urge to hold her head steady and pump into her. This was her turn, and he'd let her go for as long as he could. Give her whatever she wanted.

Right now, she seemed to want to tease him to death.

Her tongue lapped at the head of his cock, licking at the slit then flattening so he could slide farther inside. Her cheeks hollowed as she sucked on him, making his eyes snap shut at the sensation burning from his shaft to his balls and deep into his gut.

She worked his cock with a dedication that felt like a loving caress. But she wasn't greedy, didn't make him feel like he was just an interchangeable organ.

Her hands clenched at his ass then she pet him, her hands stroking from his thighs to his back. Alternately kneading him and scratching her nails against his skin.

Her rhythm steadied after her first few, quick bobs, as if she wanted to draw out his orgasm from deep in his body. As if she enjoyed his taste, enjoyed the control over him.

He forced himself to stand there and take whatever she wanted to give him. Which was quite a lot.

She sucked him for minutes, his balls tightening every time she took him all the way to the back of her throat.

When her fingers wrapped tight around the base of his cock, he had to wonder if she read him better than he read himself. Had he made some sign that he was close to coming?

Hell, he didn't want to come so fast again.

Which meant he needed to stop her.

As she worked her way back to the tip again, he tugged on her hair, getting her attention.

Again he noticed that she resisted. So he tugged a little harder and saw her eyes squeeze tighter before she opened them and stared up into his eyes as she let his cock slip from her mouth.

"I don't want to come in your mouth. I want to be fucking your tight pussy when I come again."

He saw her lips part to suck in air though he barely heard her make a sound. The brush of her breath over his cock made it bob.

"But first I'm going to put my mouth on your pussy and lick you until you come."

She swallowed hard, eyes widening. Then she sank her teeth into her bottom lip for a second.

"You look completely civilized on the outside but you're not at all, are you?" she asked.

"You're one to talk. So cool and elegant and in charge. Lie back, sweetheart, and let me make you scream."

She paused for a beat and he saw a decision flash through her gaze. "Make me."

Fuck.

His heart started to race in anticipation, blood pounding through his veins as he grabbed on to the remaining thread of his control. Then he reached for her.

Hands around her waist, he lifted her then laid her on her back sideways across the bed.

"Hands over your head. Reach for the edge of the mattress and don't let go until I tell you to."

His voice held a tone he hadn't heard in months. Mainly because he'd been Jared and Annabelle's third and Annabelle wasn't his to command.

Talia...

Right now, she was completely his.

And she did exactly what he said. Her fair skin blushed a fiery pink as she lifted her arms and wrapped her hands around the edge of the mattress, never taking her eyes off his.

The position stretched her upper body, drawing her breasts higher and tighter. Her small nipples looked peaked and tight, standing straight out from her body, tempting him to bite them.

Kneeling on the bed next to her, he settled his hands on either side of her body, making sure their skin didn't touch. Not yet.

This time, they were going to take it as slow as he could. The first time had been fast and hard. This time was going to be different, though he wasn't going to go easy on her.

But she *would* scream his name before he was done with her.

Leaning down, he licked at one rosy nipple topping a handful of a breast. Tally couldn't be more than a B-cup, but on her... she was perfectly proportioned.

And so damn sweet. Her puckered nipple felt like rough silk against his tongue as he licked at her, taking his time to make her wet.

He licked around the areolae then came back to nip at the rigid tip. Tormenting her with alternating bites and kisses, he soon had her arching her back to try and get him to suck at her.

Instead, he continued with his plan, alternating between her breasts until he literally couldn't help himself.

With a groan, he cupped one breast, plumping it so he could suck her into his mouth. The sound she made as his lips closed around the silky tip sent a shot of electricity straight to his cock. Already hard and aching, he wanted to tell her to wrap her fingers around his shaft and pump him.

He didn't. Instead, he used his teeth and lips to make her moan. Biting at her flesh made him want to growl, to mark her as his. Licking at the red marks he'd left behind made him feel like a caveman. And proud of it.

When he finally pulled back, her breasts looked rosy, like her ass after he'd spanked it.

He had a brief moment to wonder if she'd ever had hot wax dripped on her nipples. He wouldn't be surprised if she had, but he had one of those strange urges that made him want to be the first man to introduce her to that pleasure.

God, he hoped he got the chance.

"Why'd you stop?" She sounded out of breath, her lips parted as she tried to draw in air, her eyes barely open.

"Because I could spend hours on your breasts, but there are other parts of your body I want to explore, too."

Using the hand he'd had cupped around her breast, he curled it around her ribs now then dragged it down her side to her right hip. She moved under his hand like a wave and didn't protest when he slipped that hand between her thighs and nudged them apart.

She spread them willingly though not quickly and, by the time she'd bared herself completely, he wanted to fall on her and feast.

Forcing back the raging hunger, he rose to his knees then put his feet on the floor at the side of the bed. Then he immediately went to his knees between her thighs, shoved his hands under her ass and pulled her to the edge of the mattress.

Her sex was plump and glistened with moisture, and her scent made every breath he drew in a tease.

Looking up, he saw her staring back at him, her eyes glazed with lust.

Perfect.

He watched her as he repositioned her thighs over his biceps, his hands now on her hips holding her steady.

Finally, he leaned in and took his first taste.

Jesus, she tasted like heaven.

At the first touch of his mouth on her pussy, she squirmed, trying to get closer or trying to get away. He couldn't tell. Didn't matter. She wasn't going anywhere.

Not until he'd made her scream. And she would.

Using his teeth, his tongue, and his lips in concert, he pleasured her and indulged himself. He sucked on her folds, teased her clit with his tongue. Her delicate flesh melted against his tongue, and he couldn't get enough of her.

Losing himself in the scent and taste of her, he ate at her with a roughness that shocked him but only seemed to heighten her pleasure.

It made him want to give her anything she desired. And she

wanted to come. He felt it in the coiled tension in her thighs and the tautness of her abdomen as she tried to shift against him.

Every move she made increased the firestorm of desire roiling in his gut. Her soft moans felt like a physical caress, sending shivers up his spine.

He'd never had the urge to make a woman beg as much as he wanted Tally to, and it made him somewhat frantic. He used his tongue and his teeth, raking at her flesh as gently as he could but with enough force to make her squirm.

Finally, as her soft cries began to build, he speared his tongue into her sheath and fucked her, then drew back to suck at her clit.

Finally, she broke, convulsing in his hands and giving a sharp, incoherent cry.

No, it wasn't his name, but he wasn't finished yet.

Using his tongue, he licked at her clit until she went boneless and sank into the bed with a rasping sigh.

Breathing like he'd just run a marathon, he stood. The overwhelming desire to crawl over her and fuck her into unconsciousness made him growl. His cock ached with the need to be inside her again. He remembered the feel of her wrapped around him, her wet heat so damn enticing.

Splayed out on the bed, she looked spent, as if she'd fallen asleep. Or passed out.

But then she turned her head and opened her eyes, just a crack, but that blue gaze pinned him in place.

"Is that all you've got? I don't believe I screamed your name once."

Even through the burning passion making him almost insane, he smiled. He really fucking liked this woman. There'd only been one woman in the past several years that made him smile like this. And she was marrying his best friend.

This woman taunted him, even though she could barely

catch her breath. And each time she drew in air, her breasts quivered. He wanted to suck them into his mouth again, make her back bow as he bit on her nipples and watch her thighs rub together as she tried to ease the hunger he created in her.

"I'm nowhere near finished with you, Tally. I wanted to make sure you were still with me."

Her beautiful mouth curved in a smile. "I don't think I'll be going anywhere just yet."

He didn't think. He knew. "Damn right."

Then he grabbed her around the waist and repositioned her on the bed. Now her head rested on the pillows and her body lay stretched out for his pleasure.

Crawling onto the bed, he propped himself on one elbow next to her and wrapped his hand around her neck.

With his thumb under her chin, he turned her to face him then kissed her, hard, tasting her deeply. He controlled every shift of her head, moved his mouth over hers with such passion, he knew she'd have swollen lips.

But he couldn't help himself. She was a drug he wanted to OD on.

She didn't resist him at all, and that pushed him to kiss her until he felt himself start to lose control.

Pulling back, he took a couple of breaths, though they did nothing to settle him. He could still smell her desire on every indrawn breath.

Rolling to his knees, he straddled her hips, hands planted on the bed on either side of her head. She stared into his eyes through slits of blue ice, a faint dare in the tiny lift of her brows.

"Grab the rails and don't let go until I tell you to."

The beds in Haven were actual beds. This room had a bed with cast-iron rails set between mahogany panels. Convenient.

She didn't hesitate. She reached above her, wrapping her hands around the iron and taking a deep breath.

Sitting back on his heels, he reached for the drawer of the nightstand. If he knew Jared at all...

Yes. Condoms. And lube.

Later for the lube. He hoped like hell there'd be a later.

Grabbing a condom, he rolled it on while she watched his every movement.

He made sure he did it as slowly as he could.

"You're a tease."

Her voice flowed like warm honey over his skin.

"What fun would it be if you got everything you wanted when you wanted? Sometimes you need to work for it."

"I think I've done enough work for the night. I deserve my prize."

So did he.

Moving down her body, he spread her legs with his knees then stretched out full length above her. His cock nudged at her opening and she released for him even more.

"Wrap your legs around me, sweetheart. You're going to want to hold on."

"I think you should do less talking."

He smiled. "I think you like when I talk."

"I do, but I like when you talk and move. So move."

"Whatever you want, sweetheart."

His cock already lodged against her entrance, all he had to do was press forward.

God damn.

Heat surrounded him, her sex contracting around him like a fist, sucking him deeper. Even if he didn't move an inch, he might still come. But that wouldn't be any fun, now, would it?

With her slim legs wrapped around his waist and her gaze glued to his, he felt his blood pounding through his veins, straight to his cock.

Planting his elbows on either side of her shoulders, he dropped his lips onto hers and started a slow grind.

At least, that's what he tried for. He wanted to draw this out, make it last until he'd wrung every orgasm he could from her. Somehow, though, he couldn't help himself.

The heat of her mouth as she sucked on his tongue, combined with the heat of her pussy wrapped around his cock, goaded him into a faster pace.

Everything about this woman made him want more. Faster, harder. More friction. More sensation.

Every sound she made fueled his inner desire to conquer her, control her.

He wanted her to be completely open to him. Every thrust was a triumph, every retreat a promise of return.

Beneath him, she lifted to meet his hips every time, adding fuel to the fire burning in his gut. Her legs tightened, heels digging into his ass and spurring him on.

It'd been so damn long since he'd met a woman that made him feel like this. Like he could be content for a damn long time if he only had her in his bed.

His balls tightened in warning. *Too soon.*

He still hadn't heard her scream his name. And he wanted that badly.

Changing the angle of penetration made them both groan, and Talia broke their kiss to take a deep breath.

Bending his head, he nipped at her neck and increased the pace.

He heard her breathing change almost immediately, knew he was hitting a whole new set of pleasure receptors with the changed angle.

Instinct took over and his only goal became making her come. He didn't care if she screamed or didn't make a sound.

He wanted her to come so hard that she was left wanting

more. Hell, he wanted her to become addicted to what he could give her.

"Oh, my god. Dane."

Just the sound of his name coming from her lips triggered his orgasm. His cock kicked and throbbed in her clenching sex and he pressed in even farther, feeling like a superhero when she tightened and arched and came, as well.

His cock was still twitching inside her when he said, "You didn't scream loud enough. I guess we'll have to go again."

FIVE

Talia woke the next morning far too warm and way too comfortable considering the six-foot-plus man in her bed.

The fact that Dane was curled around her should've made her itchy to move, establish her own space.

She was a complete bed hog, always had been. She'd slept in a queen bed since she was a teenager and had learned the fine art of the sprawl.

Now, though, she'd woken with Dane curled around her and her first thought was not how fast she could kick him out of bed but how much time she had before she had to leave. Because she really wanted another taste of him.

And that was pretty damn dangerous.

Sure, he'd been great in bed, but that didn't mean she was going to pine after him like a lovesick puppy.

Which was ridiculous to even consider.

"It's way too damn early to be thinking so hard. It's only five thirty. Go back to sleep."

Dane's voice rumbled in her ear as his arm tightened around her waist, drawing her even closer. She shivered. She tried to cover it but wasn't fast enough to contain it.

"I actually need to get going. I've got a meeting this morning."

Totally true. The fact that she had more than enough time to get home and get ready, even if she left by nine a.m., was beside the point.

The fact that she wanted to stay right where she was, well, that was a problem. And she knew the only way to deal with a problem like this was to extricate herself.

She shifted away from Dane and he released her immediately.

And, idiot that she was, she didn't like that either.

Contrary bitch, aren't you?

Yeah, pretty much.

Rising naked from the bed, she headed directly for the bathroom. She felt Dane's eyes on her the entire way and couldn't help herself.

Before she closed the door, she turned and smiled at him.

She kept the smile as she ran through a quick shower and her morning routine. It only took ten minutes because she didn't wash her hair or apply more than a coat of mascara to her too-pale eyelashes and a layer of gloss to her lips.

Then she grabbed the robe off the door and headed back into the bedroom.

Dane had propped himself up on the bed and turned on the TV to CNN.

"No time for breakfast?" he asked as she headed for the closet.

"No, sorry." She gave him an apologetic look over her shoulder, trying not to ogle that bare chest. The man had the body of a god. And oh, god, she wished she had time to lick her way across that chest again.

Pushing that thought out of her mind, she snagged her jeans

from last night off the floor but tossed them into her overnight bag. She'd brought another pair, just in case.

She didn't think twice about dropping the robe to get dressed. He'd seen all there was to see of her last night and he'd apparently enjoyed the sight. She knew her body was toned and fit because she made an effort to keep it that way. Heart disease ran in her family and she didn't want to end up like her mother's sister, overweight and dead at fifty-one.

"Is your meeting for business?"

Strapping on a bra, she pulled the t-shirt over her head then faced him.

Did he look upset? Was he mad that she was leaving so abruptly? The thought shouldn't put a little ball of heat in her stomach.

"Yes. It's a young couple who work odd shifts. This is their only day off together."

"Nice of you to make accommodations for them."

"I'm used to working weekends. I actually enjoy being able to take off a day during the week if I need too."

Of course, she hadn't taken any days off in... weeks? A month?

Not that it mattered. She loved her job. And it wasn't like she had a man in her life to make her feel guilty working all those hours.

"Working for yourself certainly does have its perks."

"And what are your plans for the day?"

The question was out before she'd considered how it might sound. Like she was interested in his life.

Which she was, but it wouldn't do either of them any good to be. They both knew this had been a one-night stand.

A great one, but still...

"Family obligations. My niece's birthday party."

She turned and smiled as she caught him checking out her ass. Of course, he hadn't exactly been trying to hide it.

"How old?"

"Four. I'll probably need a few painkillers by the end of the day. Then again, there will be good beer. My brother-in-law owns a craft brewery."

Now dressed and ready to go, she realized there was a part of her that didn't want to leave. But that wasn't how her life worked, was it? She needed to keep moving forward, because someday it might all be taken away in the blink of an eye. And she didn't want to have to reinvent herself again.

She didn't have to fake her smile, but she couldn't allow too much heat to show. "Then I hope you have a great day. And thank you for last night."

It was probably a bad idea, but she leaned down to kiss him, lingering longer than she should have. He cupped her jaw in one hand but didn't try to hold her in place. Just let her kiss him. As if he'd realized she didn't want to be contained. Or he just didn't care.

She straightened, grabbed her bags, and left with a wave.

"See you at the rehearsal dinner."

Then she let herself out of the suite and hurried for the elevator.

DANE LACED his fingers behind his head as he watched Talia leave.

She didn't look back, hadn't given any indication that she wanted to stay longer, wanted him to call, wanted anything else to do with him.

Hell, if he wasn't careful, he thought he might be offended.

And why the hell should he be? She'd done exactly what he

would've done if he'd had somewhere to be. And it wasn't like last night had been "wham, bam, thank you ma'am." It'd been four hours of hot, sweaty sex and four hours of dead-to-the-world sleep. Until he'd felt her stir this morning and had realized he didn't want her to go.

And that hadn't happened with a woman in a really long time.

Apparently, Talia hadn't felt the same.

With a wry smile, he wondered if this was how women felt when he left in the morning.

Nice ego, Dane.

He could practically hear Jed sneer those words if Dane ever got the idiotic notion to mention his feelings to him. But that didn't negate the fact that he wanted to see her again. And now he was in the odd position of not knowing if she wanted the same.

Thoughts of Talia stuck with him all day, even through the throngs of screaming four-year-olds at a party complete with a petting zoo inside a heated tent on his sister's back lawn.

His nieces wore princess costumes so pink and frilly, his teeth hurt just looking at them.

His sister... Hell, she was dressed as the queen, gown, crown, and all.

"Jesus, can they get any louder? I swear they turn the volume up every time I see them. Good thing they're so damn cute."

Dane turned to smile at his older brother, Will, now standing behind him in the doorway to the tent. His sister had asked Dane to guard the entrance in case any toddlers made a break for freedom. So far, they were all too entranced with the baby goats, pig, sheep, bunnies, ducklings and even a tiny horse.

"Do you have any idea why they're dressed as princesses?

Shouldn't they be dressed like, I don't know, milkmaids or cowgirls or something?"

His brother gave him a bemused grin. "You're thinking way too hard about this. Livy's four. I'm not quite sure the concept of princess involves anything more than a frilly gown. As for the animals... well, doesn't everyone like fuzzy little creatures?"

"Only abstractly or at a distance."

Which went for most of the kids here, as well. Excepting his tiny princesses, who did look especially adorable today.

"I can see this is just reinforcing your commitment against children. Come on, Dane. You know Wayne and I are never going to have kids. We've got dogs. Hell, Wayne wants more than the three we've got now. But you..." Will clapped him on the back. "Our mother has big plans for you."

"Too bad she's probably going to be disappointed there."

"Ah, you're still young."

Dane rolled his eyes, thinking almost thirty wasn't really that young anymore, but his brother would never see him as an adult. "It would also mean I'd have to find someone I'd want to put up with for the next fifty years, and so far, that hasn't happened."

"Never say never, little brother."

Dane exchanged a smile with his brother who'd been out since he was twenty. No one who knew him had had to be told. Dane was pretty sure his parents had known since Will had hit puberty.

When Will, shaking and pale, had announced his orientation at dinner one night, their dad had looked up from his plate, patted Will on the back and said, "We know, son, but I'm glad you felt you could tell us."

Dane had watched his older brother fight back tears as he looked at their mom, who smiled and nodded. "Please invite your friend for dinner. When you're ready, of course. Oh, and we need to schedule your annual eye exam. I got a postcard in the mail."

Dane remembered laughing himself sick over the eye exam comment. Their mom was the queen of non sequiturs.

The next weekend Wayne had appeared at their table and had stayed for the next twenty years.

"You got lucky. Although why Wayne puts up with you is beyond me."

Will laughed and Dane noted how much he looked like their father. Practically a carbon copy at the same age. Dane took after their mother.

"That's what love will do to you. Makes you blind. Otherwise, everyone would ship their little darlings off to boarding school at the earliest opportunity. Jesus, they're loud. Step outside with me for a minute. I need to talk to you about something."

When they'd stepped far enough away from the tent so they didn't have to scream at each other to be heard, they both breathed a sigh of relief.

"I know your travel plans are starting to heat up, but we're losing Debby Bryant sooner than I thought."

Though their father headed the board of directors, Will was the CEO. Debby was Will's assistant. His pregnant assistant.

"Is she okay?"

"She will be, but the doctor put her on bed rest for the duration of her pregnancy. She was just about to get started on the annual board retreat. She's handled it for the past six years, and I honestly didn't realize how extensive the planning was. I need you to line up someone else to put it together. I figure we can hold it at Haven and you could just pass it off to Jared's planners there. I'm up to my ass in negotiations right now for that new cable station or I'd do it myself."

Dane shrugged, his mind already working. "Sure, no problem."

Will fell silent for a second. "Well, hell. That was way too easy."

Covering a long-suffering sigh, Dane settled for giving his brother a raised eyebrow.

Dane had never doubted his family's love, but being the youngest in a family of overachievers had cemented his status as a playboy who tinkered with a magazine.

Will's gaze narrowed. "Maybe it's time we give you a few more magazines to oversee. Obviously you have too much time on your hands."

Even though he knew his brother was ragging on him, Dane had the immediate urge to defend himself, which he squashed before he sounded like a whiny teenager. Amazing how your family could do that to you.

And yeah, maybe it was time to take on more responsibilities. He'd been coasting for the past year or so. Requests for his extracurricular services hadn't waned, but the network of people he worked with at the magazine had grown from a handful of people handling everything to more than twenty people around the world.

It wasn't that Dane had lost interest in providing his hacking skills. It was just that he wasn't doing multiple jobs at once. Of course, easily bored and a type A personality didn't mesh well.

"I believe I could handle a few more responsibilities. If there's anything you think I can handle."

The "Oh, shit" look on his brother's face was priceless. "Dane, you know that's not—"

Dane rolled his eyes. "Chill. Seriously, Will, you need to learn the fine art of sarcasm. At least Wayne understands me."

Will gave him a sideways glare. "That's because you and

Wayne have a lot in common. Which is really kind of weird. But you're serious, aren't you?"

Dane nodded. "Yeah, I've been meaning to talk to you, but I had a few things on my plate I needed to clear."

"Great." His brother smiled, clearly pleased, and Dane swallowed another sigh. "That's great. We'll set up a time to talk next week, okay? We just had a proposal come in, something new that I think will be right up your alley."

"Sounds good."

Will's smile grew. "Well, damn, little brother. Maybe we'll make you into a workaholic like the rest of the family after all."

"Yeah, don't get your hopes up for that. I'm not ready to tie myself to a desk completely."

Will sighed. "Don't blame you. Wayne keeps telling me I need to take it easier. I used to say I'll sleep when I die, but I'm beginning to see the error in my way of thinking."

Something in his brother's tone made Dane look closer at Will. There was an eight-year gap in their ages, so Will was almost forty. "Did something happen I don't know about?"

Will shook his head. "Nah, I'm fine. I'm just realizing that maybe you've had it right all the time. Less work, more play."

"Will."

Will smiled again. "Dane. Chill. Thanks for taking care of the board retreat. That's a huge load off my mind. Now, you want to tell me what's on your mind? You definitely look like you're working over something."

He was. It just wasn't anything he wanted to talk about. At least not with his brother. Who would tell their sister. Who would tell their mom. Who would definitely tell their father.

It'd be hard enough getting information on Talia from her friends because of the situation. But since he'd already burned that bridge with Jed and Belle...

Still, he'd never been one to look at a situation and admit

defeat at the first sign of trouble. And since he'd decided to pursue Talia, this board meeting had been dropped in his lap at the perfect moment.

"I've always got stuff on my mind."

"Usually that 'stuff' involves women or your next trip to some exclusive island resort."

"Nothing wrong with women and islands."

"Add a few cabana boys and we're set."

"What's this I hear about cabana boys? Are we finally taking a vacation?"

Wayne walked up to them, Dane's younger niece, Mariah, on his hip. Mariah reached for Dane immediately and Wayne let her go.

"Oh, sure." Wayne pulled a face at Mariah. "I'm always second-best when Uncle Dane's around."

Mariah plastered her tiny hands on Dane's cheeks and gave him a big kiss, which he returned then gave her a tight squeeze.

"I'm good with women."

Except Talia, apparently. But he was determined to change that.

Next time, Talia wouldn't be running out the door the next morning. And there would be a next time.

———

"HEY, sorry I'm late. I needed to stop in the boutique to drop off a few things and then I ran into Ty and, well..." Kate grinned. "Yeah, sorry, I'm late."

Talia leaned into her chair and grinned back. "Have you two settled on a date yet?"

Kate glanced down at the ring on her finger, her smile turning sweet. The sapphire was a Golden family heirloom that had been lost for years after being stolen. Kate and Annabelle had found the ring and the matching pin and their soul mates at the same time.

"Nope, haven't really talked about it lately, either. I'm not into all that pomp and circumstance, you know? When I get married, I want it to be on a beach on some tropical island."

Talia's mind immediately started to dress the scene, from the hurricane glass lanterns lighting the sandy aisle to the sun setting behind the couple as they said their vows.

"Don't worry." Kate's wry tone made Talia refocus on her friend. "You'll get to plan it out to your little heart's content, because I sure as hell don't want to deal with all the crap. But... you *will* be in my wedding. I won't have near as many guests as Annabelle, so you will have no excuses."

"According to you, I won't have to worry about that for a while. We'll discuss it later. So, are we all set for the bachelorette party?"

"Yep. I only had to tell Tyler we needed a few rooms at Haven for the night and he snapped his fingers and made it happen. Gotta love a man with power. Since March is a slow month, there'll only be a few other guests there. We'll have a masseuse, a manicurist, and our own bartender and chef. Dating a man who has his own hotels is a definitely a plus."

"Guess it's a good thing he's good in bed, too."

Kate's grin was blinding. "Oh, honey, you have no idea."

Not about Tyler, no. But Dane...

"What's that look for?"

Shit. Kate was too eagle-eyed for Talia's sanity. "What look? I don't have a look."

Now Kate's eyes widened. "Yes, you absolutely do have a look. The question is, why do you have that look?"

Talia huffed out a sigh. "There's no look and there's no need for questions. So what's on the menu for—"

"Oh, no. No, no, no." Kate wagged her index finger. "You're

not deflecting this time. We haven't had much of a chance to talk lately and, lucky you, I've got free time on my hands today. And I feel guilty. So spill."

"We spent most of Saturday night together."

"No, actually, we didn't." Kate's gaze narrowed. "But you did spend a hell of a lot of time talking to Dane."

And that was nothing she wanted to talk about now. "We were two of the people who weren't in a couple so, yes, we did talk a lot. He's a nice guy."

"Usually, yes. And he seemed particularly attentive to you."

Talia shrugged. "Like I said, only one of two single girls. And Trudeau seemed to have her hands full with Sebastian most of the night. Makes me think there's something going on there."

Kate cocked her head to the side. "Good try, but I'm not taking the bait."

Talia had to control the urge to roll her eyes. "What bait? I was just making an observation."

"And I know you better than you think. Did something happen between you and Dane?"

Why did Kate suddenly look worried? Was there something Talia didn't know about Dane? And did it matter? She'd spent one night with him. One really good night, but it wasn't going to happen again.

She'd been telling herself that a lot more than she usually had to after a one-night stand. Hopefully that wouldn't cause any trouble.

As for Kate's question, she didn't want to lie outright to her friend, but this wasn't a conversation she wanted to have now.

"Nothing happened." *Unless nothing includes sex.* "He seems like a great guy." *And he makes love like a freaking sex god.* "I had a really nice time talking to him."

And being under him for hours that night.

She felt the heat flush her cheeks and knew her pale skin would totally give her away. So she smiled and shrugged and waved a hand in front of her cheeks.

"And the man certainly isn't difficult to look at. I mean, what woman wouldn't want to run her hands over his chest."

Obviously, she didn't sell her deflection well enough because Kate's expression went from curious to worried again, which she quickly blinked away.

"Yes, he's definitely pretty, I'll give him that."

Talia forced a laugh, but her curiosity was starting to get the better of her. "I'm not sure he'd appreciate being called pretty."

"Dane's got a thick skin." Kate's tone became contemplative. "Pretty much everything rolls off his back."

Was that a warning? Why? And why did it matter?

It didn't. And maybe if she kept telling herself that, she would mean it. And not ask any more questions.

Now, though, she couldn't seem to help herself. "Sounds like you know him pretty well."

"Don't get me wrong, I like him." Kate grimaced. "And that just sounds like there's something wrong with him. Ah, forget it. Sorry."

But now Talia was curious. "*Is* there something wrong with him? I mean, he's Jared's best friend. And Annabelle seems to love him."

Which made Kate grimace again, before she quickly transformed it into a smile. "There's nothing wrong with Dane. He's got the reputation for being a playboy, though."

Which was nothing she hadn't been able to pick up on her own. "Best kind of man, if you ask me. They don't usually complain when you say, 'Hey, thanks for the sex, gotta run.'"

Kate shook her head. "No, Dane certainly isn't the clingy type. So you're still not in the market for a boyfriend?"

Talia mock shivered, glad to steer the conversation in

another direction, even if it was the sorry state of her romantic life. "God, no. Too much trouble."

"And sex isn't?"

"Sex is just sex. It's a release."

"But it can be so much more than that."

The look of sheer contentment on her friend's face made Talia shake her head and sigh. "You drank the Kool-Aid, sister."

Kate looked seriously pleased with herself. "Yes, I did. And I enjoyed the hell out of it." Then she nibbled on her lip for a second. "Hey, forget my ramblings about Dane. He really is a nice guy, nicer than you'd think, having that silver spoon in his mouth. And I wouldn't want you to think otherwise."

Talia had no trouble maintaining her smile. She'd had years of practice. "No problem. So we're all set for the bachelorette party?"

For a second, she wasn't sure Kate was going to let the conversation about Dane go. It was as if her friend was trying to warn her away from the man. Which she didn't have to do.

They'd spent a night together. One amazing night that had almost made Talia break her own rule about a second.

But that rule was in place for a really good reason. And considering his profession and family connections, she'd already crossed as far over her hard-and-fast line as she could.

She wouldn't be stepping over any more. Not even for a man who made her heart pound and her thighs clench just thinking about him. And if she thought about his mouth—

"Yeah, we're all set." Kate cocked her head to the side. "Shit. You slept with him, didn't you?"

Sighing, Talia shook her head. "There's still a few things we should go over for the party. I thought we could—"

"Tal, hang on a sec. I think—"

"Kate, honestly, there's nothing to talk about."

Damn it, she hadn't meant that to come out as sharp as it

had, because she'd just confirmed Kate's suspicions. And Kate definitely did not look happy. Which meant she knew something about Dane that Talia didn't.

And she wanted to know. She shouldn't, but she did.

Kate opened her mouth like she was going to argue some more, and Talia braced herself.

She loved her friends dearly, especially since she didn't have many. For so many years, she'd been afraid to make any for fear they'd find out who she really was. And the humiliation and the disgust she, her mom, and her brother had encountered had been more than enough to reinforce her belief that the fewer who knew, the better.

She'd never told Kate, Annabelle, or Sabrina. When they'd asked, she'd told them her dad had died and her mom had moved her and her brother up here to live with her parents.

It was the absolute truth. She simply had left out the more sordid parts of the story. As her mom had told her so many times, she hadn't been responsible for anything her father had done. Why should she have to live with his consequences?

Finally, after several silent seconds, Kate sighed and nodded. "Okay. What else do we need to discuss?"

"TALIA, hi. It's Dane Connelly. I hope I'm not catching you at a bad time."

The line fell silent for a long second before Dane heard Talia take an audible breath.

"Hi, Dane. No, you're not. I was just... pushing papers around, actually. I need to hire an assistant, but I'm a bit of a control freak."

"I know how you feel. It almost feels like I'm giving up if I can't do everything I need to myself."

She laughed and his gut tightened. Yes, this had definitely been the right decision.

"The curse of a type A personality, unfortunately. So... what can I do for you?"

Did he hear a hint of apprehension in her voice? Or anger?

Had she expected him to call sooner?

She'd practically run out of the room last weekend. Had she been running from him? Or maybe she just hadn't expected to hear from him. He wondered if he should be offended.

"I've got a business proposal for you. I'd like to make an appointment to discuss it with you."

Another pause. "What exactly are you proposing, Dane?"

Oh, she definitely sounded wary, which threw him. Usually he was the one dodging calls from one-night stands. He had to admit this kind of sucked.

"I need someone to organize the Connelly Media board retreat in a short amount of time. Think you can handle it?"

Another, longer pause. "Of course. I can give you references if you'd like."

"No references needed. Sorry, my question wasn't whether you could put the event together. My question was whether you could fit it into your schedule."

"What's the timetable?"

He had to admit her no-nonsense attitude was turning him on. "The week after Jed and Belle's wedding."

"Let me take a look at my calendar. Tell me a little about what you've done in the past for this event."

"From what I remember, its main function is for the board to spend time drinking, eating, and getting away from their spouses for a weekend."

"Is there an actual meeting involved?"

"A couple, yeah, strategically placed so the aforementioned

spouses don't get suspicious that there's only partying and no actual business."

Finally, he heard her huff out a soft laugh, and the sound made every hair on his body stand up. He'd never met a woman who'd evoked this response in him before.

"Look," he said, before she could speak, his brain thankfully five steps in front of his mouth.. "I think we should set up a meeting to go over the details. Can you come into the city for a few hours later this week? How about tomorrow? I know this is pretty short notice, but the woman who usually handles this for my brother is pregnant and was recently put on bed rest. We can meet, go over what she usually has planned and figure things out from there."

"Do you already have the venue?"

"Last couple of years we've held it at Haven. Debby and the conference coordinator there had started working on things, but apparently everything has been a little disorganized since Debby's health became an issue."

"So there are a few things laid out already?"

"Yes. You won't be coming in with nothing."

"That wouldn't be a problem."

No, he didn't imagine it would be. Talia had pretty much everything in her life under control.

Which just made him want to ruffle her. Make her a little flustered. Hell, make her a lot flustered.

Then he'd spread her out on a bed and spank her before he tied her on her stomach and fucked her.

Just thinking about her naked and tied made his cock twitch in anticipation.

"So, tomorrow?"

Silence. She could have been checking her schedule. Then again, she could be trying to think up an excuse not to.

"I can be free Wednesday afternoon. Does that work for you?"

He smiled but made sure his triumph didn't show in his tone. "Sure. How about we meet at Haven around one for lunch? I'll see you then, Tally."

He deliberately used the pet name he'd called her during their night together, but he didn't wait to hear her response.

Hanging up, he set his phone on his desk and looked out over the city from his window high above 12th Street.

But he wasn't looking at the bustling mess of the city below. He stared out at the murky gray sky and remembered that night a week ago.

SIX

"There's no reason to hyperventilate. It's a business meeting."

Talia stared at her reflection in the rearview of her car, making sure her lipstick wasn't all over her teeth and her mascara hadn't run on the drive down here from her office.

Exactly what she would have done to prepare for any other meeting.

Then why are your palms sweaty?

"Because I'm being totally stupid."

Which was an understatement.

She'd spent a night with the man. Had hot, sweaty, ohmygodthatwasgreat sex with the man. Then she'd practically run out the door the next morning.

Obviously, that night hadn't made much of an impression on Dane. He hadn't called afterward, hadn't texted.

She could admit to being a tad put out by that, but at least they hadn't had that awkward conversation where she had to turn down his offer to take her out for dinner and drinks and give the obligatory "It was great but I think we should just be acquaintances" speech.

No, this was much better. A business meeting.

No awkwardness there.

Right.

Why the hell had she agreed to do this?

For the resume credit. At least, that was the most obvious answer. The fact that his family owned one of the largest media companies on the East Coast should at least give her pause. The fact that she'd slept with him should have her running the other way.

Picking up her phone, she scrolled through her contacts. Her finger hovered over Kate's number, but that conversation they'd had last week made her pause.

Kate had been trying to tell her something about Dane, but she hadn't wanted to hear it.

Was that still the case?

She started when her phone began to ring, then shook her head at herself. She didn't recognize the phone number but that wasn't unusual. She gave out her cell number for business all the time.

"Hi, this is Talia. Can I help you?"

"Talia Driscoll? I'm Robert Polyak. I represent your father."

Her stomach dropped and she immediately went light-headed. Good thing she was sitting down, otherwise she might have stumbled.

"Is he okay?"

"Yes, he's fine. I'm sorry for calling out of the blue like this, but there are some papers I need you to sign."

Taking a deep breath, Talia tried to wrangle her thoughts into some semblance of sanity.

"Can you mail them to me?"

"I can. I just didn't want them to show up without advance notice. Due to the nature of the situation, I thought I'd better call."

Talia felt bitter laughter bubble in her chest. *Situation*

seemed like such a tame word. Their "situation" was so not tame.

"Thank you. I appreciate the heads-up. Can I ask... have you seen him lately?"

"I have. His situation hasn't changed." The lawyer sighed audibly. "I'm sorry, that's all I'm authorized to say." He paused. "However, if you have a message you'd like me to convey..."

Did she? And would it matter? In his state, he wouldn't hear it anyway.

"No. No message."

"I'll send the papers out today then. If you could return them as soon as possible, that would be helpful."

"What are the papers for?"

"As his legal guardian, you need to sign several documents for the hospital."

Now she really was glad she was sitting down. Maybe she'd put her head between her knees when she got off this call.

"Okay. I appreciate the heads-up, Mr. Polyak."

It wasn't until she cut the call that she allowed the tears to well. It'd been more than six years, and every time she got a call like this, she felt like she'd been punched in the stomach.

And there was no one she could call to talk this over with.

Not her friends, who had no idea who her father was. Not her brother, who continued to deny the fact that he had a father. And definitely not her mom, who didn't know Talia had legal guardianship of the man who'd ruined their lives.

It was a secret she'd never be able to tell her friends. Her story wasn't like Annabelle's. That was a tragedy.

Hers was a story of greed and consequences. Which just served to reinforce her decision.

She'd had her fun with Dane. But one night was all she got. Otherwise things got messy.

And she'd had enough mess to last a lifetime.

"HEY, YOU HAVE A MINUTE?"

Dane had been heading for the bar, leaving a message with Sabrina at the reception desk for Talia to find him there.

He stopped and turned to face Tyler. "Sure. What's up?"

"Just wanted to make sure we're set for next weekend."

Dane grinned. "Can't shut off that anal-retentive gene, can you, Ty?"

Ty's expression showed absolutely no reaction. "If it's in my genetic code then no, obviously, I can't. So, are we all set for next weekend?"

Dane sighed and crossed his arms over his chest. "Why does everyone assume I'm incompetent?"

Ty lifted one eyebrow. "I never said you were incompetent. Bad day?"

Dane shook his head, knowing he'd snapped at Ty for no reason. Guess it was better he take his pissed-off mood out on Ty rather than Talia.

"Honestly, yeah."

He'd gotten the one phone call he dreaded because there wasn't a damn thing he could do to fix the situation.

Ty's gaze narrowed. "Anything you wanna talk about?"

"No." The word came out sharper than he'd intended. "Thanks but no. Work-related."

Ty nodded. "So, we're good for next weekend?"

Dane had to laugh and he watched Ty's mouth curve in a grin. "I've heard from all of the guys. They'll be here by seven Friday night."

"Good. I've got everything else set. And Saturday?"

"Everyone's RSVP'd."

"Did you decide to bring anyone?"

Dane couldn't help but wonder if there was something

behind Ty's question other than a concern about numbers. "I'm considering my options."

Now Ty's eyebrows raised. "Interesting."

Dane smoothed out a scowl before it started. "Not really."

"You've never invited anyone in before. I'd say that's pretty damn interesting."

"Not really. And since when did you become interested in my sex life?"

Ty didn't answer right away and Dane knew that was never a good thing. When Ty put his mind to it, he could be a merciless interrogator.

And Dane had no desire to be interrogated. "I need to—"

"Dane, wait. Are you sure there's nothing wrong?"

Sighing, Dane shook his head. "Absolutely. I've got a meeting, so..."

Ty nodded slowly. "I'm sure I'll see you later. Have a good one."

Dane tipped his fingers and smiled what he thought was a pretty damn convincing smile. "You, too."

Turning, he headed again in the direction of the restaurant but stopped short when he saw Talia emerge from the elevator.

Holy hell, the woman practically took his breath away.

Tall and sleek, but not skinny. The slim black skirt she wore with black leather boots and a silky cream blouse enhanced her cool beauty but only made him remember what she looked like without them.

Jesus, he hadn't had a reaction to a woman like this since... well, pretty much never.

And it bothered the ever-loving hell out of him.

Taking a deep breath, he drew on decades of carefully cultivated charm. He'd learned from a master, after all. His dad was one of the most well-liked SOBs in the world. He could be the most ruthless businessman making a deal and also one of the most generous.

And his mom... She was the sweetest, most caring person in the world. Until you pissed her off or attempted to harm someone she liked. Then she could cut you down to size and leave you bleeding and you'd still want to beg her for forgiveness.

"Hello, Talia. Thanks for meeting me."

Stopping only inches from her, he held out his hand and watched her pull on her professional smile.

"Thank you for thinking of me for your event. I look forward to working with you."

Ah, she said all the right things. She maintained eye contact, shook his hand and kept that smile.

And yet, he felt her warm hand tremble the slightest bit in his and heard the slightest hitch in her breathing.

So she wasn't totally unaffected by him. Good, he could work with that.

Because, for the first time in years, he wanted to get to know a little more about a woman before he took her to bed again.

For the first time since Annabelle had come into Jed's life, Dane wasn't going to be satisfied with being second.

And he wanted more than one night.

TALIA HELD her smile longer than she'd thought possible, because the way Dane was looking at her made her remember exactly how he'd looked at her that night.

Not that she'd been thinking about that night. Or dreaming about it.

Nope, not at all.

"And I hope you continue to say that after we've worked

together. I thought we could meet in the bar. It's not too crowded in there this time of day and we've got a secluded booth."

Secluded, huh? She wondered if it was secluded enough to allow them to take their clothes off and—

No, probably not that secluded. And that was seriously not what she should be thinking about.

But, as she followed him into the bar, she couldn't help but notice how good he looked in a gray suit and purple shirt. His gray-and-white-patterned tied was slightly undone, giving her just a hint of skin at the hollow of his throat. The same skin she'd had her mouth all over that night. His too-long hair hung perfectly around his handsome face and her fingers curled unconsciously as she thought about sliding them through those dark strands.

Maybe this had been a really bad idea. Because the more time she spent with him, the more she thought maybe her absolute ban on second dates could be overkill.

Once they were seated, she took out her portfolio and a pen.

Dane smiled as he tapped his finger on her pad. "An old-fashioned girl, huh? Paper and pen. I like that."

"I find it works for me to take notes in longhand; then, when I transfer them onto the computer later, my brain processes the information again and I get ideas and plans I might not have thought of if I'd just transferred my notes from tablet to computer."

"Sounds like the method used by a lot of print reporters. The younger ones are all about digital recorders. I'm not sure most of them even take notes by hand anymore. But I still like to write my thoughts down on paper before I transfer them to digital."

His reminder of who he was should've killed any and all of her warm, fuzzy feelings toward him. That it didn't...

And to be totally honest, those feelings were more like hot and bothered.

"I didn't realize you wrote for your magazine."

Dane leaned back into the cushions of the booth, his lips still curved in a bit of a smile. "My dad's one of those guys who believe that if you're going to run the thing, you damn well better know how all the pieces work. I discovered I'm a fairly decent writer and a pretty shitty photographer. And I absolutely suck at layout."

She tried not to be interested. But honestly, she was fascinated.

"What did you study in college?"

His self-deprecating grin made her heart skip a beat. "Business. I know, I know, it's the major for guys who don't know what the hell they're going to do with their lives but, in my defense, there is no other course of study for third in line to a media empire."

"Is running a magazine what you wanted to do with your life?"

He laughed out loud this time and her thighs actually clenched. Thankfully, he couldn't see.

"Hell, no. I didn't have a clue what I was going to do with my life. I'm pretty good with computers and, when I was in college, I created a program that I used to hack into the college's computer system. I didn't get caught for several months. And when they finally figured it out, the IT profs brokered a deal with one of the Alphabet agencies, I apologized profusely for my misdeeds, set up a scholarship fund with the money I made off the program, and graduated on time."

"So you were a hacker?"

"I prefer 'creative systems analyst.'"

"Do you still create computer programs?"

He smiled, but there was something in his smile...

"I still like to play around with code now and then. What about you? What did you go to college for?"

"Event management."

"I bet you were top of your class."

She rolled her eyes. "Of course. Though, to be honest, there were about five other people in my major, so it wasn't all that amazing."

"I'm pretty sure you succeed spectacularly at whatever you set your mind to."

Oh, he was good. He made that line sound totally legitimate and the way he stared at her, with that warm smile...

At this moment, she *so* wanted to break her rule about seconds. That made him dangerous.

And you knew that from the moment you met him.

"So why don't you tell me about this retreat?"

He paused for a beat. "You don't like to talk about yourself, do you?"

No, she really didn't. "I just think it's better if we stick to business."

"Okay, business now. Dinner later. No business."

Her traitorous body thought that was a really great idea. Her sex moistened and her breasts tightened into sensitive peaks. Thankfully, he wouldn't be able to tell, because her bra had enough padding to hide it.

"Dane—"

"We were good the other night. Think how much better we'll be with practice."

The look in his eyes made her lips part so she could take a deeper breath. She swore he stole all the air in the room simply by existing.

Go ahead. Just say yes. What's one more night?

An image of her mom on the night Talia's dad had been

indicted popped into her head. Despair, fear, heartbreak, betrayal.

Chills made goose bumps rise on her skin. "I'm sor—"

"Just dinner, Talia." His calm voice steadied her. "I enjoyed your company. I'd like to spend some time with you. Dinner, drinks. I'll drop you at your doorstep four hours later, steal a kiss and be on my way, if that's all you're up for."

That wasn't all she was up for. Frankly, she'd skip dinner if it meant they got to the sex faster. And by faster, she meant immediately.

Damn, he was dangerous.

"Let me think about it, Dane. Okay? I've got a lot on my plate right now and not enough hours in the day. Why don't you tell me about this event?"

DANE HAD SEEN the flash of panic in Talia's eyes and realized he'd pushed her too far, too fast.

Which piqued his curiosity. There was a story here, and Dane was amazingly good at ferreting out stories.

Instead of pushing her, though, he gave her the details of the event.

Handing over the file his brother had given him, he spent the next hour going through it with Talia. He'd never given much thought to the retreat, only attending because his father expected him to be there. Dane had been content to let his brother and sister handle the heavy lifting of the family business, because that left him more time for his other endeavors, whether that was using his computer skills in creative ways or thinking up new ways to play at the Salon.

But he didn't want to screw this up in any way. This event was important for his family.

And Talia had a couple of amazing ideas off the top of her head that gave him an even greater appreciation for her skill as an event planner.

When they finally exhausted talk of the board function, he sat back as she began to pack up her materials.

When she bent to retrieve her bag from the floor, her shirt gaped open the tiniest bit and he caught a flash of creamy breast. Heat flashed through him like lightning as he remembered putting his mouth right there and biting into that soft flesh.

Christ, if he didn't think about something else and fast, he wouldn't be able to get up from the table without showing off the throbbing erection behind his zipper.

And he had the feeling that would send her running for the door. Far away from him.

"So, I'll be in touch Thursday with a preliminary agenda for approval. Then we can finalize the details."

She looked at him expectantly, and he knew she was waiting for him to get up, shake her hand, and send her on her way.

He should. She didn't want him to push her for more information, yet he saw the same heat in her eyes that he'd seen that night. Her signals were crossed, crisscrossed and recrossed.

He slid from the booth, reached for her hand to help her out and only held on to her hand long enough to make it clear he wasn't giving up.

"I look forward to it. And thank you again for fitting this into your schedule."

"I appreciate the opportunity to work for your family's company."

And wow, wasn't this just way too civilized.

Then she smiled, turned, and headed for the door.

He watched her ass the entire way.

SEVEN

"Hey, Dane." Belle's welcoming smile Wednesday night made Dane smile in return, and he bent to kiss her on the cheek. "Was Jared expecting you? He didn't tell me, and he's not here yet."

"Actually, no. I wanted to talk to you."

Her way-too-expressive face had him sucking in a deep breath as he walked into Jed and Belle's apartment. She had no idea what he wanted to talk to her about, but he knew he'd let this talk go unsaid for way too long.

He knew Jed was still in his office, and Jed knew Dane was here. He felt a little guilty for ambushing her, but they needed to rip the bandage off this situation before any more time had passed. And definitely before the wedding madness kicked into high gear this weekend.

"Okay, sure. Um, do you want a drink?" She closed the door behind her and headed for the bar. "Beer, wine, soda?"

"I'll take a beer."

She flashed a smile over her shoulder, auburn curls bouncing. "Sounds good. I think I'll join you."

Settling into a chair by the blazing gas fireplace in the wall, he watched Belle.

And realized the lust he'd felt for her from the first moment he'd seen her had tempered. Yes, he still appreciated the fact that she was beautiful and so damn sweet, but he also realized she didn't do it for him anymore. At least, not like she had.

Holding out the beer bottle to him, she slipped into the chair opposite him, curling her legs beneath her and smiling at him. He wished she didn't look so damn apprehensive.

"So, I'm guessing you don't want to coordinate our outfits for the party Saturday night."

He laughed, glad he hadn't started to drink yet. "Uh, no. You guess correctly."

"Then I guess you want to talk about sex."

He should've known she wouldn't beat around the bush or make this more difficult than it had to be.

"Yeah. I think we should."

Her nose crinkled. "This shouldn't be this difficult, should it? I mean, it's not like we didn't know it was going to end. I mean, I knew eventually you'd move on." She shook her head. "I don't mean move on, like we were in this committed relationship— Oh, wait. This isn't coming out right, at all."

Dane's smile grew at the same rate as her consternation, and finally he just started laughing.

"Oh, sure, laugh at me." She huffed. "You're abandoning me, after all."

"Sweetheart, you know I love you, right? I'm just not in love with you. And damn, when did this become a scene out of a chick flick?"

She pulled a face at him, still shaking her head. "Don't be sexist. And this isn't a movie, so none of this is going to be all wrapped up in a neat little bow in ninety minutes. And yeah, I love you, too. And I'd hate to lose you from our lives. You're Jared's best friend and he loves you. I don't know what he'd do without you to talk to sometimes. It's just..."

Uh-oh. "Just what?"

"I know this is going to sound stupid, but I'm going to be jealous. I'm sorry, but I have to be honest. I don't think I want to know about whoever it is that's got your attention now."

Yeah, that was the sticky part, wasn't it? "I never meant to hurt you."

She rolled her eyes. "Of course you didn't. I get that. You're not the villain of the piece here. It's just an odd situation, isn't it? I mean, who else do we really have to talk to about working out the end of a threeway?"

But it'd never been a true threeway relationship, because she'd never been his as equally as she was Jed's.

And he'd known that, right from the start.

"True. They don't write articles on this subject for magazines. Hell, I don't think even *Cosmo* would touch this one."

They sat in silence for a second, smiling at each other, but awkwardness was starting to creep in and he didn't want that.

"So," Belle finally spoke, "are we having this talk because you're planning to bring someone to the Salon party Saturday night?"

"Will it make you uncomfortable if I do?"

Her grimace held notes of apology. "Will you be really pissed if I say yes?"

"No way. Honey, I wasn't kidding when I told you how I feel. These next few weeks are all about you. I refuse to do anything to make you unhappy. Not only would I have to deal with Jed, but if anyone else hurt you, I'd have to kick their ass. So it'd be pretty damn stupid of me to have to kick my own ass."

"And will you think I'm a total nutcase if I tell you that I want you to bring whoever you want?"

"You're too smart to be a nutcase."

"Ugh!" She dropped her head back onto the seat cushion and huffed out a sigh. "This is hard!"

"Then let me make it easy on you. I'm not going to bring anyone—"

"No." Her head popped up and she stared straight into his eyes. "Oh, no. I refuse to be the woman who doesn't want her ex to move on and have a happy life. Even though you're not my ex. But— Ooh, see what I mean?"

He was laughing again and, by the time she'd stopped talking, so was she.

"So." Her smile still held a hint of sadness, but that actually made him feel better than if she'd simply smiled and told him to fuck anything that moved, she wouldn't care. "Who's the lucky girl?"

His gaze narrowed at the tone he heard in her question. "You already know, don't you?"

She shrugged and took a sip of her beer, closing her eyes for a few seconds. "Maybe I kind of noticed how much attention you were paying to a certain wedding planner."

"Does Talia know about our relationship?"

Belle shook her head sharply. "No, not at all. We haven't told her anything about the Salon either. I feel bad keeping secrets from her. She's one of my best friends, but..."

She paused long enough that he had to prompt her. "But what?"

"Talia's got issues."

"Don't we all?"

Her nose crinkled. "That does sound pretty stupid coming from me, doesn't it? What I mean is, she's still dealing with hers. Mine are old. I think hers are still fresh. And before you ask, no, I have no idea what they are."

"How long have you known her?"

"Since high school. She moved to the district around the same time I did. I think we became friends because we realized neither of us was going to pry into the other's life. We got closer after college, when she started working with Kate but... she doesn't really let anyone get *too* close."

"So you're telling me I should be prepared to get shot down if I pursue her?"

"There's no way in *hell* I'm going to tell you not to pursue her. I love Talia and I want her to be happy, but you've got to realize that a relationship with her might be out of the question. Then again, you're probably not talking about a relationship, are you?"

That one stung a little, but he maintained his façade. "I just met the woman. I'm pretty sure I'm not going to declare my undying love tomorrow."

Belle lifted her eyebrows. "See? That's what I'm talking about. You deflect better than anyone I've ever met."

He shrugged. "Years of practice."

"Talia's got years of practice, too. But if you're just looking for sex... well, then I guess it doesn't matter."

A cell phone beeped somewhere in the room and though it must have been hers, she didn't leap up to get it. She sat there staring at him.

"Aren't you going to get that?"

She shook her head. "It's Jared. He wants to know if he can come back."

"And why wouldn't he?"

"I'm guessing he's waiting for you and me to settle this."

"And have we?"

Sighing, she propped her elbow on the seat cushion and her head on her hand. "I guess if you have to ask... So, you want to stay for dinner?"

"Are you cooking?"

She sneered. Adorably. "Are you crazy? Why should I cook when there's a four-star chef a few floors below?"

"Then, yeah. I'd like to stay. If we're okay?"

Nodding, she hopped up but stopped at the side of his chair to smile down. "We're good. Just..." She made a face. "We're good. I'll let Jared know you'll be here for dinner." She paused. "But no dessert."

He burst out laughing.

"I DEFINITELY THINK you should get an office in Philly. If you're going to take your business to the next level, that's where you need to be. Not that there's not a market for your business in this area, but there are most definitely more opportunities to capitalize on in a bigger city."

"I know. It just seems like such a huge step. I mean I've only been in business a few years, and to take this kind of a step seems almost foolhardy. Rent is going to be so much more expensive, and there's travel expenses—"

Talia's mother frowned at her. "Wait, travel expenses? Why? I thought you'd be moving down there."

"I didn't say I was going to move."

Her mom lifted perfectly shaped eyebrows at her. "Why wouldn't you? Do you want to live in Berks County the rest of your life?"

"There's nothing wrong with Berks County, Mom."

"That's true. If you're in hiding."

"Mom."

Amelia raised delicate brunette brows at her daughter. Though Talia had her father's coloring, she looked much more like her mom. Her brother was an almost carbon copy of their father but, so far, no one had noticed the resemblance.

"I know I did my job a little too well when you were younger, honey. But it's been years, and I don't believe, after all this time, that anyone would so much as blink an eye at who your father was."

Talia gritted her teeth against the words that wanted to escape. Her mom always used the past tense when talking about Talia's dad. It made her want to scream.

"And I keep telling you. In my field, I'm supposed to be invisible. That's what makes a good event planner. When everything runs perfectly, no one is supposed to know I'm there."

"Yes, yes. I understand the concept." Her mom waved away her argument as if it were cobwebs in front of her face. "But you've been in hiding so long, I'm not sure you want to come out. And that's not good either. So what brought all this on?"

Talia blinked, swallowing hard, which made her mother's eyebrows rise again. Damn it.

"Nothing. Not really. I got a new contract today for a board retreat." She paused. "For Connelly Media."

"Ah."

"Yeah. Ah."

"For Pete's sake, Talia. It's not like they're going to investigate the background of everyone who works for them. I mean, I understand why you might be a little leery, but this goes beyond that. What's really the problem here?"

Talia grimaced. "Dane Connelly is Annabelle's fiancé's best friend."

"Okay?"

"Who I might possibly have had an encounter with."

Amelia set down the spoon she'd been using to stir tomato sauce. "And by encounter you mean..."

Talia glanced at the door, though she knew her mom was pretty fast on her feet and would probably catch her if she made a run for it.

Talia sighed. "A one-night encounter."

Amelia rolled her eyes as she picked up her spoon again. "Now why was that so hard? It's not like I think you're still a virgin. You're almost twenty-seven, not seventeen. I know you have sex, dear. Although, I'm thinking maybe you don't have enough. You never talk about guys. But you mentioned this one, so now I'm intrigued."

So was Talia. And that could lead to huge melodrama, which she *so* didn't want.

"Like I said, he's Jared's best friend. And he has the reputation for being a huge playboy."

And there it was. The one word guaranteed to set off her mom.

"Ah."

But instead of the pinched, angry look her mom's mouth usually got when any reference, even one this slight, to Talia's dad was made, right now, she just looked sad.

Maybe the years had finally softened the pain of her father's massive betrayal. It'd probably been a few years since they'd even talked about her dad, so maybe her mom had finally softened. And it wasn't like Amelia hadn't dated. She'd been seeing a local guy for years.

"So that's what you're afraid of," Amelia continued. "He really did a number on all of us, didn't he?"

"I didn't bring up Dane to talk about Dad. I'm sorry. Just—"

"No, sweetheart." Amelia put down the spoon again and rounded the kitchen island to put her arms around Talia. "Don't be sorry. He's your father. And even though what he did was reprehensible, he loved you and your brother. And me, as much as he could, anyway."

"I really don't want to talk about Dad."

"Someday we need to. We've let this talk go too long." Then her mom smiled. "But for now, let's talk about this guy who seems to have you all tied up in knots."

"TALIA, it's Dane. I was wondering if you were free tonight. I'd like to take you to dinner."

Dane had decided the best way to approach Talia was head-on.

Especially after his talk with Belle yesterday, he figured the only way he was going to get Talia to go out with him was to steamroll her with charm and determination. While his charm skills were highly evolved, his determination skills could probably use a little work.

Honestly, he hadn't really had to work too hard at anything to make most things happen.

"Hello, Dane. Nice to hear from you."

He heard droll amusement in her tone and determined that to be a good thing. "I'm glad you think so. I'm actually thrilled to hear your voice."

"I do believe we had a meeting yesterday where you heard my voice."

"True, but it's been a good twenty-four hours since then."

Now, she laughed, low and sexy and, damn, if that didn't make his cock twitch. "Wow, you just say all the right things, don't you?"

"I try. It helps if you're honest. And I'm honest when I say I'd like to see you again. Tonight, if possible. For dinner. I'll come to you if that makes the decision easier."

She paused and he wondered if she was biting her bottom lip. She did that when she thought things through. She also did it when he squeezed her nipples between his fingers.

And now he really had a raging hard-on.

"Okay. I think... Sorry. Let me start over. Yes, Dane, I'd love to go out with you tonight. I actually plan to spend tonight in the city. I have a meeting tomorrow morning and didn't want to drive down during rush hour."

"Are you staying at Haven?"

"Yes."

"Do you mind if I take you somewhere other than Haven for dinner?"

"Of course not."

"Then I'll meet you in the lobby at seven. Dress casual. Jeans and a t-shirt."

"O—Yes, that sounds good. I'll see you then."

"Bye, Tally."

He didn't wait to hear her response. He told himself he'd heard everything he needed to hear, but there was a part of him that was worried she might back out.

Something he'd never worried about before with any woman.

And now he couldn't put it off any longer.

After a quick glance to make sure his office door was closed, he called up a browser and started to search.

He was good at this and loved the clack of the keys under his fingertips as he began digging. Starting with her public face, he went through her website page by page. Then he went back.

Two hours later, he was squinting at something on his screen when his cell rang. He checked the number, just to be sure it wasn't Talia, and grimaced when he realized he probably shouldn't let this go to a message.

"Hey, Greg. What can I do for you?"

"Dane, I need a favor."

Greg was a good friend of Jed and Ty's and, by association, of his. Dane liked the guy a lot, even though he had the instincts of a shark. Greg actually reminded Dane of his dad. They had the same type A personality that put most alpha males to shame.

"What's up?"

"I need a background check on someone I'm considering for a position, but I don't want anyone to know I'm even considering the person. Tyler told me you could handle this."

Okay, now he was intrigued. "Give me the details."

"Nicky Gerhart."

"Why do I know that name?"

"He's the lead singer of Sebastian's band, Baseline Sins. And I lied. I'm not thinking about hiring him. Baz is having some issues with Nick and I think it would help to have some concrete facts."

"Anything in particular you want me to look for?"

"Yeah, there's a girl."

"Have anything more than her gender for me to go on?"

"Not really, but apparently she screwed them both over, so she shouldn't be that hard to find."

"You do know they're rock stars, right? Finding one particular groupie could be like trying to find a needle in a haystack."

"And here I thought you were good."

Dane smiled at the friendly jab in Greg's tone. "I am."

"Then I trust you to get it done. So everything's set for Friday? You need help with anything last-minute?"

"No, I got that under control too."

"Good to hear it. But if you need anything, let me know. If I can't do it myself, Trudeau will have it handled in seconds."

Trudeau, Greg's assistant, was the most efficient person Dane had ever met. And that was saying something considering the level of perfection his sister had attained.

"Thanks, but we're good."

"So, you bringing anyone Saturday?"

"Why is everyone so damn interested in my love life lately?"

"Huh. Tyler was right. So who is she?"

"Jesus, what the fuck is up with everyone? Now that you're

all seeing someone that means everyone else has be in the market. Give me a break."

"Talia's a damn pretty girl."

"Oh, for fuck's sake."

"Hey, man, just saying." Greg's amusement was plain in his voice. "You could do worse. She's pretty damn smart, too. Trudeau's meeting with her tomorrow to talk about her handling the party after the premiere."

Which was why she was staying in town tonight. He should probably thank Greg, but he wasn't going to give the guy any more ammunition.

"I'm sure you'll find her to be well-suited for the job."

Greg laughed and Dane shook his head. Bastard.

"I'm sure I will," Greg finally said. "See you soon. You have a good day."

Dane would rather have a good night. With Talia.

***

"SO YOU'RE GOING out with Dane tonight? Holy shit, that's like a major life event for you, isn't it? I mean, you already slept with the guy and now you're giving him a second chance. That's unheard-of for you."

Talia looked over her shoulder toward the bed with raised eyebrows. "Why exactly did I invite you up here to help me pick out something to wear if you're going to give me the third degree?"

Sabrina laughed, stretched out on Talia's hotel bed like a pinup. Her long, golden-brown hair fell in waves to the white down comforter, and her ample curves filled out the plain black t-shirt and jeans in ways Talia could never hope to do.

"Because you knew I'd want to talk, which means you want to talk. So talk."

"There's not really anything to talk about. Yes, we're going to dinner. It's just dinner."

"And you didn't deny the fact that you already slept with him, so obviously you did."

"There's no obviously about it."

"Yeah, actually, there is, when you're as pale as you are."

With a huff, Talia tossed the shirt in her hands on the bed and turned to face Sabrina. She had already pulled on her favorite jeans that made her ass look like it actually had some curves to it, and she knew she looked damn good in her favorite cream, lace-and-silk bra and panties.

But the shirt was giving her fits.

"He said casual. How casual is casual in Philly? I mean, should I be wearing a silk shirt or a t-shirt?"

"You are thinking way too hard about this. And where's Kate when we need her? She's the one who handles the clothes questions. I'm just here for moral support."

"I don't need moral support."

"Moral support, emotional support, whatever."

"What I need is for someone to tell me what shirt to wear."

"Oh, for— That one."

Talia held out both hands, each holding a different shirt. Plain, conservative. Boring.

God, she was totally boring.

"No, not those." Sabrina pointed at the weekend bag Talia had packed. "*That* one."

Frowning, Talia pulled out her old Roller Derby team shirt. "This? I brought this to wear home in the car tomorrow."

"That's perfect." Sabrina sounded resolute. "It's a great color on you, it's tight in all the right places, and it's fun. Seriously. That's the one."

"But—"

"No buts. You wanted my opinion. I say wear that."

With a disgruntled huff, Talia pulled the shirt over her head, tucking it into her jeans before turning to look at herself in the mirror.

"Damn, you're right."

"And, bonus, you actually look like you have some fun in your life. Why'd you give up your team, anyway?"

Brushing her fingers down the silky soft, dark green cotton, Talia sighed. "Not enough time in the day. I kept missing practices because of work."

Her team had been sorry to lose her and she'd been even sorrier to leave. The rush she got from skating and the speed and the comradery with her teammates had been amazing. Those few hours a week in the rink had sometimes felt like the only time she could completely let herself go.

"That's too bad," Sabrina said. "I know how much you enjoyed it."

Talia smiled, letting her fingers trail over the emblem of the dragon wearing quads and a helmet, his tail swiping out at a rival player.

And on the back, her nickname, BlondieBombs. If she kept her hair down, maybe he wouldn't notice. Then again, Dane pretty much noticed everything.

"Yeah, I did. But we all have to grow up and be responsible sometime."

In the mirror, Talia smiled as Sabrina fell back on the bed, arms outstretched.

"Oh, the horror." Sabrina's overly melodramatic tone made Talia laugh. "But that doesn't mean you can't have fun anymore. You just have to remember how. Oh, wow. Look at the time. You better get a move on. I know how you hate to be late." Sitting up again, Sabrina bounced off the bed. "And I've got a date, too. As long as he doesn't cancel again."

"Hey, Bree, is everything okay?"

"Yes, yes, everything's fine. I'm just feeling a little sorry for myself. I knew when I started this relationship that Greg was always going to be busy. It's just taking me a little longer to adjust to his schedule. I thought it would get better when he moved here full-time. Sometimes I feel like he has even less time for me now. But..." she drew out the word to several syllables, "I don't doubt that he loves me. We'll work the rest out. Ooh, wear that black leather jacket."

Talia was still laughing when she stepped out of the elevator into the lobby but didn't see Dane right away. She swept her gaze around the lobby and finally spotted Dane hidden halfway behind a column near the atrium entrance.

She could tell from his body language that he was talking to someone. Laughing with someone.

As she drew closer, she realized that other person was a woman.

A beautiful brunette who had her hand on Dane's arm as she laughed with him.

Talia's smile died an immediate death, and Dane chose that moment to turn and find her.

His gaze narrowed and she immediately pulled another smile.

Dane bent toward the other woman, kissing her on the cheek before making his way to her. If she wasn't positive she couldn't be, Talia would be worried that what she was feeling was jealousy.

And that would be awful, wouldn't it?

"Hi."

God, that voice made her smile more real. And that was so not good.

"Hi."

Bending down, he brushed a kiss against her cheek as if he

knew she wouldn't let him kiss her full on the mouth. Not even after the night they'd spent together.

Or maybe he just wasn't into public displays of affection.

"You look great." He took a step back and let his gaze slide down then back up. "Are you ready to leave?"

"Of course."

As they headed for the door, Dane put his hand on her lower back, just below the hem of her short jacket, letting her feel the heat of his fingertips.

A melting warmth began low in her body. She really needed to get a handle on this lust or she was going to do something she'd regret. Maybe not at the time she was doing it, but probably later.

"Would you like to know who I was talking to?"

She flushed, hating that he'd read her so easily.

"I really don't need—"

"She's one of the board members. I didn't introduce you because she would've grilled you about the retreat and I didn't want to waste our time together fending off her questions. Trust me, you'll be happy I did when you meet her at the retreat. The woman hasn't met a moment of silence she hasn't tried to fill."

"I'm sure I'll be able to handle her," Talia said as he opened the door to his car, a sleek black Dodge Challenger. "I've dealt with several brides and their mothers, all of whom have an opinion about how their wedding should be handled."

"I'm sure Belle hasn't been difficult to work with," Dane said after he'd slid into the driver's seat and got them onto the street.

"I don't think Annabelle could be annoying if she tried. Kate... She's a whole other story. Don't get me wrong, I love her, but she and I have some pretty strong opposing opinions. So, where are we going?"

"I'd like it to be a surprise, unless you absolutely have to know."

A surprise? She typically didn't like surprises unless she was the one in charge of them. They made her twitchy. But Dane looked happy and she didn't want to ruin this for him.

"Nope, I'm fine."

"Then I hope you'll enjoy it."

She was pretty sure she'd enjoy any time she spent with him.

They kept the conversation light as Dane drove out of downtown and into one of the suburban neighborhoods. The buildings were brick, older but not run down. Several showed signs of fresh renovation, and there were a few small children running up and down the sidewalks even though it was dark and cold.

It didn't take long to get where they were going and when Dane finally parked in a guarded lot in an area of the city she'd never been in, she had to admit to being extremely curious.

After getting out of the car, Dane led her to a building that looked like a warehouse. Built of the same brick as the surrounding neighborhood, the building was about two stories tall with no windows.

Music pounded through the walls and she started to smile.

She recognized this place. Even though she'd never been here, she knew exactly what lay inside those walls.

She turned to Dane, who smiled at her. On another man, that smile might have been cocky or smarmy. Dane managed to make it look sweet and sexy at the same time.

The fact that he knew this part of her background wasn't a surprise. In fact, it should be a little frightening. He'd dug into her background, at least far enough to know this about her.

The insane need to smile warred with the fear to run away. Far away. And fast.

"How did you know?"

He shook his head. "A journalist never reveals his sources."

"So you admit to poking into my life?"

His eyebrows lifted. "I don't consider it poking. I call it getting to know you."

She really wanted to be upset. Really should be worried about what else he'd found. But she couldn't be when he so obviously had gone out of his way to find something to do on their first date that she loved.

"Do you skate?"

He looked a little sheepish. "I can, but, I'll tell you right now, it's not gonna be pretty."

She laughed, as he'd meant her to, and he got out of the car to open her door and help her out.

And even though she should be angry, should feel somewhat violated, she couldn't help but be a little thrilled by the fact that he liked her enough to want to know something about her.

That he'd picked a skating rink as a first date...

Dangerous. The man is dangerous.

But for the first time in a very long time, she didn't *want* to care about someone finding out about her past. Didn't want to worry about another person she thought was a friend turning her back on her or treating her like a leper. Like she'd committed a crime... when the crime had been her father's.

Smiling up at Dane, she let herself look at him.

Under a black pea coat, his long-sleeved t-shirt was for a band she'd only vaguely heard of. His jeans were comfortably worn and not because he'd bought them that way. This man didn't always live in suits and ties. But no matter what he wore, he looked good. And he looked particularly good naked.

Thank god the temperature tonight hovered around forty degrees or her cheeks would betray her internal temperature.

Which was getting way beyond overheated.

"I thought we could eat first and then skate," Dane said. "I think I'm going to need a little fortification before I make a complete fool out of myself."

"Sure."

She looked down the street both ways but saw nothing that resembled a restaurant.

And he kept walking toward the rink.

When she looked up at him with a question in her eyes, he smiled.

"I found out about this place when one of our local papers did a feature on the chef here. She used to run a four-star restaurant in Paris before she moved to Philadelphia for a job at one of the hotels, but she was fired when her drug habit got out of hand. She got arrested in a sweep for possession and intent to purchase. She did community service in the neighborhood at the Boys and Girls Club, teaching cooking classes to the kids. One day, one of the kids told her she should apply for a job at the rink because they'd just lost their cook and she made really good grilled cheese and the kids all loved her."

"Do you know her personally?"

Dane nodded. "I've met her a few times. She's a cross between Julia Child and... that woman who cooks on TV and can't talk without her hands. I can't think of her name. Anyway, I'll introduce you. You'll like her. She's one of a kind."

Obviously Dane liked her. He had a fond smile on his face while he talked about her, and Talia had a moment to wonder if that tight feeling in her chest really was jealousy.

Then she dismissed the thought out of hand because if she didn't, she might have to admit something she wasn't sure she wanted to even consider.

Then Dane opened the door and the smell hit her.

She took a deep breath. God, there really was nothing like

the smell of a roller rink.

If you'd never been in one, it'd be difficult to describe. Old leather and well-worn wood and rubber and popcorn.

The aroma skated the line of being offensive, but for someone who'd spent hours upon hours in a rink, it smelled like the next best thing to being home.

The inside of the building was huge and the rink took up only half of the space. A wall with several openings separated the rink in the back from the front half of the building.

In the front, the food counter ran along one side, the skate rental area was on the other, and between them, mismatched tables and chairs covered the rest of the open area interspersed with benches to put on your skates.

They stopped at the lockers along the front, where Dane stowed their coats and her purse, then led her to the food counter.

"Oh, my god, the menu's huge," she commented when they stopped just beyond the counter. "And it has lobster mac and cheese on it."

"Which is fantastic, but personally I like the cheesesteaks. Not traditional at all, but they're fucking amazing."

She laughed at the fanboy awe in his tone, and they agreed to order both so they could share, along with a couple of locally brewed root beers.

As they sat and waited for their orders to be delivered, she propped her hand on her chin and stared at him.

"This isn't exactly what I expected tonight," she admitted. "When you said casual, I figured you meant sports bar and a basketball game or something like that."

Resting his arms on the table, he shook his head. "I could have, but I wasn't sure if you liked hockey. I'm not a big basketball fan, but I'm a lifelong Flyers fan. They're not in town tonight, but they will be later this week. I can get us tickets."

There was a hint of a question in his voice, but not much, and Talia wasn't sure she should let him get away with planning out more dates than she'd agreed to. But there was something about Dane that made her want to agree.

"Let me check my schedule. I'm not sure when I might be able to fit that in."

He didn't look at all put off by her hesitation. "No problem. They play Saturday and Sunday. We've got season tickets but I'm the only one who uses them regularly."

"So you're a hockey fan?"

"Played a little in high school and college but never really had the time or the inclination to take it any further. So tell me how you got into Roller Derby. Have you ever been to this rink before?"

"I've never been here, no. I don't think I've ever heard of this place so they probably have never had a team. There aren't that many teams around anymore. It's not a hugely popular sport."

"So how did you get into it?"

Ah, tricky subject. "After my mom moved my brother and me to Adamstown to live with my grandparents, I was... kind of angry. My dad had left"—huge understatement—"and my mom cried a lot and my brother was getting picked on all the time."

She didn't mention the death threats or the slashed tires or how many times their front door had been egged or spray painted or had other, grosser things thrown at it before they'd left Kentucky.

"Sounds like it was a bad time."

A bitter smile curved her lips. Bad didn't cover it. "It was. Still, lots of kids' parents split up and they get through it. We did. But my mom thought I needed a hobby. I saw a flyer at the school for a Roller Derby exhibition at a rink about twenty minutes from our house. Since I was pretty much a raging bitch at the time, I figured my mom would never agree to me being in

Roller Derby. But she caved, and I was hooked after the first practice."

Talia looked around the space with appreciation. "This is such a great place," she said.

"It's pretty much a community effort. The building was an abandoned warehouse that was attracting lowlifes and criminals until a few of the neighborhood parents banded together to get the building donated to the local community group. With donations from local businesses and a few grants, they were able to put this place together. They started a foundation to run it. Then Estella took over the kitchen and people started to come here just to eat, and things kind of snowballed. The kitchen funds most of the expenses now and the neighborhood kids have a safe place to skate."

Their dinners arrived then, and the next two hours were the most fun Talia had had with a man. Ever. Okay, maybe they were a close second to the hours she'd spent in bed with Dane.

And maybe they'd take a backseat to the hours she might spend in bed with Dane tonight.

When it was time to put on skates, she started to smile the second she stood and felt those eight wheels beneath her feet.

The sense of motion was like nothing else she knew.

Standing, she pushed off toward the rink then back to find Dane on his feet, looking pretty steady.

"I thought you told me you didn't skate very much?"

He smiled. "I said it wouldn't be pretty. I'm more used to roller blades. Played roller hockey in college for a few years. These skates seem like they should be more stable because you have four wheels each, but it takes some getting used to."

Yeah, it did. But Talia wasn't thinking about skating at the moment. She was thinking how she was getting used to him. How easy it was. How easy he made it.

"Come on, Dane. I'll hold your hand. But if you fall, you're on your own."

"I won't drag you down with me, sweetheart. Trust me, I don't want to bruise any part of that gorgeous body."

Just that easily, he made her breath catch and her body flush with heat. And she wanted so badly to tease him back.

So, pushing off from the wall, she turned and smiled at him, a hint of exactly what she was feeling, and encouraged him to chase her.

And he did.

———

"I DON'T THINK my ass is ever going to be the same. Jesus, I must be getting old."

From the passenger seat of his car, Talia laughed, the sound making his cock harden, even though the pain running down his flank made him wince.

"You did go down pretty hard, but you were doing really well up until then."

"Says the woman who didn't fall once."

She shrugged, her expression haughty and fucking hot. "What can I say? I'm just that good."

"Yes, you are."

He knew she understood his double entendre because she blushed. Even though it was too dark in the car for him to see it, he knew she was. He could tell by the way she glanced away and then back again.

"So can I take you out for a drink?" The rink didn't serve alcohol and Dane didn't want the night to end yet. "We can go to the hotel bar, or tell me what you're in the mood for and we'll find a place."

She hesitated, as if weighing her options. Had he pushed for too much, too fast?

"Would you like to come up to my room for a drink? A bar stool probably wouldn't feel too great on your abused backside right now."

"I'll be sure to thank you for that tomorrow morning." Hopefully after spending the night in her bed again. Which he was smart enough not to say out loud. "And the bruises were worth it if you had fun."

Her lips curved again. "I did. I miss skating. Thank you for tonight, Dane. I had a great time."

"I'm glad." He reached for her hand resting on her leg and lifted it to his mouth to press a kiss against the inside of her wrist.

It was an unconscious gesture but one that felt right. Especially when she shivered but didn't pull away. Her skin felt soft against his lips and her scent made him want to brush the hair away from her neck and bury his nose there.

Christ, if he didn't watch it, he'd wind up a love-struck fool like Jed. And Tyler. And Greg.

Holy hell, his friends were dropping like flies. And if he wasn't careful, he'd end up just like them.

Or maybe he'd just be very, very lucky.

They made the rest of the drive to Haven in silence, which didn't have a chance to get awkward because they were only minutes away.

They took the elevator to her floor and Dane fought the urge to pin her against the elevator wall and kiss her until she melted against him.

He realized he wasn't used to this sense of vague insecurity creeping into his gut. Especially not when it came to women.

He'd always been good with women. He knew what to say to them, how to get them to smile or laugh or fall into his bed.

He was especially good at getting them to cry out his name when he fucked them.

Talia made him work for every sigh. And damn, that made him so fucking hot.

But he'd already told himself not to push her because she'd run.

He had no idea why. His rudimentary background search had turned up her Roller Derby past, the fact that her mom had moved here with her and her younger brother when she was younger, and where she'd gone to high school and college.

He hadn't dug any deeper because he'd felt it would be a breach of privacy. And frankly, he wanted her to tell him. Wanted her to talk to him. Wanted to find out everything there was to know about her.

This was new territory for Dane, and he loved new experiences. It was one of the reasons he and Jared had started the Salon.

And thinking of the Salon made him that much more determined to get to know her better. Because he wanted to invite her into the Salon.

When they reached her floor, she huffed out a quiet laugh. "I feel like I've been staying here so much I should just take out a lease."

"Are you getting a lot of work in the city?" He followed her down the hall, realizing this was the same room she'd stayed in before.

"I am, actually. More than I expected." She pushed open the door and stepped inside, waited until he walked through, then closed the door behind him. "Since it's just me, I thought I'd have trouble getting my name out there, but a lot of people are looking for a smaller operation, which means a lower price tag."

"And the fact that you do an amazing job doesn't hurt."

She turned to flash him a smile over her shoulder as she headed for the kitchenette, but he saw nerves in her expression.

Was she nervous? Or just anxious? Did she expect him to drag her off to the bedroom and ravage her?

While that sounded like a hell of a good idea, he still didn't have a good enough read on her to do it. And that only made him more determined to find out all he could.

"Thank you. It helps that I really do love what I do."

He followed her, stopping on the other side of the breakfast bar. "Were you in charge of the bachelorette party, as well?"

She pulled out a bottle of wine from the fridge and held it up. He barely glanced at it before he nodded. He didn't care if she held up a bottle of Wild Turkey. He'd drink it because she gave it to him.

"Actually, Kate handled most of that. We're spending the night at the spa. Manis, pedis, personal chef, massages. I cannot wait. What about the boys... what are you doing?"

"Nothing half as exciting. No strippers. We'll be at Haven. We hired a dealer. Jed likes poker, so we're playing poker."

She handed him a glass of wine. "Sounds like you don't like to play."

"Actually, I love to play. Just not with cards."

He loved the paleness of her skin. She couldn't hide a flush of heat to save her soul. And he loved how her gaze dipped for a second, as if she could hide what she was thinking.

But she couldn't.

The heat in her cheeks reflected the heat in her gaze, and he heard her breath catch.

"And what do you like to play?"

"Do I really have to answer that question?"

She shook her head but he wanted to hear her voice, so he figured now was the time to test the limits. Or, at the very least, push at them a little.

"Talia. Say it. Do I have to answer that question?"

She didn't say a word but her eyes opened wide at the commanding tone in his voice, and he very nearly cursed himself out loud for forcing the issue.

The heat in her cheeks could be either arousal or anger and he so hoped it was the first. Because if it wasn't, he could lose her right now.

A split second later, her gaze latched onto his. "No, you don't."

Fuck. There it was. That combination of submission and defiance that made him harder than a damn fencepost.

"Tell me, Talia. What do I like to play?"

Come on, baby. Don't back down on me now.

Her chin lifted the tiniest bit. "I think you like to play games I don't have the rules for."

Damn it, that sounded like she was backing away. "Don't sell yourself short. You're more than capable of holding your own against me."

Her gaze dipped to her own glass of wine and she took a sip. "I'm not so sure."

Swallowing half his wine, he set the glass on the counter and made his way around it to her. She lifted her head to watch him, eyes wary but her lips parted as if she couldn't get enough air.

"Did you really only invite me up here for wine? I'm fine if that's the only reason. But I want to be clear about things. I don't want to make you nervous or do anything that might upset you. What I do want is to strip off all your clothes and lay you out on that bed again. And this time, I want to tie you to it."

He heard her swallow.

"Are you willing to play with me, Tally?"

He kept his tone even and straightforward, without an inflection of any kind. It was difficult as hell, because what he really wanted to do was lay her out on the counter, drop to his knees and put his mouth on her pussy.

She blinked several times, her skin flushed a bright pink. He wanted to spank her ass and see if it turned the same shade.

He had a hard time keeping himself from grabbing her and spinning her around so he could grind against her ass while his hands kneaded her breasts and he bit at her neck.

"I think you already know the answer to that question."

Her quiet voice still held enough backbone that he smiled. Damn, he absolutely loved strong women. He especially loved them when they gave him carte blanche to make them come.

"I want to hear you say it."

She continued to hold his gaze but made him wait for her answer.

He let her have the time, hoping like hell he hadn't misread her and that she couldn't see his sudden insecurity.

In the blink of an eye, her expression transformed and a slumberous heat infused her gaze and the curve of her lips. "I enjoy playing games with you, Dane."

Yes.

He actually had to plant his feet so he didn't grab her and bend her over the counter.

"Would you like to play one now?"

Her head tilted to the side. "I guess it depends on the game."

"I'll make sure you enjoy it."

Her lips curved even more and his blood pressure skyrocketed. He could barely control his urge to tell her to strip.

She raised her brows, taunting him. "Then what are you waiting for?"

He shot back the rest of his wine and set the glass on the table with a slight bang. She looked so damn cool and controlled. But the pulse at the base of her throat throbbed at a maddeningly fast pace. He wanted to lick it, suck it. Then he'd bite her. Hard enough to leave a mark but not enough to be painful.

"So who are you meeting tomorrow? You said you had a meeting."

She blinked, drawing in a quick, sharp breath. Then her eyes narrowed as she followed along with his change in topic.

"Trudeau. And supposedly Greg, but I doubt I'll see him. He seems to have a lot on his plate right now."

"You sound like you don't believe he does."

She wrinkled her nose and looked down at her drink for a second before she shook her head. "It's not that. I like Greg. I really do. I just don't like to see Sabrina upset."

Neither did he. He liked the younger woman. She was a sweetheart with a bright smile and a big heart who was totally in love with Greg.

"Maybe she needs to talk to Greg."

She smiled, a slightly wicked bent to it. "I'm not sure they do a lot of talking when they have time together."

Dane laughed. "You're probably right."

"So is that all we're going to do tonight? Talk?"

He controlled the urge to smile. She'd turned the tables on him and he liked that. "No. But I thought we could talk a little before I strip you naked and kiss my way down your body."

"Haven't we been talking all night?"

Was she that anxious to get him inside her? Good to know he wasn't the only one burning up. "We have, but sometimes a long buildup is just as hot as getting naked and horizontal."

She lifted her brows. "And sometimes making a girl wait too long for what she wants will backfire on you and she'll take other measures. Without you."

Fuck. "Maybe I'd like to watch."

Her head cocked to the side, as if fascinated. "Do you get off on watching?"

Yeah, he did. "Do you?"

She paused and he tried not to let on that he was holding his breath waiting for her answer. Because, holy hell, he really wanted her to say yes.

He wanted to invite her to go to the Salon with him next week. And he'd never had the urge to invite anyone solely for his own pleasure.

She held his gaze for several seconds before breaking eye contact. "Honestly, I'm not sure. I've never had the opportunity."

"Would you like to? Have the opportunity, I mean?"

A slight pause. "I guess that would depend on the circumstances."

It was the perfect opening, but he hesitated. Did he take the chance and introduce her to the Salon, now, while there was no one there? Or did he wait and risk scaring her away if he asked her to attend a sex party?

And when the hell did you start to overthink things?

Dane had been accused of being a lot of things over the years. Hedonist came up a lot. Heartless had popped up a few times, mostly from women who hadn't intrigued him half as much as this one did.

That's why he hesitated. Because he had a feeling this woman could mean more than a few nights of hot, sweaty sex. And he wasn't exactly sure how to handle the situation because he'd never been in this position before.

If a woman wasn't interested, he moved on to the next. There'd been a few over the years and he'd never given a second thought to them after they'd turned him down.

If Talia balked...

Then again, what if she didn't?

He didn't think she would. Christ, he really hoped she wouldn't.

"Dane? Is something wrong?"

He made up his mind. "No. Nothing's wrong. There's somewhere I'd like to show you. It's in the hotel so we're not going far. But... you'll need to sign a legal waiver."

Her eyes widened with amusement. "Is that a joke?"

He shook his head. "Not at all."

Her amusement faded and was replaced with curiosity.

"And you just happen to have a legal waiver on hand?"

"No, but I can have one waiting."

She shook her head, but he didn't think she was giving him an answer. "You've got to be kidding. You have to realize this all sounds a little too much like some B movie, right?"

"The waiver's necessary to protect everyone involved, you included."

"And what's so special about this place that I need to sign a waiver to even see it?"

"You'll never know unless you sign it. That's really all I can say. But I'm hoping you'll sign, Tally. Because I really want to show you. I think you'll enjoy it."

Her curiosity was getting the better of her. He could see it in her eyes.

"I swear there's nothing for you to be afraid of. You won't be hurt. You're not giving consent for anything. You're just agreeing not to talk about what and who you see."

She didn't respond right away, simply continued to stare at him.

When she didn't answer after a full fifteen seconds, he figured he'd lost her. A tight ball of regret started to form in his chest.

Finally, she set her glass on the counter and nodded.

"Okay. I'm game."

EIGHT

Talia had no idea what to expect when Dane waved her out of her room and back into the elevator.

His cryptic words and triumphant smile made her curiosity soar. But the fact that whatever he wanted to show to her required a legal waiver made her twitchy. Anything having to do with the law made her short of breath, and made her want to run the other way.

The lawyers her mom had had to deal with before and after her father's arrest and trial had made Talia wish to never see another one again in her life.

The fact that Dane wanted her to sign away her rights to talk about something should've been an automatic denial for her.

Instead, she rode with him to the fourth floor, which is where Jared and Tyler both had apartments.

When they got off the elevator, they didn't turn right toward the apartments. They turned left.

A few feet down the hall, Dane opened a door and waved her through into darkness.

A second later, she blinked as he turned on the light and an office came into view.

"This is Jared's personal office." Dane rounded the desk on the other side of the room and opened a drawer, as comfortable here as if it were his own.

"And he doesn't mind you digging around in it?"

Dane's gaze met hers for a brief second before he pulled out a sheet of paper and a pen and set them on the desk.

"He trusts me."

Three simple words said with such conviction.

"Did you tell him you were bringing me here?"

"There's no need. No one's here."

She looked around Jared's tastefully decorated office. "This is what you wanted to show me?"

He shook his head and pushed the paper toward her. "Read this and sign it if you agree. If you don't, no harm, no foul. We can go back upstairs and pick up where we left off. But... if you sign that paper, I can guarantee you won't be disappointed."

She held his gaze for several long seconds before she looked at the paper and pulled it toward her.

With deliberate movements, she picked it up and began to read.

The language was a straightforward nondisclosure agreement, basic and binding.

She read through it twice, just to make sure there wasn't anything she'd missed the first time around then signed her name to the bottom and pushed it across the desktop toward Dane, who took the pen from her hand and signed his own name as witness.

She raised her brows at him. "So tell me, what's the Salon?"

Dane smiled and her stomach did a little flip-flop. "It's easier if I show you."

Walking to the wall to the left of the desk, he pressed

against the molding. She couldn't help a tiny gasp as the wall split open to reveal a door.

"Well, damn." She looked at him with a smile. "What other surprises do you have for me tonight?"

"Quite a few, probably." He held out his hand. "Wanna get started?"

This time, she didn't hesitate. She closed the distance between them, took his hand and let him lead her into darkness that was filled with a soft light seconds later.

"Oh, wow."

Which didn't begin to describe her reaction.

She'd seen some amazingly beautiful spaces, particularly in her position as a wedding planner. But only one or two could rival this space.

The room took up at least a third of the entire hotel floor, probably more.

So much to look at, her gaze couldn't land on one thing in particular. It was visual overload.

So she forced herself to take it in pieces.

She looked up first, at the ornately decorated ceiling. Molding created interesting patterns and a chandelier hung dead center, dripping with crystal teardrops. Her gaze dropped to the silk wallpaper gleaming in the light from the chandelier, the pattern beautiful but not overwhelming. A perfect backdrop for the artwork.

And, oh, wow, the artwork.

"Those must be from Jared's collection." She couldn't take her eyes off of them. "They're stunning."

She'd seen erotic art before. Annabelle had an entire gallery full of it. The only shocking part about Jared's collection was the beauty of the pieces.

"He has an eye for it," Dane said from behind her.

"Annabelle and Jared truly were meant for each other, weren't they?"

"So you are a romantic at heart?"

The tone of his voice made her turn to give him a look. "What made you think I wasn't?"

He shrugged. "When you work in certain professions, sometimes you see the bad more than the good. It can skew your perceptions."

"Sounds like you have some firsthand knowledge of that."

"It's pretty hard to work in the news field and not be a little jaded."

That was getting a little too close to serious discussion, and she really didn't want to have a serious discussion right now. So she turned her attention back to the room.

The decadent elegance of it made her sigh.

She realized now that the room was octagonal, with several distinct areas.

Directly below the chandelier sat an octagonal game table. In one corner, a baby grand piano held court, lit by a leaded glass piano light that had to be Tiffany.

One wall was completely covered by a huge, glass-front display cabinet that held a collection of things she couldn't see from here.

Several distinct seating areas were scattered around the room and beautiful patterned fabrics covered the chaise lounges, chairs, and ottomans. One seating area sat in front of the majestic marble fireplace, now glowing with a gas fire that'd lit when Dane had flipped the light switch.

The room was a sensualist's dream. Every fabric, from the silk wallpaper to the velvet and brocade upholstery to the lush carpet beneath her feet, called out to be touched. Or caressed.

Her stomach tightened at the thought. "It's beautiful. Is everything authentic?"

She began walking toward the glass cabinet, intrigued by what she couldn't see.

"The artwork is. All the furniture are reproductions," Dane said. "We can get a little enthusiastic, and Jed doesn't want anyone to feel like they have to hold back in fear of breaking an expensive antique."

She stopped by the side of a thickly tufted chaise lounge, her fingers brushing along the curved arm, her eyes taking in images her brain hadn't yet made connections for.

This room... there was something about it that didn't add up.

"And what exactly does Jared use this room for? I've never heard anyone mention it before." Then she remembered the nondisclosure she'd signed. "And why did I need to sign a legal document to even know about this place?"

"Freshman year in college, Jed and I and a few other friends were sharing a couple bottles of whiskey and bitching about a mandatory class in world cultures. The professor was a real prick. Got off on tormenting freshmen. We decided to take him down a few pegs."

With his hand on her back, he pressed her forward, toward the case she'd wanted to check out earlier.

"Since a few of us had what you could call advanced computer skills, we hacked his private email accounts. And found a hell of a lot more than we expected."

She'd been listening intently... until her brain registered several of the items in the case.

And after several seconds, she realized her mouth had been hanging open.

Dildos filled one shelf. Glass, marble, wood, one or two made of material she couldn't identify. Beautiful works of art, some clearly antiques.

Different sex toys filled another shelf. Some had familiar shapes. Others were nothing she'd ever seen before. But some...

"Did you know there are underground Victorian erotica societies around the world?"

"No." She barely heard her own voice, and she swallowed hard.

Another shelf held whips, chains, paddles, clamps.

"Professor Kohn had this secret life as a writer and researcher for one of those societies." Dane stood right behind her, so close she felt the heat of his body seeping through her clothes, but not close enough to be pressed against her. "They're kind of like the Masons, but their organization met to discuss and reenact scenes from Victorian erotica."

She swallowed as her brain started to put the pieces together.

"So this is a sex club."

It made sense. The artwork, the furniture, the entire ambiance of the room.

And where had all the air in the room gone? Why couldn't she seem to catch her breath? Was she really turned on by all of this?

"No, not a sex club. We don't come here only to have orgies. And not just anyone is invited in. There were ten of us originally. Well, twelve, if you count Tyler and his former fiancée. We were all close friends and had been for years. We know each other, trust each other implicitly.

"With Professor Kohn's group, you had to be sponsored by at least three current members to get an invitation to be interviewed to join. Once you were in, you signed a confidentiality agreement. They had a required reading list and health screenings. Once all that was taken care of, if you were invited to join, you got to participate in 'scenes.'"

She swallowed, still checking out the contents of the cabinet. "And what are 'scenes'?"

His hands settled on her hips and she started. But he didn't release her. And she didn't want him to.

"They recreated scenes from books like *Fanny Hill* and *The Pearl*. Our scenes are more organic. We're not bound to a script. But the one trait we all share is that we're hedonists."

He'd leaned closer, his lips only centimeters from her ear. She tried to suppress a shiver but had no luck. She swore she felt him smile.

"So this is a room where people have group sex."

"No." He stepped away, and she couldn't decide if she was glad for the space or disappointed that he'd moved. Now he stood several feet away, staring at the case as if looking for something. "People have all sorts of sex in this room, not just group sex. Sometimes we use it in pairs. Sometimes in threesomes. Sometimes... yes, we have parties."

"And Annabelle and Kate... they know about this place."

He paused. "Yes."

"And Sabrina."

He didn't answer but that hadn't been a question.

"And they all participate in your... scenes?"

Another pause. "Greg's pretty possessive, so they don't participate with the group, although they have been here for a party. Tyler's not really into the parties, but he and Kate use the room on their own. Annabelle..."

"Enjoys the hell out of it." Talia shook her head, a smile forming on her lips. "That doesn't surprise me one bit."

The sensuality of this place would definitely appeal to Annabelle. And now that she'd signed the confidentiality agreement, she could discuss this place with her friends. Who hadn't even hinted about this place to her.

The thought pricked at her feelings, but she didn't want to

think about her friends now. Not while she was here with Dane. Tomorrow she'd have more than enough time to think about everything else.

Tonight...

She turned to Dane. "You helped Jared put this place together. What are your favorite parts?"

Something that looked a hell of a lot like relief flashed through his eyes before he started to smile, which made her tingle from head to toe. Then he turned to the cabinet, opened the door and grabbed a bottle.

"Sensation is such a personal thing." He tugged on her hand as he headed in the opposite direction, toward a shadowed corner of the room where a couple of chairs sat on either side of a long, low coffee table.

At first glance, the table and chairs didn't seem to match the rest of the furniture in the room. Their legs appeared thicker, sturdier. The design brought to mind a Victorian parlor, but she knew they'd been specially made for this room.

The chairs had cushioned seat pads but were higher than normal. And the seat itself curved in at the front. The longer she stared at the chair, the more intrigued she became. And the more detail she noticed. Like the three metal rings on the outside of the legs, at varying intervals.

Her body heated as she considered uses for those rings. Then her gaze switched to the table, where she saw those same rings on the legs.

"Jared had these pieces commissioned on my designs. Not as elegant as other pieces, but the company who produced them are craftsmen. They took the raw designs I gave them and created something beautiful."

His hand settled against her back again, making her breath catch in her throat. He did nothing but let it lie there, though her body reacted as if he'd caressed her.

"The same company made the larger piece in the corner."

She automatically turned to see what he was referring to, following the direction in which he pointed.

She knew as soon as she saw it what it could be used for. The images that came to mind made her wet.

Holy hell. She wanted him to strip her right now and screw her. On the floor, on the table, on the chair. On that padded, black-leather horse.

She wasn't as much of a prude as her friends obviously thought she was. She read voraciously and had acquired a taste for erotica along with the thrillers and mysteries she devoured on a regular basis.

She loved the freedom the women in those stories enjoyed and had often wished she could be just as adventurous, but she'd never met a man who made her want to give up that much control.

Until she'd met Dane.

"Which do you prefer?" She glanced up at Dane and found him watching her with blistering intensity. "The horse or the chairs?"

For a second, she thought he might insult her intelligence and ask if she knew what the pieces were used for. When he didn't, she wanted to reward him. And she would. Maybe right there on that chair.

"I don't have a favorite. Each has its own reward. I think it depends on what you're in the mood for."

"And what are you in the mood for?"

He lifted a brow at her. "Why do I have to choose only one?" A pause. "So here's how it's going to go. You're going to strip and sit on that chair."

She tried to control her reaction but couldn't, because she felt as if every bone in her body had gone liquid.

How did he know exactly the right thing to say to make her want to do exactly what he said?

Was it the tone of his voice? The look in his eyes? The memory of his mouth on her body and how she felt when he sucked on her nipples?

"Then I'm going to tie your legs to those rings with silk ropes so you can't close them."

The beat of her heart throbbed in her ears, drowning out everything but the sound of his voice and the heaviness of her breathing.

"And then I'm going to kneel between your legs and lick you until you scream. And don't worry about the noise. The entire room is soundproofed."

Oh, god. She was going to spontaneously combust.

"Do you need help with your clothes?"

She might. She wasn't sure she could get her fingers to work.

"Talia."

She reached for the hem of her t-shirt and pulled it over her head then held it out to Dane. With his gaze glued to hers, he took the shirt and laid it over the back of one of the chairs. Swallowing hard, she toed off her sneakers, unbuttoned her jeans and worked them down her legs, careful not to take her underwear along but to make sure the socks went along with them.

Dane made her want to tease, to perform for him. She'd never had that urge before with another man. Never felt such a conflicting urge to obey and to torment.

Again, she handed over her jeans and he laid them on top of her shirt.

His movements appeared almost lazy, but the intensity in his eyes made her fingers itch to curl into his hair and drag his mouth down to hers.

The bright purple lace bra and panties set looked amazing against her skin. Apparently Dane agreed.

His mouth curved in a smile she was becoming familiar with. And addicted to.

"Beautiful. But tonight I want you naked."

He held out his hand and she didn't hesitate to unclip her bra and hand it over then shimmy out of her panties.

He'd already laid her bra over the chair but he curled his fingers around her underwear when she put them in his hand. Instead of putting them with her bra and clothes, he put them in his pocket. The sight of them hanging there made her shiver with lust.

"Sit down, sweetheart. I'll be right back."

He waited until she did as he asked. She settled onto the cool, smooth wood and tried to control her breathing, which was becoming damn near impossible.

Her excitement grew every second, the evidence spilling from her body and slicking her naked thighs, which she pressed together as tightly as she could.

Dane had walked across the room to a desk, where he opened a couple of drawers and pulled out several items.

She couldn't see exactly what he had, which only added to her heightened state.

When he turned back to her, she could only focus on his face. He commanded her attention in a way she'd never experienced before. In a way that made her sit a little straighter and wonder why the hell she did.

That mix of emotions created a maelstrom of desire deep inside and made it hard for her to keep still.

She wanted to squirm but didn't want to let him see how very much she wanted him to just fuck her until she screamed. Just like he'd promised.

"I'm going to bind your hands to the chair. I want you to tell me if they're too tight."

She swallowed. "You've done this before."

"Yes. I won't hurt you, Tally."

"That wasn't a question."

He placed a condom on the chair with her clothes then cocked his head to the side as he unraveled the bright blue rope. "Have *you* done this before? And that is a question."

"No."

He nodded. "Then thank you. For trusting me. Put your hands down at your sides, sweetheart."

She did without a second thought then closed her eyes as he circled behind the chair. His hands were gentle but firm as he wrapped the rope around one wrist then attached it to one of the rings she'd seen on the chair leg. He repeated his movements on the other side, then she felt him brush by her as he came to stand in front of her again.

As her eyes opened, she saw him wind another length of rope around one hand. His gaze met and held hers just before he leaned forward and sucked a nipple into his mouth.

Her head fell back as sensation flashed through her like a live electric current, zapping her nerve endings and arrowing straight to her clit. Her thighs clenched and her arms strained against the rope as he caught the tip between his teeth and bit down until the slightest hint of pain made her moan.

Then he switched to the other side and repeated his actions.

She wasn't aware that he'd wound his hand through her hair until she tried to lift her head and came up against resistance. As soon as she did, he moved his mouth from her breasts to her neck, licking and sucking on the skin until he arrived at her mouth.

She had a brief second to suck in a breath before he covered her mouth with his and kissed her. His tongue thrust into her mouth and tangled with hers, the kiss growing more heated by the second. She wanted to sink her hands into his hair but couldn't move. Every time she tried, the ropes tightened the tiniest bit more and made her that much more frantic.

The man kissed like he had all the time in the world and no inclination to do anything else.

And she couldn't help but think of everything else he could be doing with his mouth, even while she wanted him to kiss her all night.

When he finally pulled away, she was panting, her eyelids so heavy she had trouble keeping them open.

"Spread your legs, baby."

His voice sounded a little harder, like he was having trouble controlling himself now.

Good. She wanted him to lose control. Wanted him as crazy as he was making her.

She tried to open her legs but the ache in her pussy was so great, she had to clench her thighs together again or she felt she'd fall apart.

"I see you're going to need a little help."

She felt movement and, when she opened her eyes, he was on his knees in front of her, spreading her legs.

Whimpering at the sensation of the cooler air against her burning pussy, she watched him tie her left leg to the chair and then her right.

When he finally had her almost completely immobile, he leaned back on his heels and looked up at her.

He didn't say a word but she understood what he wasn't saying.

Sucking in a deep breath, she held it as she waited for him to move again. He made her wait until she thought she'd go light-headed.

She closed her eyes as she felt his hands on the inside of her thighs. Her throat clenched and her hands curled into fists as her heart pounded against her ribs.

She'd started to pant again and she didn't know when. She only knew she couldn't get enough air and, if she wasn't careful, she'd hyperventilate.

But, oh, god, the way he made her feel. So close to the edge, and he hadn't even—

He flicked the tip of his tongue against her clit and she bit her lip through a moan as he proceeded to use his lips and tongue to drive her into the most heightened state of arousal she'd ever been in.

He teased her with slow leisurely licks that made her want to squirm. But she couldn't, and that only intensified her ache.

With her legs spread wide, she felt exposed, her throbbing pussy demanding relief. But Dane only seemed interested in pushing her toward the edge, not over it.

With her eyes closed, she finally achieved a state where her body reached for release while her mind floated in bliss.

The chair's back and the ropes kept her upright. Otherwise she might have slid onto the floor.

With every lick, Dane sank her deeper into a drugged haze that still managed to allow every sharp contraction of her pussy to reverberate through her body.

And when he added his teeth to the mix, she saw stars as she came.

His lips and tongue continued to stretch out her orgasm until the muscles in her legs and arms nearly cramped with the effort.

Through that sex-induced haze, she heard Dane muttering under his breath, felt him working the ropes away from her wrists and ankles. Her eyes opened as he lifted her into his arms and started walking. Her arms had just looped around his neck when he stopped and lowered her onto a chaise lounge.

Boneless, she lay back, her eyes barely open. But she couldn't help but watch as he started to undress.

My god, he was beautiful. In a suit, the man looked decep-
tively tame. But when he stripped away his clothes, she felt like
he stripped off the civility, and that hint of wildness was intox-
icating.

Unlike her clothes, he let his own drop to the floor. He
whipped off his shirt and her breath caught in her throat. She'd
seen him naked, but she didn't think she'd ever see too much of
his chest.

His broad shoulders and chest muscles flexed as he loosened
his belt and unzipped his pants, shoving them down his legs,
leaving him naked.

Her gaze dropped to his erection, thick and hard, and her
mouth actually watered.

She was barely able to take a breath before he practically
threw himself down on the chaise next to her. Hot, naked flesh
pressed against her own as he sealed their lips together. His
arms wrapped around her and she wriggled even closer, opening
her mouth to let him kiss her deeper.

With one smooth move, she found herself on her back with
Dane's knees spreading her legs and pushing up on his hands
above her.

She felt surrounded by him, his scent intensified by the heat
emanating from him. She wanted to run her nose along his
throat before she licked his earlobe then bit it. Hard enough to
make him flinch.

But she didn't get the chance because he lifted up onto his
knees.

She had no idea what he was doing when he turned. She'd
already started to reach for him when he whipped back around
with an oblong pillow.

"Lift."

She didn't need him to explain, just planted her feet and

lifted her hips. He shoved the pillow beneath her ass, making her feel more exposed than she had all night.

Expecting him to lean forward and thrust into her immediately, she took a quick breath.

He didn't.

Putting his hands on her thighs, he rubbed his palms against her skin. She had a brief second to be thankful she'd shaved her legs this morning before he dragged his hands down to her knees then back up again to her hips. His thumbs brushed close to her mound and she arched her hips.

She wanted him to hurry but he seemed to have no intention to rush.

"Dane."

That smile should be illegal. Her muscles tensed in preparation, though she didn't know for what.

"Do you want something, Tally?"

"I want you."

"You'll get me. But first I want to look."

The tone of his voice made heat rush through her body as her nipples tightened and peaked and her thighs tensed. She wanted to close her legs but couldn't and that simply fueled the ache.

She wasn't at all self-conscious about her body. And Dane had already seen every part of her.

But the way he was looking at her now... It went beyond appreciation.

She reached for him, wanting to touch him but she couldn't reach.

"Touch yourself, Tally. Pinch your nipples. I want to watch you."

She'd never had a man talk to her during sex as much as Dane did, and she'd never expected it to make her tingle from head to toe.

She'd also never expected herself to obey a command like this one.

But with her gaze locked with Dane's and his hands smoothing up and down her thighs, she wanted to forget every inhibition she had.

Lifting her hands, she cupped her breasts and squeezed. Her eyes closed and she bit back a moan as pleasure coursed through her.

"Keep your eyes open. I want you to see me while I watch you."

Swallowing hard, she forced her eyes to stay open. It was almost too much. His gaze burned so hot, she felt scorched. Her nipples were so tender, they *hurt* when she pinched them between her thumbs and forefingers.

The pleasure built between her thighs until she could barely stand it. Her lungs worked so hard, she had to breathe in through her nose and mouth to get enough air.

A sense of decadence wanted to drag her into a little world where only she and Dane and this room existed. And even in this state, she knew that was dangerous.

Sex. This was only supposed to be sex. Nothing more.

Dane was sex incarnate. His hair hung around his face, tempting her fingers to push it back. So dark it had blue highlights. The ends just brushed along his strong jaw covered with a dark shadow she wanted him to rub against her nipples.

Should she ask him? He didn't seem to have any trouble telling her what to do. And she loved it. She'd never expected that.

"Dane."

"Do you want something, sweetheart?"

God, yes. "I want you to rub your jaw on my nipples."

The words made her skin heat with a blush. She'd never

asked a man for anything so blatantly during sex. Had never wanted another man to do the things she'd allowed Dane to do.

His lips curved and his hands smoothed up her hips to her waist. "What else do you want?"

Just him. "I want you to do it hard."

"I already know that."

Yes, she was sure he did. But she'd needed to say it. Needed that bit of control.

His hands continued their slow glide, almost touching her breasts but pulling back just before he did.

"What else do you want, Tally? I want you to tell me."

And apparently he got what he wanted.

"I want you to fuck me. Hard."

Her words had the intended effect, and Dane finally covered her hands, which were still holding her breasts, with his and squeezed tight.

Her eyes closed as she soaked in the pleasure. It bordered on painful but... oh, god, she liked it. She'd never been with another man who gave her what she wanted. Gave her more than she wanted.

And then he rubbed his chin over her nipple and she cried out. The sound echoed through the room and she bit her lip against more escaping.

But Dane caught her bottom lip between his teeth and bit down.

The sharp sting made her open her eyes.

"I want to hear you. Every sound. I want you to scream. Trust me. No one else will hear you."

She swore his voice was hypnotic because she agreed without hesitation. His words gave her permission and she needed them.

He nodded just before he dipped his head back down to rub

his jaw against her neglected nipple. This time when she cried out, she didn't hold back.

She felt totally without chains for the first time in her life.

As if he'd sensed the change in her, he tightened his grip on her breasts, pushing her nipples out even farther then sucked the tips into his mouth.

He played his tongue over them, sucked and licked until she couldn't not move.

Her legs curled around his waist and she lifted into him, trying to rub her aching pussy against his cock. She wanted him to fuck her. Right now. She just didn't want him to stop what he was doing.

She gasped when her mound touched his cock. He groaned, the sound reverberating through her body as he sucked on her nipple.

Wriggling her hips, she managed to maneuver his cock between her legs, the tip poised at her entrance.

"Damn, Tally. You're so fucking wet."

She blinked open her eyes and saw that he'd pulled away enough that she could see his entire face.

His expression made her want to smile in triumph. He looked like he wanted to devour her. Which is exactly what she wanted.

"Then fuck me. Right now."

Her nipples still throbbed from the scrape of his whiskers on his jaw, and his hands still held hers trapped around her breasts, as tight as she could take.

"But you're not the one giving orders here, baby. You'll do what I want."

Jesus, when had she become so damn submissive? Because, holy hell, she wanted to whimper and agree to anything he said.

Instead, she forced herself to keep her eyes open. "But only if you give me what I want."

His smile made her flush from head to toe. "Trust me, I'm going to give you what you want. And I'm going to demand so much more."

Leaning back, he released her and unwound her legs from around his waist. She wanted to complain but her brain had already realized he was reaching for the condom.

"Wrap your hands around the edge of the chaise. Now."

She did, gripping it tight as she watched him roll the condom down his cock.

"Put your feet on the floor."

The motion opened her farther, the cooler air brushing against her heated labia, causing her pussy to clench in excitement.

"You're gonna be so damn tight. I can tell. I fucking love that."

"Then hurry."

"No fucking way. I want it to last. I don't want to come in thirty seconds. But whenever I touch you, I can't seem to control myself."

That sounded like the highest compliment at the moment.

With the pillow under her hips, she was the perfect height for him to enter her while he was on his knees.

With one hand on her hip, exerting pressure to keep her in place, he used the other to position his cock at her entrance.

The tip of his cock felt superheated against her naked flesh and she tilted her hips the tiniest bit until he was lodged at the entrance. The fat head spread her puffy, sensitive lips, but her pussy needed that thickness to clench around before she went crazy.

He had both hands on her hips and he held her so tight, she would probably have the mark of his fingers on her skin tomorrow morning. Which she'd love.

Now, she only wanted him to provide the friction she needed.

His first thrust was shallow, not enough to satisfy any of her out-of-control cravings. Looking down, she could see he hadn't gotten more than half of his cock inside.

"You make me want to fuck you hard and fast." He shook his head. "And that's not how I wanted this to go."

"Dane, just fuck me. I don't care about how you wanted this to go. Just do it."

His fingers tightened and he yanked her closer, impaling her farther onto his shaft. Each inch he gained spread her wider, made her ache a little more.

When he withdrew until only the tip of his cock made contact with her clit, she wanted to scream at him. She bit back that impulse.

And he pushed down on her hips until his cock wasn't touching her at all.

"I told you. I want to hear you."

Panting, she nodded, ready to give him whatever he wanted.

And when he shoved the entire length of his cock inside her, she gave him exactly what he asked for.

She cried out as he stretched her so deliciously far, she thought she'd break.

"There you go. That's what I want." His voice had deepened to a raspy growl, and she tried to lift into his body to make him sink even deeper. "Plant your feet, Tally, because I'm going to fuck you hard. Now."

He made good on his word. He pumped his hips with such leashed power she couldn't help but wonder what he'd feel like if he ever completely let loose.

She wasn't sure she'd be able to take it because, right now, she could barely breathe.

Each time he thrust home, his balls slapped against her ass, and each time he withdrew, she tried to lift into him.

But he controlled her movement to such a level that she found herself straining against her self-imposed limits. He'd told her to keep her hands locked around the edge of the chaise and she did, even though every muscle protested.

He kept his pace punishingly slow, his control showing in the rigid muscles of his arms and thighs. With dazed intent, she watched his abs clench and ripple. The motion became mesmerizing.

But she couldn't keep her eyes open for long. As they closed, she felt every inch of his flesh in different ways more intensely.

As if she'd given him permission, he groaned, a low rumble of sound that made her shiver, and increased his speed.

Now, he didn't pull all the way out. He only withdrew far enough to build friction before he shoved back in. His motion had become a little less controlled, a little rougher.

She heard his breathing over her own. Heard him groan, felt his hands leave her hips and felt him grab the cushion on either side of her.

And then he loosened the reins and fucked her exactly how she needed.

Powerful. Strong. Perfect.

She couldn't keep her feet on the floor any longer. She had to wrap her legs around his waist and hold on.

As her heels dug into his thighs, he leaned down and sealed their mouths together. His tongue lashed against hers and she swore she heard the chaise creak as he pounded into her.

She felt her orgasm building, felt her body tensing in anticipation.

As if he knew she was nearing the edge, he thrust and held deep inside her, pinning her to the cushion under her hips.

Then he pulled away and looked down at her. Her body responded deep inside to the look in his eyes.

He held her gaze as he started to move again, and the connection felt so deep and so strong, she wanted to look away.

She couldn't.

Now his every thrust held one purpose. To make her come.

Already so deep in lust she didn't know which way was up, she felt anchored by his gaze. Every nerve in her body dedicated to the overwhelming desire drowning her in sensation.

A slight adjustment and the base of his cock hit her clit at the perfect angle.

Her head bowed back as she came, his name a sharp, short cry from her lips, as her pussy spasmed and clenched around him.

He managed a few more thrusts before she felt him groan and his cock pulsed inside her.

Then she closed her eyes and let herself go boneless.

———

DANE FELT TALIA'S body go slack, though her pussy continued to clench around him.

No problem. He wasn't going anywhere fast. If he had his way, he'd stay here all night, buried deep inside her.

No one would disturb them. Jared knew he was here and would make sure of it.

Still, he wanted to lay her out on a mattress and curl up around her and wake up in the morning ready to kiss her awake and slide back into her, this time slow and easy.

But he didn't seem to be able to do slow and easy with this woman.

Why the hell was that?

Still unable to catch his breath, he figured he'd leave that one question to ponder tomorrow.

First, he better make sure he could still move and that he didn't crush her.

Rolling, he took her with him until he lay on his back with her draped over him. He loved the way she seemed to sink into him. Loved the warmth of her body and the press of her skin against his.

With her face tucked into his neck, he turned his head to the side to rub his nose against her hair.

"You okay?"

He had to ask, just to be sure.

"I'm not sure I'm going to be able to move. Ever."

He laughed at her deadpan delivery then shuddered as he felt her lips brush against his neck.

"Well, we could live on room service, but you'd have to get used to being an exhibitionist."

He felt her still against him. Damn it. Had he just pushed her over the edge?

He'd already made the decision to ask her to Annabelle and Jared's pre-wedding Salon party, but now wasn't the time.

"Who says I'm not?"

His cock twitched at her quiet response and he had to fight back a triumphant grunt.

"So if I ask you to accompany me to a party here, would you say yes?"

She paused. "Am I allowed to ask who'll be there?"

He'd never felt the urge to bite his tongue more than he did right now, but he answered. "You read the waiver and signed it, so yes, I can tell you who'll be there. But..."

"I'm bound to silence by the waiver. I get it, Dane."

He sighed at the slight hint of pique in her tone. "It's not

that I don't trust you. You wouldn't be here if I didn't. It's just...
I've never invited anyone."

She shifted against him until she had herself propped up on
one elbow and could see his face. "Seriously?"

He let his silence speak for him.

Her eyebrows rose and her lips curled with the barest hint
of a smile. But it wasn't sly or knowing. She look slightly
stunned.

"I think I'd still like to know who'll be there first."

"Jed, Annabelle, Tyler, Kate, Greg and Sabrina. Mel and
Geoff Black and Cory Shirk and Liane Ryder. You met them at
Jed and Annabelle's dinner the other night."

Her steady gaze held his. "Are you going to expect me to
have sex with someone else?"

His immediate response was "Hell, no," followed fast by
"Only if I allow it."

None of which he spoke aloud. He knew that, as submissive
as she was while having sex, Talia would balk if he pulled that
last one on her.

"Is that something you would enjoy?" he asked instead.

She didn't answer right away, and he could tell she was
considering his question carefully.

"Never having attended a sex party, I can't tell you if I
would or not."

"The parties aren't just for sex." Which contradicted what
he'd said earlier. Shit. "They're not orgies. They're... for people
who enjoy letting go of their sexual inhibitions."

"But you do have sex with people in this room. Several
people have sex in this room at the same time."

"It honestly depends, but yes. Some people get off on watching. Some like to participate more fully. Some like to perform."

"And you've done all three."

"Yes."

Her gaze narrowed, but he didn't think she was judging him. "Which do you enjoy most?"

"I like to participate."

He could see her rolling that one around in her head, trying to figure out all the angles. "And by 'participate' you mean you bring a partner here?"

"I told you I've never invited another woman here."

Her gaze narrowed and he wanted to kick himself for revealing more than he'd wanted. "So you have sex with the women who are members."

She was making connections faster than he could keep up. "Yes."

Her lips parted in preparation for another question. He knew exactly what it would be and mentally braced for it. Because how he answered could break their relationship before it'd started.

Instead, she settled her head back on his shoulder and draped her arm across his chest.

"So when is this party?"

"Next Saturday. After the bachelor and bachelorette nights."

"Ah. I'd wondered."

"About... ?"

"The night before the wedding is typically the rehearsal dinner, but Jared and Annabelle are having that on Thursday. And no one said anything about plans for Saturday night, so I figured there weren't any." She shrugged. "I thought Jared and Annabelle were going to spend it together."

"They couldn't tell you anything. You know that, right?"

She hesitated for a second. "I understand the severity of the nondisclosure."

"Then you should understand why they couldn't say anything, even if they wanted to."

"Then why could you?"

"Because Jared and I have the final say on everyone who gets to know about the Salon. We're the only ones who don't have to put new members to a vote. Well, technically, Tyler doesn't either, but we figure after Kate, he'll never invite anyone again."

She pulled back again to look at him. "And why haven't you invited anyone else?"

"Because I hadn't met a woman I thought would be interested."

She nodded, though he had no idea what she was agreeing with. Then she leaned forward and kissed him.

Sweetly sensual and most definitely meant to end the night.

And he let her.

"I'll let you know this week, if that's okay. Now... I don't want to move but I need to get some sleep. I do have a meeting tomorrow morning, and I don't think Trudeau will be happy with me if I'm late."

"I understand."

She smiled as he rolled off the chaise to collect their clothes. He delivered hers first then dressed himself. Shoving his hair out of the way, he caught her watching him though her gaze dropped as soon as she realized. So he got to watch her shimmy into her bra and sighed when she finally pulled her shirt over her head.

Running her hands through her hair, she fluffed it then tossed it back over her shoulders. He couldn't wait to wrap it around his hand again, this time while he took her from behind.

"Let me walk you back to your door."

She agreed with a smile then let her gaze roam the room one last time before she turned and walked for the door.

He stopped her with one hand on her shoulder before she could leave.

"Are we still on for next Saturday?"

Her bottom lip disappeared between her teeth for a brief second. "Yes."

He managed to contain the urge to pump his fist. "Let me take you out to dinner this weekend, too."

"I have two events this weekend."

"Then how about tomorrow night?"

She glanced up at him. "I'm staying in Harrisburg tomorrow night for a weekend wedding. And Sunday I have a fiftieth anniversary party for friends of my grandparents."

"Monday night."

Her smile made him want to strip her jeans down her legs, hold her up against the wall and fuck her hard and fast.

"I'll call you Monday?"

No, he wanted her to say yes now. "Sounds good."

Turning, she leaned her back against the wall and stared up at him. "I want to see you again, Dane. It's just that I have a weird schedule. I can work until midnight one night and be up the next day at seven for a business meeting."

"I will have no trouble working around your schedule. I just want to make sure I get myself on your calendar."

"I have no doubt you'll find a space on my calendar."

"Glad to hear it. Now, about Monday night..."

NINE

"So do you think you're up for the challenge? I know I can throw a lot at a person right away, which sometimes makes them run screaming. But I find it's helpful to lay everything out up front so there are no misconceptions."

Tru finally stopped to take a breath, and Talia barely managed not to make it obvious she felt like she'd just gone through the spin cycle in a washing machine.

Talia considered herself a competent multitasker and, by competent, she meant she fucking rocked at multitasking.

Tru made her feel like a total slacker. And made her feel ancient.

Tru looked about nineteen with her light brown hair scraped back in a perfect ponytail, that adorable pug nose and those freckles that looked like she dotted them on her face every day. Today, she wore square, blue-framed glasses that managed to make her look both nerdy and cool with her blue-and-cream-striped sweater dress that fit her perfectly.

Her sky-blue eyes held a sharp intelligence that made Talia sit a little taller in her chair.

Tru's office in the building Greg had bought to house his

new film production company that he'd recently moved from Hollywood to Philadelphia was organized so well, not even Martha Stewart would be able to find a fault.

"Yes, I'm up for the challenge. I've handled several large events and honestly, I think I have a good handle on what you're looking for."

For the next several minutes, she rattled off the ideas she'd been turning over in her head since Tru had first approached her about handling the opening-night party for Greg's newest film. Tru had given her all the promotional materials and sent her a few clips from the film that gave her a sense of the tone, and she'd been able to put together some ideas from that.

The fact that the film was basically a romance was a huge point in her favor. And that it was an unsentimental romance made it that much better. From what she'd seen, Talia knew this was something she'd spend her money to watch.

When she'd laid out her plans for the after-party, she waited for Tru to say something.

Instead Tru closed her eyes and let her head fall back on her shoulders.

Okay, maybe she'd been totally off base—

Tru bounced off her chair, rounded her desk and bent down to give Talia a huge hug.

"Oh, my god! Thank you so much for being exactly what Sabrina and Kate promised."

Laughing, Talia returned Tru's hug as best she could, since the angle was a little awkward.

"You're welcome. I think. Maybe I should ask what they promised first."

With a heartfelt sigh, Tru sank into the chair next to Talia's and let her head rest against the back cushion. "They promised me you were brilliant and I'd be grateful I hired you. And everything you said just allayed all of my fears.

With everything going on, I was really worried about this party."

Nice to know her friends actually did believe in her. Which was totally bitchy to even think and she pushed the thought away. "Then you're very welcome. Honestly, I'm thrilled to have the opportunity to work on something like this. I love a challenge."

"Damn, I am so fucking glad I don't have to tell Bree we aren't going to hire you. She's been telling me for weeks we need to get you to do this."

Turning her head toward the masculine voice behind her, Talia saw Greg leaning against the door frame.

"Hi. I didn't realize you were there."

Greg grinned as he pushed away from the door to walk over to Talia. "I wasn't until a few seconds ago, so if you talked about specifics, I didn't get them. But when Truly gets that blissful look on her face, I know all is right in her world. Therefore, all is right in my world."

Sitting on the edge of Tru's desk, Greg nodded at his former assistant, now partner. "Of course, you're gonna hate me for this, but Baz is in the studio and he needs to talk to you about some mixer or something."

Tru's gaze narrowed and that sweet, girl-next-door face of hers screwed up into a frown that made Talia's eyebrows rise.

"That man is going to..." Tru huffed out a breath and pushed away from her desk. "Sorry, I'll be right back, Talia."

Then Tru left, grumbling under her breath something about smashing equipment over Baz's head.

When the girl had disappeared, Greg began to laugh.

"If they don't kill each other first, they're gonna be two of my biggest assets in this company."

"They don't appear to get along at all."

"Well, Tru thinks Baz is a fucked-up rock star, and Baz

thinks she's an uptight control freak. They both happen to be right."

Talia's back immediately went up. "Tru is one of the sweetest people I know. And Baz is one of the funniest. I think they're both great."

Greg smiled. "And that's all true. I love them both. But you don't like me very much, do you?"

Taken back by his blunt statement, Talia blinked up at him, her lips parting but she had no idea what to say.

"That's not true."

He continued to smile. "Yeah, it is. I appreciate the fact that you're trying to save my feelings, but I'd rather you be honest. The thing is, Bree loves you. And I think you honestly care about her."

Her eyes narrowed. "I do honestly care about her. She's one of the absolute best people I know."

"Which is why you're not too sure about me."

She drew in a breath, ready to refute him... and stopped. Greg just continued to smile at her.

Because he was totally right.

While Bree thought he was the most amazing man on the planet, Talia saw way too many similarities between his personality and her father's. Though Greg wasn't slickly handsome like her dad had been, he was attractive in ways that made women flock to his side whenever he smiled. And made men want to throw money at him, whatever his plans were.

"I don't *not* like you, Greg. It's just..."

"You don't think I'm good enough for her."

Was that it? "I don't want to see Bree get hurt."

He nodded. "And if I told you that's the last thing I ever want to do?"

"Then I guess I'd give you the benefit of the doubt." Now

she smiled and made sure he saw the edge on it. "And cut off your balls if you ever do."

Greg threw his head back and laughed, and now she saw the genuine side of him that she might have possibly been over-looking because of her protectiveness of Sabrina. And because of her dad, who'd colored so much of her perception of men since she was a teenager. She knew most men didn't stand a chance in her eyes.

Greg met her gaze again and, yeah, she totally got what Sabrina saw in him.

"Bree said you don't pull your punches and I like that about you. Which is kind of why I wanted to talk to you. You know, I don't feel the need to explain myself to any of her other friends. Not Kate, not Annabelle. But you... you're the one I need to win over."

She shook her head, a bemused grin on her face. "You don't need to win me over. I'm not the one you're seeing."

"But you're the one she looks at and thinks, 'I wonder what Talia would do.'"

Rolling her eyes, she held up one hand. "If that were true, she never would've gone near you."

And there was that damn mouth of hers, getting away from her again.

Greg just continued to smile. "See, that's what I like about you."

Sighing, she leaned back in her chair. "Honestly Greg, you remind me of someone, but that's my issue, not yours."

"I hate to think I remind you of someone who hurt you, but I get it. It's human nature, hon." He shrugged. "It's hard to let go of the past. Anyway, I just thought we should talk. I needed to get that off my chest so thanks for listening. And I'm anxious to see what you do with the premiere party. I know you'll pull together something amazing."

He got up to leave and she reached out to touch his arm as he passed by.

"Greg... Thank you."

He snorted. "Yeah, don't thank me yet. You haven't actually had to work with me. Talk to you..." Greg slowed as he got closer to the door then stopped just short of walking out. "Well, shit. They're at it again. I swear I'm going to have to hire a referee to handle those two. If I didn't know better, I'd think they hated each other."

Though she hadn't before, now Talia heard Tru and Baz arguing in the hall and getting louder every second.

Turning, Greg headed back toward her. "I'm getting the hell out of Dodge, babe. I love those two, but there's no way you want to be between them when they start arguing. I suggest you find a back way out." Stopping by her side, he dropped a kiss on the top of her head and made quick time for the door on the other side of the room. But he stopped before he left and turned to look at her.

"We good?"

She nodded. "We're good."

He smiled and she totally understood why Sabrina would fight tooth and nail to keep him. "See you soon."

She blinked as he disappeared out the door, her brain snapping with questions.

Did he know that Dane had invited her to the Salon? Was that what that smile of his meant? Or had she totally read something into his expression that wasn't there?

Was she really going to go?

If she did, there was a damn good chance Greg would be seeing her naked or at least could watch her having sex with Dane.

While her brain was scandalized, her body went tight and hot all over. Because that really didn't turn her off. At all.

"Jesus Christ, Truly, you are going to fucking kill me. Just get the goddamn—"

"Don't you dare use that language with me, Baz. You know—"

"—mixer I want in the first place. Christ, you're such a priss. You know I don't mean—"

"—I'm not going to respond. This is what they had when I called, so I figured you'd rather have this than nothing at all. I'm sorry it's not up to your exacting standard, but the one you wanted is on its way now."

"Then why the fuck didn't you just say that to begin with? God—"

"Because you still would have felt the need to run your mouth. Now, if you don't mind, I'm going to continue my meeting."

"Oh, for fu— Ow!"

Truly reentered her office, her smile fixed and brittle. "I'm so sorry, Talia. I—Never mind. Is there anything else you need to go over?"

"Uh—"

"Hey, Talia. How goes it?"

Standing, Talia turned to Baz with a smile. Unlike Tru, Talia had no problem with Baz. Smart, funny and, yeah, occasionally crude and loud and totally inappropriate, Baz had wormed his way into her good graces by being such a good friend to Sabrina. Talia had secretly hoped Sabrina would fall for Baz.

Which probably went to show how screwed up she was about her dad.

"Pretty good, actually." She gave him a hug, which he returned tightly. The guy was a total sweetheart. Obviously, he and Tru were oil and water.

"Don't let the taskmaster get to you." He nodded in Tru's direction but never glanced her way. "She's just never happy."

Trudeau raised her eyebrows at him. "And you're such a joy to work with all the time."

Baz laughed, but she heard an undercurrent of self-disgust in his tone. "You know I totally am. But it looks like I'm not getting any work done so I'm outta here. Have a good one, Tal."

Then he was gone and, behind her, Tru took a deep steadying breath. "That man is going to be the death of me. Unless I strangle him first." Shaking her head, Tru switched gears on a dime. "So, let's run with the ideas you've already presented and we'll set another meeting for the Monday after Jared and Annabelle's wedding, if that works for you."

That was two days after the Salon party.

"Absolutely. I'll see you then."

If she survived the weekend.

———

"HEY, YOU GOT A MINUTE?"

Looking up from his computer, Dane found Jed standing in the door to his office.

"What are you doing here?"

"Nice to see you, too. And I wouldn't have to show up if you'd just answer your damn phone."

Glancing at his desk, Dane realized he'd missed a few calls from Jed and more than a couple of texts from several others. None of which mattered because none of them were from a certain blonde who was formerly a Roller Derby girl, a fact he found utterly fascinating.

"Sorry. I lost track of time. What's up?"

Jed leaned against the door frame and tapped his watch.

"Appointment at the jeweler's. You said you wanted to go with me to get that necklace for your mom. You also mentioned something about bracelets for your sister and the girls. After 'necklace for Mom,' I tuned you out because you were talking about jewelry."

"And if it doesn't have anything to do with Belle, you don't give a shit right now."

"What can I say, man? I found the woman I want to spend the rest of my life with and she loves me back. Amazing."

Jed's smile made Dane shake his head. "The amazing thing is she hasn't tossed you out yet because she's sick of you."

"Let's hope that never happens."

Dane nodded in agreement. "She's the best thing that's happened to you in a damn long time. So don't screw it up."

"Don't plan to. So what's got you so wrapped up you don't even answer your phone?"

Dane paused, wondering if he should admit what he'd been up to, because he wasn't sure how Jed would react. Then again, it wasn't like he was doing something illegal. At least, not yet.

"Come in and close the door."

Jed's eyebrows lifted but he did what Dane had asked.

"Okay, you wanna tell me why you're all cloak-and-dagger? Is it one of your cases?"

Dane shook his head. "I'm checking out Talia."

Jed's eyes widened. "Come again?"

"You heard me the first time."

"Yeah, I did. But I'm pretty sure there's more to the story." Jed dropped into the chair on the other side of Dane's desk and leaned his elbow on his knees, blue gaze intent on Dane's. "Because I'm pretty sure you had her sign the nondisclosure and I know you. You already checked her out. So what's with the double dip?"

Good question, and one he couldn't answer. Which was bugging the hell out of him.

"I'm not sure."

"And..."

"And I'm not fucking sure."

A frown wrinkled Jed's forehead. "Wait, did you find something?"

Had he? He honestly didn't know. "No. I don't think so. Talia's parents divorced more than ten years ago, but someone went to a hell of a lot of trouble to wipe her father out of her history. Now, that could be because the guy was an abusive bastard. I've helped a few people with stuff like this. I know how to do it so someone like me can't find anything. Someone did that to Talia's dad."

Jed's gaze narrowed. "You said it yourself. Maybe the guy was a total dirtbag and it's better to let him disappear than dig him up."

"This coming from the guy who had me dig into his future wife's history to find out if she was the daughter of a famous murdered painter."

Jed shrugged. "Old news, buddy. I'm marrying the girl, remember?"

"And you're damn lucky to have her."

"All of which I know. What I don't know is why you're digging into Talia's background like a man possessed."

He wasn't possessed. "I'm curious. It's in my blood."

"You're also hot as hell for her. You're an idiot if you think you're hiding that from anyone."

"I'm not trying to hide anything." He wanted to add "fuck you" to the end of that statement but kept his mouth shut because he knew Jed would torment the hell out of him for that.

"I know you and Belle talked the other night, but did you mention the fact that you're screwing around with one of her best friends?"

"We're not screwing around, for chrissake. We're..."

"Fucking."

No. "Seeing where things go. Slowly."

"And when was the last time you decided to go slow with a woman?"

"What the hell is your problem? Jesus, Jed. I like her. All right? I'm trying not to be an ass and screw things up. And apparently that's harder than I thought. You ready to go?"

Jed rose and headed for the door, a slight smirk on his lips. "After you."

They headed for the elevator through the offices that housed most of the staff of Connelly Media's magazines. A few people nodded as they made their way through the office but no one stopped him to ask a question or show him a layout.

Probably because he looked like he wanted to tear someone's head off.

The cab ride to Tiffany's in Rittenhouse Square was thankfully short, and Jed managed not to piss him off any more by mentioning Talia again.

When they entered the store, he headed for the counter where he'd seen the bracelets he'd wanted to get his sister and nieces for his sister's upcoming birthday. For some reason, when he'd been here with Jed to look at rings a few weeks ago, those bracelets had caught his eye.

Delicate silver links connected with genuine gemstones. His sister's bracelet would have a stone for each of her children. The girls' bracelets would have only their birthstones.

"Hey. Come look at this."

Jed called him back, holding out his hand, palm up with a ring in the center.

"She chose the matching ring to mine."

Dane picked up the delicate gold band inlaid with yellow and white diamonds.

When he glanced at Jed, Jed's smile made Dane shake his head. "You really are a sap."

"Sue me. I love her."

"Yeah, I know. And you're damn lucky she loves you just as much."

Jared took the ring from Dane and held it up in front of his face, his smile softening. "I never thought I'd do this. Never thought I'd find a woman I wanted to wake up beside every morning or go to bed with every night. I thought I'd be bored out of my skull having to spend so much time with one woman. And here I am, thinking I just won the lottery."

"If you start to cry, you're on your own. I'm all out of hankies."

That made Jed laugh, as it was supposed to. And when Jed turned to smile at him, Dane couldn't help but grin back as he shook his head.

"There's still hope for you," Jed said.

No way was he giving Jed ammunition. "I never said I didn't want to get married. Hell, my parents are the poster children for marriage. For that matter, so are my brother and sister."

"So you do think about it?"

Dane shrugged. "Honestly... No. I've never had the urge to ask anyone to marry me."

"At the risk of sounding like a Hallmark commercial, when you meet the right woman, you'll know it."

Nodding, Dane tried not to laugh in his best friend's face but finally lost the battle. Jed didn't take offense, though.

"Go ahead and laugh, buddy. Someday the shoe will be on the other foot."

"Not sure there're any more like Belle out there, so don't be fitting me for new shoes just yet."

"So, you're gonna ask Talia to the party."

"I already did."

Jed didn't bother to look surprised. "And..."

"She's going to let me know."

"Ah."

"Don't make me tell you to fuck off again."

Turning back to the counter with the bracelets, he ignored Jed's quiet laughter and ordered the damn bracelets for his family.

TALIA TAPPED her fingers on the back of her phone as it lay on her desk, trying to decide if she was going to make the call or not.

She wanted to make the call. Felt like she'd crawl out of her skin if she didn't make the call. And yet...

What?

She hadn't had much time to think about Dane this weekend. She hadn't been kidding when she'd said she'd be busy.

And yet... he'd crept into her thoughts more than she'd liked.

Which meant she'd been debating calling him, because any man who took up this much of her brainpower was a man who had the potential to have way too much power over her.

And isn't that what you loved about Thursday night?

She sighed, spinning in her chair to look out her office window, which basically looked out over Penn Avenue. This time of day there was a lot of traffic. At least, a lot of traffic for Wyomissing.

If she moved to Philly, which was still a big if, she'd have to get used to a lot more traffic. A new apartment, a new office. She'd have to pay to park everywhere and, and oh, my god, there were so many more people.

Which made her sound like a total hermit, when, in reality,

the only reason she was having any kind of second thoughts was because of Dane.

Ugh.

She should call and tell him no for tonight and the weekend.

But... she wanted to say yes. Which was why she was having this silent argument with herself.

With a huff, she picked up her phone and made a call.

"Hey Tal, what's—"

"You busy?"

A pause. "No." Kate drew the word out to about five syllables. "But you sound like you are."

"Not busy, just... I need you to be honest."

"About what?"

"Dane. The man is driving me crazy, and I need to figure out what to do."

Kate fell silent for several seconds. "About what?"

"He invited me to the Salon Saturday night."

Another pause, this one longer. "Ah."

"Seriously. That's all you have to say?"

Kate snorted. "Well, you could give me a few seconds to process. Shock will do that to you."

"Should I be worried that you're shocked?"

"Oh, jeez. I think this conversation requires alcohol, and I'm working with lace at the moment, so no alcohol for me. I take it things have progressed with Dane."

"I don't know that *progressed* is the right word."

"So what is the right word?"

"I'm not sure yet."

A short pause this time. "Fair enough. And don't take this the wrong way, Tal. I like Dane. He's the kind of guy you want on your side if you're in serious trouble, because he will find a way to get you out of it. But... I've never heard of him being in a, ah, monogamous relationship."

"Then I guess I'm glad we're nowhere near the relationship stage. We've had sex a couple of times and gone to dinner once. It's not like we're declaring everlasting love."

"Uh-huh. Okay."

The amused scoff in Kate's voice made Talia want to stick her tongue out at her friend, even though she wouldn't be able to see it.

"Now you're deliberately pissing me off."

Kate's laugh rang through the line and now it sounded more like Kate. "It's my goal in life. You know that. Sorry, Tal. I don't mean to be a bitch. And, honey, if the sex is good enough to keep you coming back for more, then more power to you."

"Now tell me why you're shocked that I know about the Salon. Apparently my friends are all in on the secret."

"Talia—"

"Sorry, sorry, sorry. That came out way bitchier than it should have."

"For the record, I want you to know we didn't keep it from you intentionally. You obviously signed the nondisclosure so you know how restrictive it is."

"I know. And I understand. I do, really. It's just... now that I do know, I've got so damn many questions, I don't even know where to start."

"So just ask the first one that comes to mind."

"Have you and Tyler had sex in front of other people in there?"

Kate's laugh was a sharp bark. "You've met Ty. Do you really think he's gonna let other people watch him get busy?"

"So that's a no."

"That's a big no. But that's not to say we haven't used the room, because we have. That black leather horse in the corner? Let's just say I've probably logged more hours on that than I have on any other piece of furniture in that room."

"That good, huh?"

"Please. If I had my way, I'd be tied to it at least three times a week."

"Dane had me tied to one of the chairs."

"We haven't had the opportunity to try those out yet. They're fairly new. So... are you coming Saturday night? Oh, wait," Kate said as Talia started to laugh. "Maybe I should rephrase that."

"Don't bother. And I'm not sure. I'm afraid I won't be able to participate the way he'll want me to."

"Honestly, I don't know what to tell you about that. Sometimes I think you have to jump in with both feet and damn the consequences, you know? But if it's not for you, don't do it because he expects you to."

"Maybe I'm a little afraid I'll like it too much."

"With this crew, Tal, trust me, that's not a bad thing."

DANE GRABBED HIS RINGING PHONE, checked the name and started to smile.

"Hey, I'm glad you called."

Actually, he felt like beating his chest like a caveman but decided Talia probably didn't want to hear that.

"Hi, Dane. How are you?"

"Better, now that I hear your voice. How were your events this weekend?"

"They went well. The anniversary party, especially. After fifty years together, the couple still likes each other. I call that a win."

"I'm sure your party was perfect for them. And I'm hoping you called to tell me we're on for tonight."

"Actually, I did. If you're still free."

He'd actually turned down an invite to go drinking with friends on the chance that she would call, but he wasn't going to tell her that. "I am. So what time can I pick you up?"

"You want to come up here?"

"If that's okay with you. I thought we could grab dinner at the Retreat."

And have sex until they passed out in the Salon. He'd already checked with Jed and no one had reserved it for the night. Not that he would mention that now. Didn't want her to think sex was all he wanted from her.

Even though she was all he'd thought about all weekend. Not that he was obsessed with her or anything.

"Sure, that sounds great. I haven't actually eaten there yet. It's only a few minutes from my apartment. Do you want to pick me up there?"

"Sounds good. I'll pick you up at seven. See you soon."

DANE HUNG up before she realized he hadn't asked for her address, so she figured he already had it. Which reinforced the fact that the man had checked her out.

And while he definitely had more resources than she did, she'd admit to Googling the hell out of him.

She managed to stay on task the rest of the day, getting as much work done as she possibly could. She tied up a few loose ends for Annabelle's wedding, worked out a schedule based on the information Dane had given her for his company's board meeting, and set up a meeting in two weeks with a bride for a Christmas wedding.

By the time six forty-five rolled around, she'd changed her clothes twice, put her hair up, taken it down, and picked up her phone to call Sabrina, only to put it down before dialing.

She had no idea what she would've said. She wasn't a teenager who needed affirmation before her date with the football quarterback.

Of course, she'd never gone out with the quarterback. The quarterback of her high school football team had been way more interested in the cheerleaders, and Talia had still been way too angry at life to consider going out for squad.

Instead, she'd played field hockey and soccer and gotten a job at one of the local supermarkets when she'd turned fifteen.

She realized now that she'd needed to have some control over her world, and making her own money had helped with that.

When her bell rang, she took a deep breath and tried to tame the wide grin on her lips.

Which died a fast death when she opened the door.

"Ms. Driscoll?"

The man was fortyish, balding and slightly rumpled, as if he'd spent all day in his car. And he looked as if he hadn't slept all night.

"Yes?"

"Certified letter."

A clipboard and pen appeared before her eyes before she could blink. And once she'd signed the paper, he whipped a letter out of his pocket faster than her brain could process.

He was already turning away when he said, "Have a good one," and left her staring at his back holding a business envelope in her hand.

Since the door to her apartment opened onto a small outdoor courtyard that provided a buffer between the building and the parking lot, she could see the man get into his small car and drive away. She watched as Dane pulled into the very next spot seconds later.

Since he could clearly see her, she squashed the impulse to

slam her front door closed and hide the letter. Because she knew what it was. The lawyer had warned her it was coming, but she'd forgotten. How the hell had she forgotten?

The answer to that was easy and walking toward her with a smile on his face.

Which disappeared as he came closer.

"Hey. You okay?"

She forced her lips into a smile though her heart had started to pound and her stomach rolled a couple of times.

"I'm fine. Come in. I just need to"—*hide*—"stick this in my office, then I'll be ready to go."

He walked by her into the apartment, but she knew she hadn't fooled him.

"Did something happen?"

She managed a more convincing smile this time because he seemed truly worried about her.

"No. Just work."

Tossing the letter on her desk in her office as if it meant nothing, she grabbed her coat out of the closet in the hall then headed back to the living room.

Dane stood in the center of the room, hands in the pockets of his black slacks, a thin gray sweater lovingly molded to his chest under a black leather jacket.

He almost made her forget the contents of that letter.

Almost.

An uneasy guilt rolled in her stomach. Why she felt guilty, she had no idea. She didn't owe this man her life story. If he knew...

Hell, he'd probably want to make a front-page story out of her. Her dad's name got mentioned in the media whenever there was a huge scandal in the banking world. She tried not to read the financial news, but sometimes it made its way onto the front pages and the morning news and she couldn't help seeing it. And it would dredge up everything she'd tried so hard to forget.

And now this...

She took a deep breath, trying to get a handle on her emotions. She'd taught herself to control the anger by the time she was a teenager, which had pretty much sealed her fate as "the ice bitch" in her high school.

But locking down everything had been the only way to stop the fury that would overtake her.

She'd have attacks of rage that she'd only been able to contain by running and, later, by skating.

She hadn't had an attack in years, and she thought she'd outgrown them. Now she had the sick feeling she was about to have one.

God, not in front of Dane.

She wouldn't be able to hide it from him. He saw way too much.

Maybe she should plead illness. Tell him she was coming down with a stomach virus, the flu, anything.

But she didn't want to lie. Except for the identity of her father, she refused to lie. About anything.

"Talia."

She couldn't tell him. She couldn't tell anyone. Couldn't betray her mom. Couldn't subject her to the hell she'd been through before.

"Talia." Dane walked over to her and cupped her shoulders. "I think you should sit down."

"Sorry, no. I'm fine."

"You don't look fine. You look like you're about to pass out. Are you sure you feel okay?"

"Actually, no. I'm not."

"Come on. Sit down. I'll get you a glass of water."

She sat and let her head fall back onto the cushion. Closing her eyes, she focused on her breathing. She heard a cabinet door open and close then the sound of water pouring into a glass.

"Here. Take a sip."

She opened her eyes to see Dane standing over her, a genuinely worried look on his face and a glass of water in his hand.

Lifting her head, she took it. "Sorry. That caught me off guard."

"What caught you off guard?"

Taking a sip of water allowed her to shift her attention away from him for a moment. Otherwise, she'd find herself staring into his eyes and losing herself there.

"I'm sor—"

"Hey, no need to be sorry." He eased onto the couch next to her. "You're not feeling well. It's not like you can chose to be sick."

Which wasn't entirely true. She'd brought this on herself.

"Do you want—"

"Would you like to stay in tonight? Order pizza or Chinese?"

She didn't want him to leave. The thought that he might was adding even more stress to her situation. Already she could feel her lungs wanting to hyperventilate. She had the insane urge to grab his hand so he couldn't get away.

His eyes narrowed as she made a conscious effort to control her breathing. Passing out would be way too embarrassing.

"I'm feeling Chinese? Okay with you?"

She smiled and now it felt more natural.

When he smiled back, she felt the knot in her throat loosen. "Sounds good."

And suddenly the night was looking up once again.

DANE HAD the brief thought that Talia had staged her bout of dizziness to get him alone for the night but immediately dismissed it.

They would've been spending the night together at Haven, so it didn't make sense for her to fake an illness to stay in. If she'd wanted him to leave, maybe then he would've thought she was trying to get rid of him.

But she'd wanted him to stay.

And he didn't want to leave her.

Something had spooked her. Something to do with that letter.

He wanted to ask but he wouldn't. Instead, he helped her choose which dishes to order. She liked spicy food, a taste he shared.

And when she offered him a beer and told him to help himself, he was pleasantly surprised to find more than a few good microbrews in her fridge. Another taste they shared.

The food only took twenty minutes to get there and, by the time it arrived, she looked like she was back to her normal self.

Which just made him wonder what the hell was in that letter. But he wasn't stupid enough to ask. If she wanted to talk, he wanted to listen.

Actually, he didn't care what she wanted to talk about. He'd listen.

Throughout dinner, she'd talked about her most recent weddings. About the bride who'd wanted doves released in the church so they could coo from the rafters during the ceremony, and the one whose dog ripped her dress the day of the wedding, requiring Kate to make emergency repairs.

He'd told her about the last island he'd visited, about the way the owners had made the cottages modern and self-sufficient but still made them feel isolated and rustic.

He wanted to take her there someday, wanted to show her what he'd loved about the place.

The thought was straight out of left field and completely, fully formed.

It should've made him twitchy to even think about taking a woman with him on a business trip. And yet it didn't.

Because it was her.

"Do you want another beer?"

Pushing herself to her feet, Talia motioned to his empty bottle on the coffee table.

"I probably shouldn't, if I'm going to drive home tonight."

Which he didn't want to do. He wanted stay right here. He'd understand if she wasn't feeling up to it, but the overnight bag he'd packed and had stashed in the backseat of his car was proof that he'd been thinking about this moment all day.

She stilled, looking down at him. "Do you want to drive home?"

No sense in being coy. "No. I want to stay with you."

Her lips curved in a way that let him know she was about to tease him. He liked that, too.

"And if I ask if you planned on spending the night... ?"

"I'd tell you the truth. I want to spend the night with you. In bed. Naked. Hot. Sweaty. Making you come. But if you're not up—"

"I think I can handle anything you dish out. Do you want that beer now?"

"Only if you join me."

She walked toward the kitchen and threw him a look as she opened the door to the fridge. "You don't need to get me drunk. I did just ask you to spend the night."

"But I don't want to drink alone. If you're done for the night, so am I."

She walked back to the couch with a beer in each hand. "I guess one more won't hurt."

Halfway into this beer, he said, "So do you want to talk about what happened earlier?"

She huffed out a laugh. "Ah. I see you had an ulterior motive all along."

"Not at all. But if you want to talk..."

And he really wished she would. He wanted her to trust him with whatever it was that had sent her over the edge earlier.

Staring down at her bottle for a few seconds, she finally lifted her gaze back to his.

"Family stuff's always complicated, isn't it?"

"Usually, yeah. Is everyone okay?"

She grimaced. "Like I said. Complicated."

Resigning himself to being in the dark on this one, he was about to change the subject when she sighed.

"I don't mean to be difficult. It's just... My mom, my brother, and I, we had this traumatic event happen when I was a teenager. My dad... wasn't the man we thought he was."

"I'm sorry."

She smiled up at him and his body gave that kick deep inside that meant his libido had kicked in. All night he'd managed to keep it under control, to simply enjoy her company without allowing sex to dictate the entire conversation.

Yes, he'd wanted to prove to her... and himself... that this was more than just sex.

But apparently, he'd reached the end of his patience.

Her smile held a heat he hadn't seen in her all night. A heat he wanted to explore. In her bed. With her under him. Or over him. Hell, he didn't care, so long as he was able to get inside her at some point tonight.

"Nothing for you to be sorry about. My dad... made our lives hell. But the worst part was, we didn't realize until it was too late to do anything about it. And after he—when he died, I thought everything would be better. It wasn't. It was just... different."

"That's not your fault."

"I know. But that anger... it's a bitch. I was an angry teenager. I'm sure my mom wished she could ship me off to boarding school many times."

"But she didn't."

"No. I think my mom deserves a medal for putting up with me. Of course, back then I thought everyone else was the problem. Not me."

"Teenagers are good at seeing only what they want to see."

She continued to hold his gaze, though she didn't say anything for several seconds. "So what do you see when you look at me?"

He should've seen that one coming and he was surprised she'd asked. "A smart, beautiful woman who's so fucking hot she makes me want to keep her naked and tied to a bed."

She blinked and her lips parted but no words emerged.

"I'm fairly civilized on the outside," he continued. "But it's a front most of the time. Your turn now. What do you see when you look at me?"

Her pause lasted long enough that he thought she might not answer.

Finally, she cocked her head to the side. "I see a man who makes me want to break a few hard-and-fast rules I've set for myself."

Sounded good so far. "And what are those?"

"I saw the hell my mom went through with my dad, and I never want to have to deal with that. I'm not looking for a man to complete my life. I never want to be one of those women whose lives revolve around men."

He smiled at the thought of Talia ever blindly pursuing a

man at the cost of her business. "I don't think you have to worry about that. You're too focused."

Her answering smile made his cock twitch. "High praise coming from you, I think."

"Which doesn't mean I don't think you're sexy as all hell."

Rising up on her knees, she put her hands on his shoulders and leaned down until her lips were only inches away from his. "I want you to know I didn't plan on this happening."

"What? You weren't planning on seducing me into your bed tonight?"

"No. I might have been planning to seduce you into a bed at Haven.. But I guess we'll just have to make do with my plain old queen bed tonight."

Picking her up by her hips, he lifted her over him, her knees falling on either side of his hips.

"I think I can manage to get over my disappointment. Now kiss me, Tally."

Leaning forward, she settled her lips over his and kissed him so hard, she took his breath away.

But it was the emotional force behind the kiss that made his hands tighten on her hips then slide back to cup her ass.

He loved her ass, so tight and sleek. Wanted it naked beneath his hands so he could pet her.

Wanted to fuck her ass because he was pretty sure no other man ever had. He wanted her to trust him enough to let him have her that way.

The primal instinct made him kiss her deeper. He let her believe she had the upper hand for several minutes as she licked at his tongue and put her hands on his jaw.

Her fingers felt so small against his face. So delicate. But he knew how strong she really was.

He began to remove her clothes. No pretense, no tease. Just

stripped her down to the skin, her clothes dropped on the floor wherever they happened to land.

She didn't protest, let him do what he wanted.

And there was that submissive streak again that made every ounce of his protective nature rise up.

He should've been confused, but he wasn't. He knew exactly what she needed and how to give it to her.

He sensed her spiraling desire in the frantic motion of her hands over his body. She'd already shoved her hands under his shirt and was pulling it up his torso. Leaning forward, he let her pull it over his head, breaking their kiss for just a few seconds before she sealed their lips together again.

Her naked breasts pressed against his chest, nipples tight and hot against his skin. She moaned as he shoved his pants down his legs, toeing off his shoes so he could get his cock free.

Her frantic heat infected him and he barely remembered to grab his wallet before he kicked his pants free.

Going by touch, his mouth still engaged with hers, he retrieved the condom, ripped it open and rolled it down his aching shaft.

"Hurry."

He barely heard her but he felt her words like an electric jolt.

She'd already started to roll her hips against him by the time he grabbed her hips and brought her down on his cock, seating himself to the balls.

The cry she gave could've been pain but he knew it wasn't because she immediately took over the rhythm and began to fuck him hard and fast.

He didn't have to move at all. All he had to do was sit there and let her take him.

But it wasn't in his nature to do nothing.

His hands moved to her breasts, cupping her, kneading her,

making her moan into his mouth and slam down even harder. Every time her ass hit his thighs, his cock jerked, he was already so close to coming.

And every time she lifted in preparation for slamming back down, her fingernails dug a little deeper into his skin, until he was pretty sure she'd drawn blood.

Two minutes, tops, and he felt her shatter around him on a downward thrust, coming so hard her entire body shook.

Wrapping his arms around her, he held her in place as he pumped his own orgasm into her.

TEN

"No, I never said I didn't like to be tied up. I just said we've never done that, and I only wanted to know if rope or silk scarves would be better. Damn, you guys really know how to make me feel like a newb."

As Kate and Annabelle laughed, Talia took another sip of her exquisitely wonderful rum punch and looked Sabrina right in the eyes as she answered her.

"Ropes. Definitely ropes."

Three pairs of widened eyes pinned her in place.

Talia rolled her eyes and lifted a shoulder. "What? It's not like I'm a virgin."

"That's not why we're looking at you like this," Kate wagged her index finger in front of Talia's face. "And you know it."

Talia blinked slightly hazy eyes because it was close to midnight and they'd been drinking rum punch since they'd finished with dinner around nine. During which they'd polished off two bottles of wine.

Talia would admit to feeling no pain whatsoever, although she knew tomorrow morning would probably be a different story. Which was why she was switching to water after this last drink. Probably. Maybe.

"Then why are you looking at me like that?" she demanded.

"Because you, miss, have been holding out on us." Annabelle sounded slightly more slurred than Kate, but then Kate was almost as good as Talia at covering. "When was the last time you used ropes during sex?"

"I don't think I should answer that on account of incrimp— incriminating myself."

"Ooh, you really have been holding out on us, haven't you?" Sabrina pouted, setting her glass on the coffee table in front of her, which separated the matching couches, then leaning her elbows onto it. Kate sat next to Talia while Annabelle and Sabrina shared the one across. "I wanna know what you did with the ropes. Were you the tie-er or the tie-ee?"

Talia shrugged, slumping further into the fluffy couch in their suite at Haven as she did.

Warm blue walls glowed in the dim light from the crystal fixtures around the room. The brochure listed this as the Crystal Suite. Girly without being overly feminine, and elegant without being stuffy or uncomfortable. The deep purple fabrics and dark wood furniture made her want to stay for days. With Dane.

She gave Sabrina a wry glance. At least she tried. Her muscles seemed a little out of her control. Good thing she wasn't moving any farther than the next room tonight. "I don't think those are actual words."

Sabrina scoffed. "How would you even know, considering you're just as drunk as we are?"

"I'm not drunk." Talia tried for haughty and probably only attained confused.

Annabelle snorted. "Yeah, right. And I *know* how you used those ropes. And," she drew the word out impossibly far for someone who had the amount of alcohol in her that she did, "I know who used them on who."

"And how do you know that?"

Annabelle's lips curved in a knowing smile. "Because I know Dane. And I know you."

Something niggled at Talia's alcohol-soaked brain, but said alcohol wasn't letting her grasp it, so she shrugged.

"And what do you know about me?"

Annabelle leaned forward across the table separating the couches. "I know you're not as straightlaced as you think you are."

Talia rolled her eyes, though maybe they were closed the whole time, which is why everything went dark. "And I don't think I am very straightlaced, considering I let Dane tie me to one of those chairs in the Salon."

Dead silence greeted that statement. Three pairs of eyes stared at her with varying stages of fuzzy shock.

And then Sabrina began to laugh. "Oh, my god, you're a freak too. I mean, that makes me so *happy* to hear!"

Talia grinned at the squeal in Sabrina's voice. "We all have our kinks. And we are not freaks. A healthy sex life can involve all kinds of different activities, and you shouldn't be ashamed of any of them."

"Oh, hell." Kate shuddered. "Now you sound like my dad... if my dad ever mentioned anything about sex to me. Which he hasn't. Ever. Thank god."

"Can we *please* not talk about your dad at my bachelorette party?" Annabelle started to laugh. "I don't want that image in my head tonight. Of course, now I've got an image of Talia tied to one of those chairs..."

They all started to laugh again and Talia joined in because she knew they weren't laughing at her.

"Y'all do realize when I first saw that room, I couldn't stop imagining you in there... using all that furniture." She paused. "And let's not forget the toys."

"Yes, please let's not forget the toys." Annabelle's plea was heartfelt. "Have you tried that little—"

"TMI!" Sabrina started waving her hands in the air, having put her glass on the table in front of her. "TMI, seriously. I don't want to know which toys you use. Because I would never be able to look at any of them again. We don't use them too much, but still..."

Talia had to ask, the hold on her curiosity loosened by the rum. "Don't you like them? Or does Greg not like them?"

Sabrina got a sly little smile. "We just haven't found the time to use them yet. Usually we're too happy to have the time together to even think about going to the Salon. We rarely leave the bedroom in Greg's apartment at Haven when we have a few minutes together."

"So what's the freakiest thing you've done?"

Talia's question produced a noticeable lull in the conversation, but when she looked around at her friends, she was pretty sure they were all thinking and not avoiding her question.

"Giving Tyler that much control over me." Kate's quiet voice sounded sober. "I never thought I'd like being tied to a bed and having all control taken away. But I realized, it's not that I don't have control. It's that I'm giving my control to someone I trust."

Talia nodded. "Yep. That. And the fact that I have to be in control of so much during the day. I like not having to always be the one who handles everything."

Annabelle's soft smile gave her away. "I like the fact that Jared loves me enough to allow me to try different things."

Talia smiled at the amount of emotion in Annabelle's voice when she spoke about Jared. "Like what?"

"Like having sex with Jared and—"

As Annabelle stopped abruptly, Talia blinked, trying to bring her eyes into focus. "And? And what?"

"And having others watch."

"Just watch?" Sabrina's quiet question made Talia shift her gaze. "Because sometimes, I wonder... if Greg wanted to ask someone into bed with us, would I say yes?"

"It depends on the person." Annabelle's lips curved in another one of those mysterious smiles. "I'd have to trust them just as much as I trust Jared. But... I love Jared and I can't imagine living without him." She opened her mouth to say something, but Talia knew she'd switched gears before allowing the words to slip out. "That other person doesn't affect those feelings I have for Jared. If your relationship is strong, even if you have feelings for that other person, it won't be a problem."

"Wow. You sound way too sober right now. And Tyler doesn't share." Kate shrugged. "I'm totally okay with that."

"Baz watched Greg and me have sex once." Sabrina spoke so fast, Talia almost didn't understand her at first. "It was the most exciting sex I'd ever had up until then. I love Baz... I mean, not in the same way I love Greg, but still. And I gotta admit I could probably be talked into having Baz join in. But it wouldn't be the same as with Greg. Does that make sense?"

Talia nodded. "Yep. Of course, I may forget you said that by tomorrow morning because I'm still trying to process the fact that Baz was watching you and Greg." She paused and let her lips curl in a smile. "How do you know Baz wasn't just watching Greg?"

Sabrina's mouth dropped open for a second before she started to laugh and threw a pillow at Talia. "I don't. And now I'm going to have to ask him. Baz. Not Greg."

Kate and Annabelle joined Talia as she started to laugh.

"I can honestly say I think I'd rather watch Greg."

Annabelle sighed. "No offence, but the man certainly is nice to look at."

Sabrina and Kate exchanged a smile that confounded the hell out of Talia. She was just about to ask what it meant when they caught her attention.

"So, Talia, are you coming to the party next Saturday or have we scared you away?"

Talia took another sip of punch. Maybe she would have one more. "I wouldn't miss it for the world."

DANE HAD SWITCHED to water after four Macallan doubles.

Most of the other men were still downing alcohol, knowing they didn't have to drive home.

Tyler had started to lose at poker to Jed, which meant Tyler had polished off way more alcohol than he usually did. Greg and Baz sat on the other side of the table, beer glasses in hand, as Greg laughed at something Baz had said.

Geoff Black and Cory Shirk stood at the bar in a private room off Frank's Bar at Haven.

Jed had wanted to play cards at his bachelor party and had forbidden any entertainment that involved strippers. Dane had privately thanked him for that.

Of course, none of the men here, with the exception of maybe Baz, would've wanted them.

"Dane, hey. It's your bet, man."

And he'd lost the last four hands. "Hell. I fold. I'm getting fleeced here."

"You just don't know how to play the game." Baz grinned at him, a pile of chips sitting in front of him.

"And if you had sleeves, I'd say you were cheating."

Baz shrugged. "Nah. I'm just that good."

"I'm gonna go drown my sorrows. Deal me out next time, guys."

He headed toward the bar. Cory and Geoff nodded to him as he gave the bartender an order for water.

Cory nodded toward the glass the bartender set in front of Dane. "Saving yourself for tomorrow night?"

"Definitely not interested in ending up with a hangover tomorrow. We're not as young as we used to be."

"And you're still younger than me." Geoff laughed. "I think I'll take your seat at the table. I'm feeling lucky."

He walked away, leaving Dane and Cory to hold up the bar.

"So you're bringing someone new tomorrow night."

"News travels fast." Dane settled onto the stool next to Cory's as the bartender discreetly moved to the other side of the bar.

"Big deal for you to bring someone."

"First time for everything."

Cory laughed, not buying Dane's obvious attempt to shut him down. Dane and Cory had known each other for years. They had more in common at first glance than Dane and Jed did. They'd known each other just as long as Dane and Jed, but Cory and Dane shared a love for skiing that meant they took several vacations together throughout the year.

They also had a similar taste in women, which translated to a few legendary stories of their European exploits in certain circles.

"I heard she's a friend of Annabelle's."

"Yep."

"Gonna be awkward."

"No, it's not."

Cory still didn't take the hint. "Remember that time in Switzerland? The twins. Did everything together. Dressed alike, did their hair the same. Could barely tell them apart until you got them naked."

Dane remembered, which is how he knew where Cory was going with this. "Not the same. They were sisters. Of course they were going to be competitive. Talia and Annabelle aren't like that."

"True. But they're women. Women don't like when you fuck their friends."

"Why is my love life suddenly so interesting to you?"

"Because I know you, Dane. You wouldn't have invited her if you didn't have feelings for her. And that alone is amazing."

He was trying not to get pissed off, but Cory was pushing his buttons. He knew why Cory was doing it and, if he thought about it rationally, he'd realize the guy wasn't trying to be a dick.

Because he wasn't saying anything Dane hadn't already thought about.

But, damn it, he didn't want to lose her. He wasn't ready to declare his undying love either, but he wasn't ready to give her up.

And he knew there was a really good chance that he'd have to when Talia found out about the nature of his relationship with Belle and Jed.

He looked over to the poker table to make sure Jed hadn't moved, wasn't close enough to hear. "I do have feelings for her, but I'm not asking her for a list of men she slept with before I met her."

Cory shook his head. "You know that's not gonna hold water, because it's Annabelle, and they're friends. Talia finds out, she's gonna be hurt."

"So you think I should just say, 'Hey, just so you know, I've been fucking Annabelle with Jed?'"

"Yep, because if you don't, you know she's gonna hold it over your head."

Shit. "Have a little experience with this?"

Cory sucked back the last of his drink, a club soda because he'd been in AA since he was twenty. "A little."

"And how'd that work out for you?"

Cory gave him a sidelong glance out of glacial blue eyes that could melt women's inhibitions in less than a minute.

With cover-model looks, wavy auburn hair, and rough-edged features, he'd been able to get exactly what he wanted since he'd been born.

His parents had been a Philadelphia power couple until their spectacularly brutal divorce when Cory was fifteen. The resulting battle for the Shirk billion-dollar empire and the control of Cory, who, at fifteen, owned more than half of the global company shares due to his grandparents' deaths, had given Cory a taste for living on the edge.

Extreme sports had been his rebellion, but he'd still managed to get a business degree from Wharton and a law degree from the University of Pennsylvania. "Live Fast, Die Young" had been Cory's motto... until he'd nearly died in an avalanche climbing Mount Kilimanjaro when he was twenty-two. The woman he'd been climbing with hadn't been as lucky.

"She died pissed off at me, and her parents and sister think I'm the devil."

"Shit. Sorry."

Cory shrugged. "Long time ago. Water under the bridge. I just don't want to see you standing on that bridge. Not a good place."

No, he didn't expect it would be. "So what the fuck am I supposed to do? I can't tell her now. At least not until after the wedding."

"Do you think Annabelle will tell her?"

"No. I think she'd check with me first."

Cory's gaze focused on the alcohol on the bar. "This used to be fun."

Dane's gaze narrowed at his friend, wondering, for the first time in a very long time, if Cory might be thinking about falling off the wagon.

"What used to be fun?"

"Going out, getting drunk, having sex with anyone I wanted. Now Jed's getting married. Don't get me wrong. I think Annabelle's wonderful. And she's good for Jed. But... maybe we're just getting too old."

"For what? Sex? Fun?"

Cory laughed and Dane watched his friend's expression lighten. "Yeah. Bringing the mood down, huh? Sorry. Not the time or the place."

"That's not what I'm saying. Is everything okay?"

Cory's eyelids lifted. "Are you asking if I want a drink?"

"No. That's a stupid question, isn't it?"

Nodding, Cory saluted him with his club soda, the look in his eyes hard. "Absolutely, because yeah, I want a drink. Especially now. And I know I can't touch the stuff or I'll be right back where I was nine years ago."

"No, I'm asking if there's something bothering you that you want to talk about."

Cory clapped Dane on the shoulder, his expression easing into a grin. "Yeah, sure. But not tonight. It's not my night."

A loud groan from the card table made them turn in time to see Greg toss his cards on the table as Jed threw his head back and laughed.

"I thought Geoff was crazy when he and Mel got married," Cory said. "Couldn't imagine being tied to just one person."

Dane nodded in agreement. Geoff had shocked the hell out of all of them when he'd announced his engagement five years ago to a girl the rest of them had never met. But Mel had fit into their group like the missing piece in a large machine. A few of the female members of the Salon at the beginning hadn't appreciated her presence, mainly because Geoff had been pretty damn popular. The guy had the stamina of a teenager and the creativity of a world-class artist.

And Mel hadn't been willing to share. Although she had been more than willing to let them all watch.

On the other hand, Liane enjoyed sharing. She and Cory played together a lot, but she wasn't averse to spending time with Dane or other single Salon members. Of which there weren't too many left.

Dane, Cory, Jim Newkirk, Ian Sommerhall, Blake Grantham. And even fewer women... Liane, Deirdre Brant, and Chrissy Fennici.

"Now we're falling like flies. And they look so fucking happy, it's almost pathetic."

Dane knew exactly what Cory meant and he laughed like he was supposed to. But...

"It's not all pathetic."

Cory's smile settled into a grin. "Apparently you're going down, too."

Dane shook his head, unsure about everything and not liking the fact that he didn't have any answers. "Not sure, but I'll let you know."

"YOU LOOK AMAZING."

Despite the nerves making her stomach cramp, Talia smiled. "I really didn't know what to wear. I've never been to a sex party before."

Dane smiled and those cramps became butterflies that fluttered in a flock. "It's not a sex party, and you don't have to do anything you don't want. We can leave early—"

"No. No, I wasn't suggesting we don't go. I want to go. I just don't want to... impede your fun."

"Haven't you figured out yet that I am having fun? With you."

Her smile widened as she joined him in the hall, making sure the door to her suite at Haven closed behind her. She'd arrived only an hour ago, close to nine p.m., and hadn't seen anyone yet. "So am I. With you."

"Good. Then you don't have anything to worry about tonight. Tonight is all about having fun."

He stuck out his elbow for her to take and she did, walking with him to the elevator.

"I guess I just wonder how this works. I mean, do we all just sit around and talk until someone gives the signal and everyone picks a partner and starts to go at it?"

Dane stopped at the elevator but didn't push the button. They were alone in the hall, but she couldn't help herself. She kept her voice pitched low, worried someone might hear her.

She'd been going back and forth in her head all day. She wanted to go. Her curiosity was huge, but she didn't want to get there and be paralyzed. And ruin Dane's night.

"There's no signal since everyone is paired off. We'll have some food, a few drinks, and let things progress."

Progress, huh? Sure, she could do that. She wanted to let things progress. It was just going to be weird.

Yeah, if that's true, why are you so excited?

And she was. Absolutely no denying that.

"Okay."

She looked up at Dane, who still hadn't pushed the button and was staring down at her.

His eyebrows lifted and he stared down at her with a look

she was beginning to recognize. The one that questioned without being judgmental. He had that one down to an art.

"Seriously. I'm fine." She leaned closer, and he bent his head until her lips were only centimeters from his ear. "I'm actually looking forward to seeing you out of those clothes."

Now his lips curved in a way she'd grown addicted to, and she couldn't help but smile back.

And that excitement continued to grow.

Now he pressed the elevator button.

"I like the dress."

She looked down at the pale purple sweaterdress that had a line of functioning buttons up the side from the skirt hem to her waist and another set on the opposite side from the waist to below the raglan sleeve.

It looked good on her and was simple enough that she didn't look like she was trying too hard.

Looking back up, she returned his smile, letting her excitement seep into it. "Thanks. I figured... easy access."

His grin got a little naughtier. "I appreciate the gesture."

When the elevator arrived there were already several people in it, so Dane waved it on with a smile and they waited for the next one, which was empty.

When they got on, he swiped his card again and pressed the button for the fourth floor.

As soon as the door closed, he had his arms around her waist and pulled her full against him.

In the next second, his mouth closed over hers, and he kissed her with enough heat to set off the fire alarm.

Breathing in through her nose, she gave as good as she got, kissing him with her fingers digging into his back, kneading the muscles and longing for the moment she could get him naked. If that was in a room full of people... well, at the moment, she didn't care.

When he finally let her up for air, about a millisecond before the elevator stopped on the fourth floor, he was breathing just as hard as she was.

He tugged on the ends of her hair, a short, sharp yank meant to get her attention, and his smile made her long to tug his head back down.

"Hold that thought, babe."

"I plan to."

The walk to the Salon was short and silent, but Dane's arm around her shoulders held her tight against his side. When he opened the door to the Salon, she took a breath, as if she were going underwater.

But the sight that greeted her was so normal, it almost felt anticlimactic.

They were the last to arrive and everyone else had gathered in the main sitting area. Greg and Sabrina sat on one of the chaise lounges, Greg sprawled back with Sabrina between his legs. Sabrina looked animated and happy, talking with Kate, who sat draped over Tyler's lap on a large, overstuffed wing chair. Tyler's head was turned to the side so he could talk to Jared.

The soon-to-be-married couple shared a love seat big enough for three as Annabelle talked with the other two couples she'd met at dinner.

But when Annabelle noticed her, she popped off the sofa and came to give her a hug.

"I'm really glad you came." Annabelle pitched her voice low enough that no one else could hear. "But please don't feel like you have to stay if you're at all uncomfortable. I know this scene isn't for everyone and—"

"Annabelle, seriously." Talia grinned. "I'm a big girl. If I didn't want to be here, I wouldn't be."

Annabelle's smile widened and the wicked edge to it made Talia smile in return.

"I knew that. Just had to check. Get a drink, you have some catching up to do."

For the next hour, the party was no different from any get-together she'd ever been at. They talked, they drank, they laughed.

The jokes got more risqué as the alcohol loosened inhibitions. But Talia didn't drink enough to make her sloppy. And it did nothing to dull the desire beating through her body.

Every glance she exchanged with Dane fed that desire. Every time his hand brushed against her hip or her back, a shiver ran through her. They shared a small sofa on the other side of Greg and Sabrina and the conversation flowed with an ease she wouldn't have thought possible.

About an hour into the night, during a brief lull, Annabelle bounced off Jared's lap and held out her hand to him. "Come dance with me."

Jared smiled up at her and took her hand. "I thought you'd never ask."

Kate stood, pulling Tyler with her. "Which means you're playing the piano. Come on, big guy. You haven't played for me for a while. I miss it."

Ty bent to press a kiss against Kate's temple. "Your wish is my command." They moved toward the piano in the corner.

Greg snorted out a laugh. "You're so whipped."

A second later, Sabrina's hand smacked him in the chest. "Hey. Just because he gives her what she wants doesn't mean he's whipped. If I ask you to—"

Her words cut off with a short, girly laugh as Greg grabbed Sabrina by the hips and hauled her around to face him. Her knees spread on either side of his hips and she smiled as she dropped her head to seal their mouths together.

Talia blinked as Greg's hands immediately molded to Sabrina's ass and he pulled her down until Sabrina's groin was pressed directly over his. If they weren't wearing clothes, they could easily be having sex.

Talia's breath caught in her throat at the blast of lust that swept through her. It felt like a heat wave and made every part of her tingle and ache.

As she watched, Greg's hands began to move down her thighs, still on top of her loose skirt, but she knew that was just the beginning.

When Greg did reach the hem of Sabrina's skirt, Talia sucked in a deep breath as his hands slid beneath. Though she couldn't see, she knew when he reached his destination because Sabrina moaned. Not loud but the sound still made Talia want to cross her legs against the pulsing in her own pussy.

Blinking, Talia glanced away... and found Cory and Liane blatantly watching the other couple. Cory's hand had found its way to Liane's neck, where he had a strong grip on her. Commanding. Liane's hand lay on Cory's thigh, her fingers slowly flexing.

"Do you want to dance?"

Swallowing hard, Talia turned away from the other couples and locked her gaze with Dane's. So dark. So intense. And so very hot.

Not trusting her voice, she nodded. Tyler's piano-playing hadn't registered, but now the sexy, sultry tune heightened her response.

Dane stood with a smile and held out his hand to her. She took it and let him pull her to her feet. He led her to the space that'd been cleared out in the center of the room.

She hadn't noticed before that the game table was missing. Or that someone had lowered the lights.

As she stepped into Dane's arms and let him lead her

around the floor, she pressed herself against his hard chest and sucked in a deep breath.

Just his scent made her thighs clench again, and she nearly made a fool of herself by tripping over her own feet. Dane steadied her with his hand spread across her back and she turned her face into his neck.

Damn, he smelled good. And felt good. And he even danced well.

"You're very good at this. Dancing, I mean."

"Too many years of formals where I quickly learned I got laid a hell of a lot more often if I actually danced with a girl before trying to get her in bed."

She laughed, shaking her head. "At least you're honest."

"I try. I find it helps when you don't have to remember a lie."

Yes, she absolutely knew that for a fact but wasn't going to open herself up to more questions at this moment. "I knew Tyler played, but I didn't realize how well."

She caught sight of Tyler now, though the lights had been dimmed so much, she couldn't make out more than his form at the piano. And Kate sitting behind him on the bench, her arms wrapped around his waist and her head nestled against his back.

Talia could just imagine where her friend's hands were and what she was doing with them.

Dancing in a tight circle several feet away, Annabelle and Jared had their lips sealed together as they swayed. Jared's hands cupped Annabelle's ass and pressed her into his hips. Though she couldn't see, Talia was pretty damn sure Jared had an erection and was going to use it sooner rather than later.

And the way Annabelle moved against him, she wanted him to speed up his plans.

"Tyler could've been a concert pianist. He chose not to."

Dane's voice drew her attention back to him, although he'd

never really lost it. She'd been completely aware of his every move, even as she looked around.

"What about you?" She pulled away enough that she could smile up at him, watching his gaze drop to her mouth then back up to meet her eyes. "Do you have hidden talents you haven't told me about?"

"Like my ability to juggle while riding a unicycle?"

The amusement in his eyes made her realize he wasn't kidding. "Seriously?"

"What can I say? I'm good with my hands."

Yes, he was. One of which was stroking up and down her back at the moment, spreading liquid heat. It seeped through her body, from her back through to her chest and into her nipples, which tightened into painful little points that rubbed against the lace of her bra.

Lust burned through her body. Her breasts ached, her lungs felt compressed and lacking air. Her thighs clenched involuntarily and her underwear dampened and clung.

Her fingers cramped with the need to brush along his naked skin, to spread open the button-down shirt he wore, a silky, gray-black cotton that molded to his chest and matched his eyes.

She wanted—

Her gaze caught and held on Mel and Geoff. She blinked, twice, just to make sure her eyes weren't deceiving her.

They weren't.

The married couple hadn't moved far from the loveseat they'd been sitting on before. In fact, Geoff hadn't moved at all. Mel, however, was now on her knees in front of her husband. Her hands worked at his pants as she stared up at him with a sultry smile.

Talia considered not watching but realized how foolish that would be. Everyone here had absolutely no desire *not* to be watched. Otherwise, they wouldn't be here, and they wouldn't be doing what they were doing.

And watching Mel and Geoff made her burn even hotter.

"They're really good together." Dane's voice in her ear made it clear he knew she was watching the other couple. "They've been married for several years but have dated since college. Complete extroverts, always have been. Helps they're so in love with each that they enjoy other people watching."

Mel finally released Geoff's zipper completely and slid her hands inside his pants, releasing his cock.

Talia saw every move they made so clearly because they sat in a pool of light from the lamp on the table next to their loveseat. Geoff's face was shadowed but Talia saw Mel's smile as she wrapped her hand around his shaft.

The guy had a short cock but what it lacked in length, Jesus, it totally made up for in width.

"And Geoff loves to get sucked off."

Moving slowly, Dane turned her until her back rested against his chest. And his full erection nestled between her ass cheeks. One arm wrapped around her shoulders, pressing against the tops of her breasts, the other around her waist, keeping her ass tucked tightly against his groin.

Dane was tall enough that he could almost rest his chin on the top of her head. Now though, he rubbed his whiskers against her temple.

They'd basically stopped dancing but continued to sway as Talia watched Mel lean down and take her husband's cock in her mouth. She lavished all her attention on the tip at first, tongue flicking out to play with the slit.

Her fingers, wrapped around his shaft, barely met, the guy was that thick. And Mel's mouth stretched so wide, Talia could only imagine the burn at the corners of her mouth.

God, her own jaw ached just watching. And her mouth watered in response.

What would Dane do if she dropped to her knees right here and took him into her mouth? Is that what he wanted?

Her gaze skittered to her right and caught on Cory and Liane, who were also watching Mel and Geoff. Liane's hand had shifted to rest on the bulge behind Cory's zipper and she stroked her fingers along the denim. Cory's one hand remained on her neck, the other had slipped into the V-neck of her sweater to caress her breasts.

They seemed more than content to watch at the moment.

Talia's gaze moved again, this time back to Greg and Sabrina.

Greg's shirt had disappeared and Sabrina had her hands all over his broad chest. Talia hadn't realized how well built the guy was. Or that he had so many tattoos. She'd have to ask Sabrina about those later.

Right now, Sabrina was a little busy. Her shirt had disappeared as well, and now she wore only a lace bra that barely contained her beautiful breasts. The girl was totally slapped together, something Talia really envied.

Greg seemed to enjoy that, too. With Sabrina leaning over him, Greg was able to get his mouth on her breasts, sucking on her nipples right through the bra.

He still had one hand under her skirt, and Talia watched as the muscles in that arm bunched and, a second later, his hand emerged to drop a scrap of lace to the side of the chaise.

Sabrina gasped, though Talia couldn't hear her, and stared down at Greg. Her scolding look was a total fake and, in the next second, she laughed as Greg let his head drop back so he could smile up at her.

In a flash, Sabrina followed him down to kiss him, hard and hot, both their jaws working. When Sabrina sat up again, she tossed her hair over her shoulders then deliberately sat back onto Greg's thighs. But she wasn't teasing now. She was deadly serious.

Brushing aside her skirt, her hands worked at his jeans, undoing the button fly, not at all careful or slow.

Then she yanked them down his hips, barely giving him time to raise his ass before she had his cock exposed.

What was it with the guys in this group? Damn, not a pencil dick among them.

The funny little thought flitted through her mind for a brief second, making her lips curve until Sabrina moved again.

Even though the skirt covered her from waist to thighs, Talia knew exactly what she couldn't see just from the look of ecstasy on Sabrina's face and the answering expression on Greg's.

Sabrina sank down, her head falling back and her golden-brown hair hanging down until it just brushed Greg's thighs. She stilled for several seconds as Greg's hands gripped her hips. Finally, she started to move.

Slow and teasing, her body undulated above his, her gaze locked with Greg's the entire time. She rode him deliberately, each motion designed to drive him crazy.

From the look on his face, he apparently was most of the way there.

Talia didn't know how Sabrina managed to keep that molasses pace because, even in the low light, Talia could tell she wanted to go faster. And Greg wanted her to go faster, his hands trying to get her to ride him harder.

Instead, Sabrina smiled and Greg groaned. He muttered something to her but Talia couldn't hear him. Then he moved one hand up her back and pulled her close enough that he could get his mouth on her breasts again.

Now, Talia did hear Sabrina moan, such a wanton sound Talia very nearly blushed. And her pussy dampened even more.

She looked around to see if anyone else had been as affected, but Cory and Liane had progressed from fondling to fucking.

Liane had stripped off her jeans and now sprawled on the coffee table at the center of the conversation area.

Talia couldn't believe she'd missed them moving. Then again, she'd been so totally focused on Greg and Sabrina...

Oh, god. She shifted back against Dane, wanting him so badly in that moment, she wasn't able to breathe.

As if he sensed her distress, Dane tugged her even closer, though she couldn't believe that was possible.

His cock felt like an iron pike against her ass, and she wanted to be the woman sprawled on a chair or a table for his pleasure and hers.

"Talia."

"Yes." To anything. Everything.

"That's the word I wanted to hear."

In the next second, she found herself scooped up into his arms and he was moving. Into the shadows.

Some part of her breathed a sigh of relief. Another part of her wanted to protest. But that part was quickly silenced by her last shred of better judgment.

He took her across the room to the darkest corner, away from the fire. A chaise surrounded on two sides by walls and on a third by a short wall topped with marble. She'd seen it earlier but had no idea what it could be used for. Now, she was simply happy it was there.

It offered the illusion of privacy she needed at the moment. It offered her freedom.

As soon as Dane's ass hit the chaise, she twisted in his arms, maneuvering until she had her knees on either side of his thighs and her hands on his shoulders.

She knew he thought she was going to kiss him and he'd

already started to lean in. Instead, she shoved at his shoulders until he got the hint and let her push him down to the chaise.

Smiling at him, which she was sure he could see even in the dim light in this corner, she sat there for several seconds simply staring down at him.

And the view certainly was spectacular.

Dane looked good no matter what he wore, but tonight he took her breath away. Sprawled on the chaise, he looked huge, imposing, and oh so sexy. His narrowed gaze followed her every move, as if he couldn't get enough of her.

Well, she certainly couldn't get enough of him.

That warning bell in her subconscious started to ring but she ignored the hell out of it. No way was she going to allow anything to interrupt her pleasure tonight.

They'd go their own ways soon enough and—

Fuck it. Kiss him.

Leaning forward, she settled her lips over his and kissed him hard and hot, releasing all of her pent-up desire. Practically devouring him.

He tasted like the whiskey he'd been drinking, smoky and sharp. His tongue tangled with hers as she linked their fingers and drew his hands up beside his head, as if she actually could control him.

She felt that leashed power coiled in his body, felt it in the strength of his hands and his thighs. Damn, she wanted to feel it all over her.

But she didn't want to move. Not yet. Not while his lips parted beneath hers and his tongue stroked into her mouth.

Her pussy ached and she found herself rocking back and forth against him.

Her dress had slid up to her hips and only her underwear and his pants separated her clit from his cock. Pressing that aching nub against the ridge beneath his pants, she eased a bit of the ache but only for a few seconds. And then that ache intensified until she fucked him through their clothes.

And he let her. He allowed her to set the pace, to direct the force. Allowed her to dominate him.

And then he didn't.

One second, she was above him, so close to getting off simply by rubbing her clit against him. The next, he released her hands, gripped her hips and reversed their positions.

Moaning at the sudden motion, she bucked against his hips, now spreading her legs wide, trying to get the same friction she'd had before. But Dane obviously had other ideas.

"Not so fast, Tally. You're gonna come, I promise. But the first time is gonna be around my fingers. The second around my cock. The third... well, we can discuss that one."

Third? God, yes, please.

"We'll leave the dress. You're always so completely put together. I like seeing you a little undone."

The edge in his words made something tighten deep in her gut, and she dragged in an unsteady breath. He was the only one who'd managed to undo her in her entire adult life.

She couldn't tell him, couldn't give him that much power.

Instead, she lifted her hands to his shirt and began to push the buttons through the holes.

"And I love the feel of your skin against mine."

When his shirt gaped open, she ran her fingertips down his chest to his nipples. Tweaking the hard nubs, she brushed her fingers through the soft smattering of hair on his chest.

She was partial to men with chest hair. Those guys who shaved always felt stubbly and it turned her off. But Dane had the perfect amount over his pecs.

His abs were smooth, though, and he only had a small thin line of hair that arrowed straight to his groin.

She followed that line now until it disappeared into his pants.

Unbuttoning his pants took less than a second, and the zipper made a satisfying sound as it released.

And when she slipped her hand into his black boxer briefs and wrapped her fingers around his cock, she watched his expression contort with pleasure.

He didn't move as she explored the silky softness of his cock with her fingers, wrapping them around his shaft and allowing their skin to drag together.

"I think the first time should be around your cock."

She hadn't spoken above a whisper, but he heard her.

And she realized Tyler was no longer playing the piano. Soft music now filled the air but above them, she heard soft sighs and pleasure-filled moans. Which meant everyone else could hear her.

Instead of making her self-conscious, it fueled her desire to another level.

Staring up at Dane, she tightened her fingers and tugged at him while her other hand worked his pants down to his hips.

"I think that time should be now."

"Front right pants pocket."

He didn't need to say anything else.

Slipping her free hand into the pocket, she pulled out the condom, each breath getting harder and harder to take.

"But I still think you should come around my fingers first."

Without hesitation, he slid two fingers into her pussy, so wet already, he entered her easily.

Eyes closing on a moan, she felt every inch as he pushed high, one finger stroking at the perfect spot to make her shudder.

She nearly lost her grip on the condom but managed to hold on as he pulled out all the way then shoved back in. Each thrust got harder, almost to the edge of pain. But she liked it. So much.

And he was right. She came around his fingers in seconds, moaning as her pussy clenched and her back arched off the cushion.

Adrenaline buzzed through her body, heightening her pleasure, making her hungrier for more.

"Dane." She opened her eyes when she could, finding him staring down at her, jaw clenched. Waiting.

"All you have to do is ask, sweetheart."

Instead, she lifted the condom between them and ripped the foil. The sound barely registered through the beat of her pulse in her ears.

His cock already bared, she reached for him, rolling on the condom with shaking fingers. When she was finished, he gripped her hips with both hands and slid her closer. It was a short trip, but the friction of the crushed velvet beneath her back and ass further heightened her senses.

The hungry look in his eyes pushed her over the edge.

"Please."

"Anything for you."

The words were a growl, low and fierce, and accompanied by his cock pressing against the outer lips of her pussy.

She expected him to shove inside hard and strong. Instead, he took his time. And tortured her just as much as if he wouldn't fuck her at all.

Grabbing on to his wrists, she levered her hips up, trying to make him sink deeper, faster. Instead he stopped.

And smiled.

Bastard.

God, he drove her crazy and made her want so much more than she could have.

No. No, that wasn't true.

She had him right where she wanted him now.

Smiling up at him, she twisted her hips, working the tip of

his cock inside her. "Come on, Dane. You know you want to move."

"Jesus, do that again and I'll give you anything you want."

The strain in his expression fed her own desire, her pussy tightening around him and making his eyes close for several seconds. Then she repeated the motion, her fingernails digging into the skin at his wrists, not enough to break the skin but enough to mark him. She wanted to mark him, make him hers, even if it was only for this short window of time.

"Now give me what I want."

His head dropped to cover her moan as he pounded into her.

Hard, fast, almost painful. Not hard enough.

Her back arched but his hands pinned her shoulders to the cushion, his hips keeping hers pinned to the chaise.

The wild desire that spread through her body nearly made her incoherent. It short-circuited every functioning brain cell and reduced her to a creature of pure sensation.

Every thrust made her cry out into his mouth, every retreat felt like a devastating loss. So much need inside her, it was almost frightening.

But she couldn't shove it back in that black hole she normally kept it in. Her hunger was well and truly off the leash.

As was Dane's.

She loved the sense that he couldn't quite control himself. That his desire for her was too strong, too unruly. She loved the sound he made every time he pumped back inside, as if he was in pain and couldn't get enough of it.

"*Fuck.* Tally, baby. Move with me."

She obeyed without thought, lifting into his thrusts, making the base of his cock hit her clit at a different angle, one that made her body tighten with pure pleasure.

She struggled against his hands but didn't want him to

release her. She liked the struggle. And it seemed to turn him on. Though he didn't hold her any tighter, his hips moved even faster.

Her clit felt like it might burst, so overstimulated from her first orgasm and from the one she was building toward now.

Still kissing him, she bit at his tongue, just a quick nip, and heard him groan. Ripping his mouth away from hers, he shoved his face into her neck and bit her at the soft curve into her shoulder.

Electricity zinged, pinging pleasure points through her body. She wanted his mouth on her breast, on her stomach, between her legs. Wanted him to shove his cock in her mouth and her pussy and her ass. To give her so much pleasure, she couldn't stand it.

She already couldn't.

After his last, huge thrust, he hit her clit at the exact right spot and she broke.

Oh, god, it felt like her entire body got zapped by an electric jolt, flowing through her until she couldn't take it any longer.

Her body went boneless, even as he continued to pump into her. Even though she was spent, she still felt her body respond until finally, he stiffened, holding himself deep inside as he came.

Long seconds later, he lowered himself to stretch out on top of her.

Still trying to catch her breath, she wrapped her arms around his waist and let herself cling.

ELEVEN

An unfamiliar droning sound woke Talia from a deep sleep.

She wanted to ignore it, but her subconscious wouldn't let her. It kept prodding her.

Can't be late. Get up, get up, get up.

She didn't want to get up. She was warm and comfortable and wrapped in Dane's arms—

A more familiar alarm began to sound. The bleat of her cell phone.

And her eyes flew open as she gasped and sat straight up in her bed at Haven.

"Oh, thank god."

The words were out of her mouth before she realized she'd said them, but they were totally heartfelt.

She had a pathological fear that she'd sleep through her alarm one day and miss someone's wedding.

And after last night... well, she'd set the bedside clock alarm right before she'd left for the Salon last night. She'd also set the small travel alarm and her phone.

Turning her head, she looked for the travel alarm, grimacing

KEEP MY SECRETS   215

as she realized it was on the bedside table next to Dane, still sleeping like the dead.

Which he wouldn't be when the alarm—

BEEP. BEEP. BEEP.

Scrambling out of bed, she made a beeline for the alarm but wasn't fast enough.

Dane's hand emerged from under the covers to swat at the little plastic clock. Which flew across the table and off the other end.

"Shit."

She froze at the end of the bed, biting her lip as Dane flopped onto his back and sighed.

With his eyes still closed, he looked adorably rumpled. His dark hair messy and covering his eyes. She knew he was naked under those covers and wanted nothing more than to crawl back beneath the sheets with him even though she knew she couldn't.

No, she had the most important wedding of her life today. And that had nothing to do with the fact that it was for the heir of the Golden fortune and so much more to do with the fact that one of her best friends was getting married and had trusted Talia to handle the details.

"I'm really sorry I woke you," she said to the unmoving lump of Dane beneath the covers. "I'm going to jump in the shower and get downstairs."

After a huge yawn, which simply made him that much cuter, Dane ran a hand through his hair, settling it back into place in one swipe. Amazing.

Then he opened his eyes as he pushed himself up onto his elbows so he could smile at her.

Damn, she really didn't have time to take care of the constant ache between her legs whenever he was around. Was there anything about the man that didn't make her want to crawl all over him?

"Big day. You want some coffee?"

And he offered her coffee, too?

Be still my heart.

"I would love some coffee. Thank you. You don't mind if I get in now, do you?"

"Not at all." He flopped back onto the pillow. "What time is it anyway?"

"Seven," she said as she continued for the bathroom. Naked and getting a little chilled, she started the shower and turned, intending to go back out and tell him to go back to sleep.

Instead, she gasped a little as she realized he'd come up right behind her. The next thing she knew he was kissing the last of the sleep away and making her body tingly and horny.

His hands spread across her back held her tight against him, his erection stiff and heated against her belly.

Moaning, she opened to him, not wanting to turn him down but knowing she couldn't allow herself to be distracted this morning.

And still she wanted more, because he ended the kiss way too early.

"I know you've got a full plate today and I don't plan to get in your way. I just wanted to give you something to remember me by. And to ask you to save a dance for me tonight."

Aww, her insides got all gooey and her heart fluttered so much she thought it might be growing wings.

Damn the man, there had to be something wrong with him.

Then he smacked her ass, just hard enough to sting, widening her eyes as she stared into his. "I'll order coffee but then I'm catching a few more hours of sleep, if you don't mind. Brunch isn't until eleven and if I get up now, I'll just be in your way."

"No problem."

His smile took her breath away just before he leaned down for another kiss that took what breath she had left.

"Last night was amazing, Tally." He ran a finger along her jaw, making her nipples pucker. "I sincerely hope we get a chance to play again tonight."

He left without waiting for an answer, and she watched his naked, perfect ass until he closed the door behind him.

Holy shit.

Seriously. Holy shit. The guy was way too perfect. Too good to be true.

Shaking herself out of the fairy tale starting to unroll in her head, she jumped into the spacious marble shower stall, separate from the garden tub where she would love to spend hours lounging in hot, bubbly water.

Just not today.

Today, she had a wedding to run. And a routine to stick to.

After her shower, she rubbed herself with scented lotion, dried and styled her hair up and out of her face, and applied her makeup.

When she was happy with the finished product, she slipped on the underclothes she'd laid out last night then retrieved the dress she'd hung in the small wardrobe.

She usually wore a suit for her events, or if it was going to be warm and outdoors, a blouse and skirt.

Today, yes, she was working, but it wasn't all about work.

Today was about celebrating her friends' marriage. So she was breaking tradition and wearing a beautiful dress Kate had made for her last year for her grandmother's eighty-fifth birthday party.

Sky-blue silk that perfectly matched her eyes in a retro fifties style that made the most of her slim frame and average cup size. She loved it and had had absolutely no chance to wear it since that party.

Open-toed silver pumps, diamond studs in her ears, and a two-carat diamond solitaire necklace her grandmother had given her for her twenty-first birthday completed her outfit. No perfume. Too many people had a sensitivity to fragrance these days.

Stepping back to look in the full-length mirror, she inspected herself with a critical eye. She looked good. Even better, she looked confident. Sometimes, that was half the battle. At least her dad had taught her one good thing.

A familiar guilt cropped up, one she'd learned to deal with simply by ignoring it.

Now, she pushed it out of her brain with practiced ease. She needed all her faculties firing in perfect order.

Deeming herself prepared, she took a couple of deep breaths, not because she was nervous but because this was part of her routine and, for days like today, sticking to the routine made sure she didn't forget anything.

All she needed was her tablet, and that was in the other room.

Opening the door silently, she moved through the dark bedroom, resisting the urge to peek at the bed because if she did, she was afraid she'd get off track if she saw Dane.

The thought rankled, drawing a frown. That wasn't her. She wasn't like that, the kind to get bogged down with a man. She was smarter than that—

The lights flicked on and she turned to see Dane sitting up in bed, staring at her intently. "You look gorgeous. Damn, I didn't think you could look any better than you did last night, naked and screaming my name. I gotta say, this is a damn close second."

She couldn't help that flutter again. Damn him. "Thank you. I think."

"Oh, no. Thank *you*. Seriously."

When he smiled like that, she wanted to shake her head at him and throw up her hands in defeat. And crawl back into bed with him.

"I really need to go.'

He grinned, lacing his hands behind his back so his naked chest flexed. "Don't let me stop you. I actually enjoy watching you leave, as long as I know I'll see you again later."

Dangerous. So dangerous. "And you know you will in about four hours."

As if he sensed her impatience—with herself, not him—his eyes narrowed but he didn't say anything more.

But he did smile. "I'll see you at brunch. Sit with me."

It wasn't a request but it wasn't quite a demand either. "I'll see what I can arrange."

After a quick smile and a nod, she headed for the front room and her tablet, which she'd made sure had been charging all night.

Just before she left the room, she closed her eyes, took another deep breath, then opened her eyes and the door, ready to wrestle any problem to the ground.

DANE WATCHED Talia stride through the private dining room where the bridal couple was holding the rehearsal brunch.

There'd been no rehearsal dinner because there'd been no rehearsal. Belle and Jed had spoken with the judge who was going to marry them a few days ago in the atrium, where the wedding would be held.

Annabelle had insisted on keeping the wedding small and, even though the Goldens occupied a spot on the list of the top 500 wealthiest American families according to *Forbes*, Jed's parents had immediately agreed.

There'd be no press and only close family and friends, including Dane's parents. The guest list topped out at a hundred and twenty.

No circus.

"You have the ring?"

Letting his gaze slide away from Talia, Dane turned to look across the table at Tyler and Jed, just in time to catch Ty's rolled eyes.

"Yes, for the fourth time." Ty patted his suit pocket. "I have the ring."

Jed nodded, shaking slightly, which Dane knew was caused by his foot tapping under the table.

Dane couldn't help smiling. He'd never seen his friend this rattled. Not even when they'd been called in front of their college's morals committee. Dane had been sure they were going to be kicked out. Jed had smiled through the entire hearing.

"Jesus, are we going to need to medicate you?" Dane asked. "What's got you so rattled?"

It was close to one p.m. and they'd already eaten. Belle, Kate, Sabrina, and Talia were talking in a circle with Jed's parents and grandmother and Annabelle's grandmother, Aurelia.

Belle was smiling, which was all that mattered, so Dane shifted his focus to Talia.

Who looked completely in charge.

Total turn-on.

Jesus, he hoped he didn't get a hard-on now. Totally inappropriate. But damn...

"I'm not rattled," Jed shook his head. "There are just too many moving parts to this damn thing and I don't want anything to go wrong for her."

"I don't think you have anything to worry about." Dane nodded toward the group. "Talia has everything in hand."

Ty and Jed turned to look at him and so did Greg, sitting to Dane's left.

Damn, he'd walked right into that one.

Jed began to smile and even Ty cracked a grin. Greg just laughed. Which made Jed start to laugh.

"Dude." Jed shook his head. "Thanks. I needed the laugh."

Dane sighed and nodded. "Glad to be of service."

"So things are going well with you and Talia?" Jed's gaze now focused intently on Dane, who had the distinct impression he'd just thrown his friend a lifeline by diverting his attention onto a different topic.

"I don't know what you mean by well. We're dating."

"Is that what they call it these days?"

Ty's dry question made him laugh again. Dane didn't think Ty was expecting an answer so he didn't offer one.

But Jed seemed to be fixated now. "But you like her?"

"Of course I like her. What's not to like?"

"Not a damn thing from where I'm sitting," Greg said. "She beautiful, successful, and she looks like she's got it all under control, even though you know an event like this has got to have more screw-ups behind the scenes than you will ever know about. But that's what makes a great producer. And her events are most certainly productions."

Dane agreed wholeheartedly. The brunch had gone off without a hitch, not a glass or a fork out of place. Each course served at exactly the right moment, and the room looked amazing. Hell, he'd even noticed the beautiful flowers on the table.

"I have no doubt she can handle anything you throw at her." Jed smirked at him. "Including you."

Dane just smiled back, letting Jed take his nerves out on him. Dane didn't think Jed was nervous about marrying Belle, but there was definitely something else going on. Or maybe it was just the fact that it was finally happening that had him slightly freaked.

Didn't matter. He'd get through it. Dane would be there to make sure he didn't bolt before the ceremony.

Of course, when Jed looked at Belle the way he was now, having transferred his attention back to her, Dane had no doubt they'd be fine.

He and Talia, however...

Watching Talia work, whether it was dealing with the wait-staff or talking to the catering manager and the florist at the same time, made him realize just how in control she was most of the time.

And how she lost that control with him.

He liked that. A hell of a lot, actually.

As if she'd felt his gaze on her, her head popped up and she looked straight into his eyes. At the moment, they were the calm blue of the Mediterranean. Last night they'd been closer to stormy gray with passion.

He couldn't wait to make them that color again tonight.

FOCUS, *focus, focus.*

Talia knew she shouldn't be thinking of Dane today, but her subconscious had different ideas.

All through brunch, which she'd forced herself to sit through when all she wanted to do was double-check the decorations and the seating in the atrium, make sure the sound system worked for the third time, and that the specially made drapes covering the atrium windows had no gaps, giving the wedding party complete privacy.

Yes, the hotel staff was amazing and she was sure they'd

done their absolute best, but Talia was still going to check every last thing.

She had a list, after all. And that list was king today.

Brunch had been the only item on her list that required her to sit down for more than a few minutes at a time.

And even though it'd been difficult to switch hats midstream, she'd managed. For Annabelle.

She might be biased, but Annabelle was the most radiant bride-to-be she'd ever seen. And she'd seen her fair share.

Annabelle had greeted her with a huge smile when Talia had knocked on the door to Jared's apartment at ten this morning. Kate was already there. Jared had been banished to Ty's apartment across the hall.

They'd run over a few last-minute details while Kate helped Annabelle out of the gorgeous, candy-pink lace dress Kate had made for her for the brunch. Since the stylist wouldn't arrive until three—which Talia had double-checked with a phone call this morning—to do her hair and makeup, she'd left it down, auburn curls so pretty against the pink.

Kate wore lace as well, but her dress was an understated ruby red that looked amazing against her pale skin and dark hair.

Annabelle had seemed remarkably calm. Excited but not hyper. Some brides she'd worked with had to be medicated to make it through the day without collapsing in a puddle of nerves.

Not Annabelle. She seemed to be taking it all in stride.

After making sure everything was on track there, Talia had knocked on Tyler's door across the hall. Ty had given her an apologetic smile when he'd waved her in. She hadn't understood why until she'd talked to Jared, half-dressed and pacing in front of the window.

She'd never seen Jared nervous or otherwise ruffled, and she hadn't quite known what to do with him. She'd attempted to reason him down but that just made Tyler laugh as he steered her toward the door.

"He'll be fine," Tyler had said. "Trust me. Even if I have to stuff his head under a cold shower for a few minutes, he'll be fine."

Rolling her eyes, she'd said, "Just make sure he's not in his tux when you do it."

Ty had bowed, his amusement with his brother clearly visible. "I wouldn't dare."

Now that brunch was over, she wanted to plunge back into making sure everything was set for the six p.m. start of the wedding.

She'd almost made it out of the dining room without complication when she felt Dane brush her elbow with his fingers. She knew it was him just by his touch.

"Tally."

Her mouth dried at the caress in his voice and the pet name he usually only called her in the bedroom. And even though she knew she should smile and continue on her way, she stopped.

"Hi."

His smile was totally worth it. "Hey. Everything was great."

And the praise in his voice made her smile widen. "Thank you. But I've got a lot more to do so..."

"I know. I just want to remind you that I want a dance and I don't want any excuses."

She wrinkled her nose at him but she was charmed. "Bossy."

His gaze heated. "You like that about me."

Yes, she did. But there was no use in letting it go to his head. "I'll see you later."

And she headed back out into the whirl.

She went to the atrium, where she checked everything she could possibly check, to the kitchen to make sure no problems had come up while she'd been at brunch, back to the atrium, where the floral designer was making last-minute adjustments and the trio playing the service was setting up. After that it was into the banquet room directly off the atrium, where she checked in with the band playing after dinner. She stopped at the back of the room, closed her eyes then let herself simply look.

And couldn't see anything glaringly wrong.

Good. That was good.

Then she looked at her watch.

"Shit."

She only had five minutes to get back upstairs to Annabelle before the hairstylist arrived. And the photographer should be here any minute as well.

Annabelle hadn't wanted every second of the day documented, but she had wanted the photographer with her and her bridesmaids while they were getting ready.

Minutes later, hairstylist, makeup stylist, and photographer in tow, Talia knocked on the apartment door.

"Oh, yay! You're back."

Dressed in a white silk robe that matched the ones Talia had gotten for Kate and Annabelle, Sabrina grabbed Talia's arm and practically yanked her through the door, waving the other women in behind her.

"What's wrong? Did something happen?"

She looked around but didn't see Kate or Annabelle.

"No, no, nothing's wrong," Sabrina said. "We were just missing you. If I ever get married, I'm having your assistant run everything the day of the wedding, and you will take the day off to enjoy being a bridesmaid."

With a sigh of relief, Talia shook her head at Sabrina. "That'll be a good trick, considering I don't have an assistant. Where's Annabelle and Kate?"

"Oh, you will soon enough. You're going to have more work than you can handle by yourself after everyone starts talking about this wedding."

"Yes, well, let's not get ahead of ourselves, now. Annabelle. Where is she?"

"Oh, she's in the bedroom. Kate made her put her feet up for a while so she can dance all night."

Which Talia had suggested to Kate just before she'd left the brunch.

"Then she needs to get her ass out of bed."

Sabrina laughed and, from the bedroom, Talia heard Kate snort and Annabelle giggle.

Clapping her hands, she turned Sabrina toward the bedroom and gave her pat on the ass.

"Let's get this show on the road, people. Shit's about to get real."

"ARE YOU REALLY THIS WORRIED? What the fuck's wrong with you?"

Forty-five minutes before the wedding, they were waiting for the photographer to get there to take some pictures before they headed downstairs for the ceremony.

Jed shrugged as he continued to wear down the carpet in Ty's living room.

Jed's nervous energy had started to make Dane wish he'd forced some whiskey down the guy's throat before they'd donned their wedding suits. They'd all bought custom-made matching tuxedos for the occasion, but Jed kept fiddling with his coat like it didn't fit right.

Which it did, of course.

"I'm fine. I just want to get started. All this buildup is fucking with my head."

"All what buildup? Are you seriously getting cold feet?"

Jed looked at him sideways, disgust in the twist of his lips. "Of course not. I'm just... Forget it. It's stupid."

"What's stupid?"

Jed shook his head. "Nothing. Forget I said anything."

"Jared." Dane put his hand on his best friend's arm, causing Jed to stop. "What's stupid?"

Jared's smile finally looked like himself. "Me."

"Why?"

"Because I'm worried she won't be there."

Dane rolled his eyes. "Okay, yeah, you're an idiot."

Jed shook his head as Dane laughed at him. "I know, I know. Laugh it up, asshat. I'll remember this when it's your turn."

Dane didn't immediately deny that would ever happen like he normally did, but Jed was too distracted to notice.

"Jed, trust me. She'll be there."

Rolling his shoulders, Jed started to pace again. "I know she will. I also know I'm being an idiot. I also know I don't know what I'd do if I lost her. I can't imagine living without her."

"And you won't have to." Ty came up behind Jed and bumped his shoulder against his brother's. "She loves you, which makes you one lucky sonovabitch."

The knock at the door made them all turn toward the entrance.

As Ty headed for the door, Jed turned to Dane.

"Thanks. For standing up with me today."

Dane nodded, his smile easier now that Jed seemed to be a little steadier. "I wouldn't be anywhere else."

"All right, gentlemen." The tiny redheaded photographer dressed completely in black hustled into the living room, one hand pulling Ty along with her. "Line up. On the couch."

Fifteen minutes later, after being bossed around by a tyrant with a camera who must have taken at least a thousand shots, they were in the elevator heading down to the atrium for the ceremony.

As soon as they stepped out of the cage, they were met by a smiling Talia.

Though her focus was on Jed, she did meet Dane's eyes for a quick moment, giving him a smile that threatened to give him an erection. And now really wasn't the time.

Talia disappeared again after issuing strict instructions on exactly where to stand.

The next half hour flew by in a blur and, in no time, he found himself standing in a line with Jed and Ty next to the judge. He'd had a few seconds to take in the beauty of the atrium, and then the musicians began playing "The Wedding March."

Belle began her walk down the aisle.

The smile on her face radiated joy, and Dane snuck a glance at Jed, who finally seemed to have lost his nerves. His confident grin probably inspired several women in the audience to sigh.

And the vision Belle made probably had a few of the guys calling Jed one lucky SOB. Which he was.

When Belle finally took Jed's hand and they turned to face the judge, Dane had a quick second to look for Talia.

He found her slipping into the end of the second row on the left, her gaze glued to Belle.

Beautiful. Absolutely beautiful.

His.

TWELVE

"Oh, my god, Talia. You outdid yourself today. You deserve a bottle of champagne all for yourself and that's exactly what I'm going to get you. Ty, honey, Talia needs her own bottle. Stat."

Draped across Ty's lap, Kate was feeling no pain.

The clock had just struck ten p.m., and Talia's last official duty for the wedding had passed. The band would play for another hour as Annabelle and Jared made their final rounds, saying thank you and good night to their guests.

Then the newlyweds would head back upstairs to their room before leaving tomorrow morning for two weeks in Italy.

Sitting next to Dane at the head table, Talia finally released the breath she felt like she'd been holding for the past thirteen hours.

Smiling at her friend, she nodded her head. "You know what? I think I'm going to take you up on that. Although I will share. If you're nice."

Kate shook her head, eyes closing for a moment. "I know I've had more than enough already. Nope, you earned it, it's all yours. Ty, baby, make it so."

"Yeah, Ty, be the man. Do as your woman tells you."

Greg's jab produced no response from Ty except the middle finger of his right hand pointed in his direction. With his other hand, he signaled for one of the waiters.

Everyone at the table laughed, Talia included.

Kate's compliment, though, made her all warm and fuzzy inside and she'd barely had anything but water to drink.

But by god, she deserved that champagne now.

The ceremony had been beautiful and everything had gone like clockwork. Sure, there'd been a few near-misses. But if she was honest, those had been minor compared to other wedding disasters she'd had to correct.

She wanted to take a victory lap around the dance floor but she didn't want to move.

No, that wasn't true. She wanted that dance Dane had promised her.

And now was the perfect time because the band had started a slow song.

But before she could get the words out of her mouth, Dane stood and held his hand out to her.

"You owe me a dance. The champagne will still be here when you get back."

"Well, most of it anyway." Sabrina gave her an impish grin.

Taking Dane's hand, she let him pull her to her feet, which immediately protested.

"Hang on. I've been sitting too long." Kicking off her shoes, she sighed again. "Much better."

"And here I thought you were the Bionic Woman, able to leap tall buildings in a single bound and spend an entire twenty-four hours in four-inch heels." Kate winked. "My illusions are crushed."

"Yeah, and so are you, sweetheart." Ty covered her mouth with his and kissed her so hard and so long, a few people actually stopped and stared. "Come on, dance with me before you can't stand."

Laughing, Talia allowed Dane to tug her onto the dance floor.

"Hey, I'm not crushed," Kate claimed in a haughty tone. "I'm slightly smashed. There's a difference."

More laughter from behind them but the second Dane took her into his arms, she was aware of nothing else.

Oh, she still heard the music, was aware of the other couples on the floor. None of it mattered.

Only the fact that Dane held her in his arms and danced with her in slow circles, as if he'd realized she was too tired for more than that.

Sitting down for those few minutes had allowed the fatigue to kick in. She'd been running on adrenaline all day and she was afraid she was going to crash as soon as she hit the bed.

And she totally didn't want to do that.

She wanted him. Slow and easy. Hard and fast. Didn't matter. She had this insatiable hunger for him that ate her up inside.

And there went those warning bells again. Which she totally ignored.

Without her heels, the top of her head barely reached his chin so she couldn't wrap her arms around his neck. She settled for laying her head on his chest, wrapping one hand around his neck, and laying the other on his shoulder.

He had his hands splayed across her back in total possession, keeping her tight against him.

Heat radiated from him, sinking deep into her body, making her crave more. His naked skin against hers. Her breasts pressed to his chest. His cock thrusting between her thighs.

Apparently, she wasn't too tired to be horny.

She wanted to leave now, but she always stayed until the

band packed up and left. Usually, they were turning the lights out when she walked out the door.

So she let him sway her around in this little circle.

"I think I'm lucky I booked you for the company retreat when I did." Dane finally broke the silence surrounding them. "I have a feeling you're going to be busy in the coming week."

She smiled, rubbing her cheek against the fine material of his shirt. He'd lost the coat a couple of hours ago.

"I did get a few business cards slipped into my hand today, but we'll have to wait to see what happens."

"You did a great job."

Amazing how just a few words from the right man could make her smile even more as her eyes welled with tears.

It had to be the adrenaline leaching out of her system.

"Thank you. I hate to say this, but I'm glad it's over. Of course, tomorrow's Monday and I've got another event later this week, and the guy I'm working for is a real taskmaster."

Dane laughed, a short, hard bark that widened her smile.

"Yeah, well, this taskmaster is about to order you back to your room for some sleep. You're practically dead on your feet."

He wanted to take care of her. Damn, the man was sweet.

"As soon as the band plays the last song, I'm out of here. But not until then."

She didn't know how long they danced after that, but they were still on the floor when the band finally announced the last song. It could've been an hour. Could have been ten minutes. She had no idea.

She only knew, the second the music stopped, Dane was hustling her back to the table.

Everyone else had gone and Dane stopped to grab her shoes and bag and his coat. With his arm wrapped around her shoulders, he steered her through the lobby toward the elevator.

Dane stopped to shake hands at a larger group, introducing

her by name and making sure to announce that she'd been the wedding planner.

All of the women complimented her on a lovely event, and one woman who said her daughter was planning a January wedding asked for a card, which Talia gave her.

And then they were alone, staring at each other as they leaned on opposite walls.

When the doors opened, Dane swept her into his arms and carried her down the hall to her room.

She should have protested. She was perfectly capable of walking. But... she liked it. She'd allowed no other man to treat her the way Dane did. As if she was his.

For tonight... she was.

He didn't bother with lights when he opened the door. He must have left a light on this morning because a soft glow illuminated the front room. Enough for him to navigate.

He didn't stop until they reached the bedroom, even though she'd started to kiss her way up his neck.

Nibbling kisses that must have stung because she couldn't keep from using her teeth on him.

The desire she'd been suppressing all day began to surge, making her heart race and her lungs strain for air.

Sinking her fingers into his hair, she tugged on the strands until he dipped his head and sealed their lips together, taking her breath away.

She couldn't get enough of him. His taste, the feel of his hands on her body, the sense that he wanted to devour her. Only her.

That he wanted only her. It was a heady feeling and she couldn't be bothered to care right now that that was dangerous territory.

Right now, she only wanted to have him.

Laying her on the bed, he came down on top of her,

covering her completely. She reveled in the sensation of being surrounded by him for several seconds until he rolled. Now she was on top of him, their lips still pressed together, tongues entwined, breathing the same air.

His hands roamed up and down her body and on his last downward stroke, he caught the zipper at her back and pulled it down.

Cool air brushed against her bare back. She hadn't worn a bra because she hadn't needed one with this dress, and she couldn't wait to shed every scrap of clothing and roll around on this bed naked with him.

But Dane didn't seem to be in any big hurry. He stroked her skin through the opening of the zipper, making her shiver and moan. His fingers spread heat that tingled through her, stoking the blaze already firing through her.

Wriggling her hips against his, she wanted to hear him as she rubbed against his thickening cock.

He rewarded her with a groan, his hands tight on her hips. In the next second, she found herself on her back again, smiling up at him as he sat back on his heels.

"Don't move." He stripped off his shirt as she watched, and she was pretty sure he'd practically torn a button off it while he did.

She had no trouble obeying his order as he got rid of his clothes until he finally stood by the side of the bed after discarding his pants.

Naked. So beautifully masculine.

"Your turn now."

She smiled up at him, though she could barely breathe at the lust chiseled into the lines of his face.

Slowly sitting up, she let the dress fall from her shoulders and down her arms. Keeping her gaze locked to his, she got it over her hips then handed it to him, leaving her in a tiny pair of bikinis and thigh high stockings.

"I like those." He put one knee on the bed and touched a finger to the lace trim on her stockings. "Keep them."

"So bossy."

One side of his mouth kicked up. "Yeah. And you like it."

She did. Maybe a little too much.

Shaking the thought out of her head, she pushed herself up onto her knees. "I think you should stop talking and start making me come."

He lifted one hand to cup her breast and squeezed, making her suck in a deep breath. "It's not gonna be that fast and easy tonight, sweetheart."

"I certainly hope not."

He caught her nipple between his thumb and forefinger and squeezed until she shuddered with pleasure. "I fucking love your mouth."

Lifting his other hand to cup her jaw, he ran his thumb along her lips, his eyes narrowing when she flicked her tongue at the tip.

"Then lie back and let me use it for something other than talking."

His chest expanded as he drew in a deep breath and she put her hands over his pecs, feeling his tight nipples press into her palms.

He stared down at her for several seconds before he threw himself on his back, hands behind his head.

"Suck me, babe."

There was no grin on his face now, only lust, and her chest tightened. There was a demand in his voice she hadn't heard before. One that backed up to the edge of cliff.

He was ordering her to do something to him. There was no hint of a question.

And she had no second thoughts about giving him what he wanted.

Without hesitation, she leaned over and sucked his cock into her mouth.

She took him down as fast as she could, no tease, no build up.

His grunt of approval and the hand he shoved into her hair to hold her to him made her pussy ache. And made her suck him harder.

She worked him with her mouth, sucking him deep then pulling up until only the tip remained. She used her tongue to tease the slit, feeling his hand tighten in her hair until she could barely move.

When she did, the burn on her scalp made her moan.

As she took him back down, she felt his free hand slide down her back to her ass, smoothing against the skin before he lifted away.

And returning with a smack that made her shiver in reaction and swallow around him.

"Fuck. Yes." His hand returned to stroke her ass again but this time, he slid a finger between her cheeks until he found her tight entrance.

She'd never had anal sex, and right now, with his finger circling that tight pucker, it was the only thing she wanted in the world.

For him to own her completely.

"You like that. Good. Because I'm taking that ass tonight."

She shivered, taking him even deeper and swallowing.

"God damn, Tally."

She had no other warning. In a flash, she found herself flat on her stomach with a pillow shoved under her hips.

"I'm only going to ask one question."

His voice sounded so calm, but she knew beneath it, there

was so much command. Her bones went limp and her hands latched onto the bed frame in front of her unconsciously.

"Have you ever had a man take your ass before?"

She sucked in a deep breath. "No."

"Good answer." He ran a hand from her right hip to her thigh, a hard caress. "Only gonna ask once. Yes?"

"Yes."

"Thank you."

She felt him press his lips to the base of her spine then he shifted around. She heard the bedside table drawer open and close, then he was back with his knees on either side of her thighs.

When he put his hands on her back, her eyes closed. For the next few minutes, he ran his hands along every inch of skin he could touch. Kneading, massaging, making her feel boneless and weightless. And so turned on she could barely breathe.

When every inch of her was sensitized and she felt ready to vibrate out of her skin, he shifted again, rearranging the two of them until his knees were spreading her thighs apart.

Cool air rushed against her burning pussy, which he quickly covered with his hand. His middle finger pressed against her clit and she moaned as if on cue. Flicking the little nub until she squirmed beneath him, panting, Dane pulled his hand back and pressed one long, thick finger inside her pussy and fucked her with it.

She tried to cry out in relief but all that emerged was a moan. Her fingers tightened around the slats in the headboard until they hurt, but she didn't release them. Not even when he stroked the exact spot inside that made her come.

"Yes, that's good, baby. Come for me."

He continued to thrust his fingers inside her for several more long seconds but before he withdrew, she felt something cool and slick dribble between her cheeks.

"Dane."

"Soon, baby. Gotta take this slow."

Using his fingers, he spread the lube, rubbing at that little hole until she felt herself loosen up for him.

Only him.

Her breath caught as she felt him press one finger into her, just the tip, and even that felt way too big.

Jesus, this would never work.

"Trust me, babe. Press back."

Without really knowing what she was doing, she moved, and his free hand smoothed down her ass, petting her.

"That's right. I swear this will feel amazing. Trust me."

She did. More than any other man in her entire life.

And she wanted this. Wanted to be completely owned by him.

"Good. Jesus, Tally. Yes."

His finger started to pump, slow and gentle. Widening her.

When he pulled out completely, she groaned, needed more.

"Slow. Gotta go slow."

She wasn't sure if he was talking to her or himself. She only knew she didn't want him to stop.

"Now," she panted. "Now."

He made a rough sound in his chest that made her pussy clench and ache.

And then she felt the broad head of his cock pressing against that tight rear entrance.

She didn't think it would ever fit. It couldn't. He was too big, and yet she wanted—needed to be filled.

The steady pressure increased until it almost became pain. But a pain so pleasurable she knew she wanted more. So much more.

Finally, that tight ring of muscle released and he was inside. And now the pressure made her gasp.

Wow, too much. She couldn't take more.

Still, she didn't release the headboard to push him away. She wanted it all.

"Relax, baby. It gets so much better."

Then he showed her just how much.

She'd never imagined how sensitive those nerve endings were, how much that slight bit of pain made her want to scream and beg for more.

And when he finally started to move and the pleasure jolted through her like an electrical shock, she became a creature dedicated only to pleasure.

And the man who gave it to her.

TALIA WOKE WITH A START, feeling as if there were an elephant sitting on her chest.

Blinking sleep out of her eyes, she sat up and slid to the edge of the bed, not even trying not to wake Dane.

The second her feet hit the floor, she made a beeline for the bathroom.

All she knew was she had to get behind a closed door before she had a panic attack. She knew them intimately, though she hadn't had one in years.

Why now?

Hands clenched around the edge of the sink, she concentrated on her breathing.

She'd had the best sex of her life last night. Why would that have triggered a panic attack?

Because it wasn't about the sex. It was about him.

It was all about Dane.

She didn't want to leave him. Wanted to blow off everything

in her life and spend every moment with him. Her heart was engaged, and that was a disaster waiting to happen.

The worst part was, she'd let it happen. Opened herself up to it and went down without a fight.

And yet, part of her couldn't breathe. Part of her wanted to run.

Part of her knew she needed to break this off now before she couldn't find a way out.

It wasn't fair to Dane.

Yes. Absolutely, it wasn't fair to Dane that she took what he offered but gave nothing in return. She didn't have anything to give in return. Not now. She couldn't. He didn't know who she was and when he did...

No, better to leave now.

Then why did the rest of her feel like she wanted to cry?

"ARE YOU FREE TONIGHT? We could get some dinner."

Talia smiled over her shoulder but quickly looked away as she buttoned the last button on her sweater.

"I'm not sure. Can we play it by ear? I've got so much to do today, I'm just not sure where I'll be with everything by dinner. I may need to work all day."

Dane's gaze narrowed. That had sounded legit, but he heard something in her voice... "How about tomorrow?"

She shook her head, not bothering to turn this time. "Can I let you know tomorrow? I had a great time last night, Dane, but I've just got so much work..."

Finished with her sweater, she turned toward him with an apologetic little smile.

And his gut clenched. Under the bland smile, he saw a little fear. And that made no sense whatsoever.

What the fuck?

"Everything okay?"

Rolling her eyes, she ran her hands down her sides, smoothing her clothes, but Dane was pretty sure it was out of nervousness.

"Yep, fine. Thanks again for last night. I had a wonderful time."

Yeah, now he knew something was definitely wrong.

"Tal, wait."

She did, giving him more of that same smile, but there was a hint of desperation to it now.

"Spend the weekend with me. I don't care if we do nothing but sit in my condo and watch TV and eat delivery. I want to be with you."

Her eyes widened and her lips parted in stunned shock.

He'd shocked himself, but now he couldn't think of anything he wanted more. He'd never asked another woman to do nothing at all with him except spend time. And he wasn't above using the command she seemed to love in bed.

"Pack a bag and be here Friday. Tell me when you'll get here and I'll make sure we have the entire weekend to ourselves."

She blinked and, for a second, he thought she was going to give in.

Then she shut down. He couldn't think of any other word for it. She simply went blank.

Her smile totally fake, she sighed and grabbed her overnight bag and the garment bag hanging from the armoire door.

"I'm sorry, Dane. I really need to check my schedule before committing to anything. I'll let you know. Talk to you soon."

The door closed behind her, leaving him feeling like he'd been kicked in the gut.

THIRTEEN

"Will, you got a few minutes? I need to talk to you."

Tuesday morning after the wedding, Dane stuck his head in his brother's office. With Jed gone, Dane needed a sounding board.

Because he'd fucked up good, and he wasn't sure he could fix it.

"Of course, what's up?" Will didn't bother to look up from his computer, just waved Dane into the room.

"I need advice."

Will's head popped up and, before Dane had even closed the door behind him, Will was asking, "Jesus, who died? You look like you're gonna be sick."

"No one died. But I think I fucked up pretty good and I might've ruined my relationship with Talia."

Will's eyebrows shot sky-high. "Whoa, you used the word *relationship*. I don't think I've ever heard you use that word when you're talking about yourself. Ever."

Dane took a deep breath as he walked to the window overlooking the city. He wanted to kick the glass, but he'd freak out his brother and he didn't want that.

"Shit, Dane. What'd you do?" Will's phone signaled a text. "Hold that thought. Wayne's here."

"Good. That's good. I think I'm gonna need all the help I can get."

"Damn, that sounds really bad. What the hell—No, just... hold the thought. Wayne will be here in a minute."

Dane used the time to get his thoughts in order, though that was pretty much a lost cause. Jesus, he'd been so stupid. And arrogant.

Christ, if she ever found out...

Behind him, he heard the door open.

"You ready to head out—Oh, hey, Dane," said Wayne. "I didn't know you were here."

"He wasn't until a minute ago," Will said. "Close the door. Dane's got a problem."

"Oh, yeah? What kind of problem? Are you okay? What happened? How can we help?"

Even without seeing their faces, Dane heard the worry in his brother's and brother-in-law's voices. The fact that they were so seriously concerned for him helped steady his nerves a little. Not much, but some.

Because, Jesus Christ, he'd screwed up.

Turning, he found Will leaning against his desk, arms crossed over his chest, his brows drawn down hard. Dane recognized that look. He'd seen it more than once during contentious editorial meetings. Wayne's expression held a world of compassion. And that perfectly explained the difference between them and why they worked so well together.

"It's about Talia."

"Okay," Wayne encouraged. "What about Talia?"

"I'm pretty sure I fucked up pretty good."

"Okay," Wayne said again, even more patience in his voice

this time, as if he understood Dane's precarious state and didn't want to push him over the edge. "And..."

Dane sighed, trying to find a way to say what he needed to say without coming off as a complete asshole.

"Dane, just spit it out," Will barked at him. "Whatever it is, we—"

"I dug into Talia's background and came up with a mother lode of shit. And I think I set something in motion, and I don't know how to *fucking* undo it now."

Will and Wayne exchanged a glance before their narrowed gazes landed back on him.

Finally, Will said, "And by shit, you mean..."

"I mean I found out something that's gonna make her hate me."

Wayne frowned. "I'm sure she won't—"

"Yeah, she will. Damn it."

He wanted to kick the desk, kick the chair, punch a hole in the wall. Anything to alleviate some of this miserable, angry frustration. And he only had himself to blame.

Sighing, he threw himself into the closest chair, elbows on his knees, fingers laced together until they turned white.

"I found out she changed her last name around the time she turned thirteen. Her parents were divorced and I didn't really give it much thought. And then yesterday morning..."

"Yesterday morning... what?" Wayne prompted when Dane shook his head, shoving a hand through his hair.

"Yesterday morning, she started to pull away, physically and emotionally. And I—"

He cut off, unable to find the right word.

His brother had no problem. "You panicked."

"I didn't panic. I... got concerned."

Will rolled his eyes. "You panicked and decided you needed to know all her secrets."

"No. Yes. *Shit.* Maybe."

"Jesus, Dane." Will sighed and rubbed at his forehead with his fingers. "I thought you learned your lesson in college."

"What happened in college?" Wayne looked between them as Dane sank back into a chair.

"I almost ruined one of my professor's careers by exposing his private life."

Will rolled his eyes. "Yeah, the operative word being *almost.* Still, I thought you learned your lesson."

Dane snorted. "You would think, right?"

"So what'd you find out that's so awful?" Wayne asked. "Is she a closet serial killer?"

Dane shook his head then stared directly into Will's eyes. "Nothing we say can leave this room. You have to swear."

Will and Wayne exchanged a quick look then nodded slowly.

Dane took a deep breath. "I told you her parents were divorced and her mom changed their names back to her maiden name, but that wasn't all. Someone did a thorough and careful wipe on her first thirteen years. They basically wiped her father out of her existence."

"And, of course, your curiosity got the better of you." Will shook his head. "Jesus."

"Damn it, I had every intention of leaving it alone. I swear. And then yesterday morning... She basically told me it'd been fun and she'd call. And I'm pretty sure she meant she wasn't going to call."

"Ooh." Wayne winced. "I can see how that would sting."

"So I thought if I knew what'd happened in her past, I could figure out what I needed to do to get past this. I just wanted to know what happened."

"And you found out." Will settled into the couch across from Dane, where Wayne already sat. "I can't imagine you went out and shouted it from the windows. And please tell me you weren't stupid enough to confront her with it."

Dane grimaced. "Of course not. But when I hit a certain level in my, um, investigation, it triggered an alarm. Someone knows I went after that information. Of course, that just made me more determined to ferret out the information."

"And obviously you did." Will looked more intrigued than upset with him now, the newshound in him coming out. Will had the heart of an investigative reporter and, even though he hadn't worked as a reporter for more than ten years, the guy still had all the instincts pointing him toward a good story.

"Yeah, but it wasn't what I thought."

Wayne lifted his brows. "So," he drew the word out to at least four syllables. "Are you going to share with the class?"

Dane looked straight at Will. "You gotta promise me, Will. You can't run with this. Seriously. Now that I know why she changed her name... You have to give me your word."

Will paused. "Before I do, am I right in guessing this is newsworthy?"

Dane didn't have to answer. He only had to stare at Will.

"Fuck."

Wayne looked between the two of them. Then he put his hand over Will's and squeezed. "Will."

Will sighed. "Of course. But you know, if the story breaks, I can't—"

Dane nodded, his stomach taking a dive at the hell that it would cause Talia. "I know."

"You have my word."

Dane closed his eyes for several seconds. Damn it, he was such an idiot.

"She's Frederick Van Dyke daughter."

Will closed his eyes and leaned back in his chair, sighing.

"Who?" Wayne's brow furrowed. "Why does that name

sound familiar?"

"*Fuck.* Only you, Dane. Jesus."

"Hello?" Wayne knocked on the table between them as Will opened his eyes and shook his head at Dane. "Someone want to clue me in?"

Finally, Will sighed and turned to Wayne. "Remember the Dawson Savings and Trust failure?"

"Yeah, but I don't— Oh. Oh, *shit. That's* her father?"

"Jesus. You still can't mention his name in certain parts of the South without risk of being stoned. He went to jail, got shanked, and has been in a vegetative state for the past several years. An interview with Talia or her mom would be a fucking gold mine."

"Even after all this time?" Wayne asked.

"Hell, yes. There were a few congressmen who wanted to indict his wife, as well, even though they never turned up any evidence that she knew what her husband was up to. I also remember the huge controversy when a local reporter used a connection with a friend of the daughter to ambush her for an interview. The girl tried to keep her cool but ended up looking like a spoiled, delusional brat and the video went viral. She was thirteen and she got savaged."

"And this just keeps getting worse." Wayne shook his head. "You have to tell her you know, Dane."

Dane grimaced, closing his eyes in disgust. "I haven't told you the worst part yet."

"Spill it." Will leaned back into this chair. "It's not gonna get any easier the longer you wait."

"I think I tipped off one of your damn reporters about the fact that she's living in the area."

Will dug his fingers into his temple, as if trying to rub away the pain. Dane knew the feeling. "How the hell did you manage that?"

"I needed background info. I was digging through the online archives and Jason Kelly was looking something up at the same time. He's a goddamn investigative reporter and of course he wanted to know why I was digging into a decades-old case from Kentucky. So he started to follow my trail and I'm pretty sure he thinks he's got a lead on the mother. Thanks to me."

Wayne's indrawn breath was a hiss. "Kelly's a pit bull. When he's got his teeth in something, he's not gonna let go."

"I know that." Dane could barely get the words out from between his clenched teeth.

Wayne laid his hand on Dane's shoulder. "You have to warn her."

"I'm not sure Jason'll be able to dig out the info he needs. It's buried to hell and back. I think the only reason I kind of knew where to look is because I know her. Hell, I might just be paranoid and completely off track. But my gut says I'm not wrong about this."

Wayne shook his head. "Christ, Dane. You really know how to make a mess, don't you?"

Dane slumped back in the chair. "Not helping."

"Yeah, sorry." Wayne's grimace made Dane feel even worse. "Okay, so how are you going to fix it?"

"I don't have a fucking clue. If I tell her I was digging into her past, she's going to hate me. If I don't tell her, I'll feel like shit for keeping it from her. If anyone else finds out, she's going to be in the center of a shit storm that I brought down on her."

"Yeah, anyway you look at it, you're fucked."

Will held out his hands. "Let's not get too far down the rabbit hole yet. Can you do anything to fix this?"

"Other than making sure Jason doesn't track down her mother, you mean?"

"Can you do that?" Wayne asked.

"Short of having Will tell him straight-out to stop?" Dane took a deep breath and shook his head. "No."

Then again...

Maybe there was something he could do.

"I know that look on your face," Will said, regaining Dane's attention. "Maybe you want to get a second opinion this time before you go off half-cocked."

"I don't think half-cocked is the problem. I think his whole cock got him into this one."

As Will rolled his eyes, Dane actually smiled for the first time in what felt like forever.

"Okay, here's what I'm thinking."

DANE HADN'T CALLED.

Of course, she'd told him not to when she'd left. She'd told him she'd be in touch.

Although she'd meant about the board retreat next weekend and she knew he'd realized that.

Wednesday morning, Talia sat at her desk, setting up last-minute details for Connelly Media's board retreat, staring at her phone as if she could make it ring.

Which was stupid because she didn't want him to call.

If he called, she'd break down and answer it and that would totally contradict what she'd said Monday morning. When she'd told him she'd had fun but it was time to move on.

Groaning, she leaned forward, resting her forehead on her arms crossed on her desk.

The headache she'd been trying to hold off for hours wasn't letting up, and she was going to have to move to dig out some pills for it in a minute.

But for now, she just wanted—

"Knock, knock. I brought hot chocolate and cupcakes from that shop in West Reading. Oh, my god, I think I died and went to chocolate heaven. Just the smell put ten pounds on my ass, I swear. Hey, what's wrong? Too much partying last night? Were you out with Dane again? Get your head back in the game. We've got work to do, girl."

With a long-suffering sigh, Talia looked straight at Kate and said, "I hate you."

That was the good thing about friends. They knew how to read you.

Kate hmphed and set the box of to-go cups and a pastry bag on her desk. "What's up your butt this morning? Did you forget we had this appointment? Nice to know I'm so—"

"I wasn't with Dane last night. And I've got a slight headache. Sorry."

"Did you take something for it?"

"No."

Kate dug around in her purse, withdrew a pillbox and set two pills in front of Talia. Then she waited with her arms crossed until Talia swallowed them with a sip of water from the glass on her desk.

"Satisfied, Mom?"

"Not yet." Kate divvied up the cups and set a decadent-looking chocolate cupcake with a mound of white icing dusted with more chocolate in front of her. "Tell me what's wrong. And don't screw around and say 'nothing.' We still have business to discuss, so let's get this out of the way now."

"It's just the headache."

"Bullshit. That's not why you look like death warmed over."

"And thank you so much for making me feel even better."

Kate rolled her eyes. "Oh, please, even your death warmed over looks better than me on a good day. Are you coming down with something?"

"Other than a case of indigestion if you don't stop asking all these questions, no, I don't think I'm coming down with something."

No, she'd already had her episode of utter stupidity for the year. Pneumonia on top of that would be anticlimactic.

"Okay, now I know something's up. Is it work or personal?"

"It's personal and I really can't talk about it."

After a few seconds, Kate nodded. "Fair enough. But you know you can tell me anything, right? No judgment, and I'll even keep my mouth shut as long as I can, if that's what you want."

Until this moment in her life, Talia had never considered telling anyone her secret. For so long, it'd been too raw, too painful.

But she'd realized, after she'd cried herself to sleep last night, that if she didn't get over the guilt and shame and fear stemming from a part of her life more than a decade in the past, she might never get beyond it.

And that scared her more than the thought of her life being destroyed again.

But she had no idea how to keep her secrets and still let people inside her walls. Kate, Annabelle, and Sabrina had gotten closer to her than anyone in her life, and they still didn't know who she really was.

Kate frowned at her. "Okay, now you're starting to freak me out. What happened? Did something happen between you and Dane? Did he... tell you something?"

Something about the way Kate asked the question sent a warning signal through Talia's brain. It wasn't the first time she'd gotten this vibe that there was something about Dane that everyone was tiptoeing around. Of course, she'd been keeping more than her fair share of secrets for so long, she certainly didn't have the right to judge anyone else.

"What should he have told me?"

Kate grimaced. "We've all got secrets. But they're ours to tell, right? Not anyone else's. And if you don't want to tell me this one, which is obviously eating you alive, that is totally up to you. I just want you to know, unless you eat kittens or like those stupid 'Real Housewives' shows, there's nothing you can tell me that will make me think you're an awful person, Tal. Because I know you too well."

Talia blinked away tears and tried to hold back the all-out blubbering she wanted to indulge in. But before she could, Kate wagged her finger in front of her face.

"Don't you dare. My makeup is perfect today and you are not allowed to mess it up, because I've got a date with my man tonight."

Talia huffed out a laugh and shook her head, her amusement allowing her to get her tear ducts under control.

"Bitch."

"And proud of it." Kate nodded. "Now, eat that damn cupcake and tell me what the hell's going on."

Twenty minutes later, Talia had polished off the two-thousand-calorie icing bomb, and Kate couldn't stop shaking her head, her expression full of pained sympathy.

"That is some major suckage, Tal. Damn, I'm so sorry. How'd you manage to keep this all a secret for so long?"

"I asked my mom that a few years ago, when I realized just how much of a task it must have been, and she told me there are still a few decent people left in the world and she hired one of them to wipe my dad out of existence. It helped that my grandparents hated him and basically disowned my mom after she married him. They didn't attend the wedding, and they never told anyone their daughter had gotten married. Guess Granny and Pop knew what they were doing after all."

"No offense, but your grandparents give my dad a run for

the 'chilliest people in the world' award."

True. "But they took us in when we needed them. And they never threw it in my mom's face that my dad was a criminal. At least not while my brother and I were around."

"So how does this all tie into you mooning over Dane?"

"Because my last words to him Monday morning were along the lines of 'It's been real, have a nice life.'"

Kate's eyes widened. "And why would you do that?"

"Because he asked me to spend the weekend with him and then to consider moving in."

Her mouth hanging open, Kate looked almost comical. "Holy. Shit. Seriously?"

"That was the gist of it, yeah."

"And I say again... Holy shit." Kate just shook her head. "Wow, Tal. I've gotten to know Dane over the past year and I have to say, if he even hinted at the fact that he wanted you to move in with him, he is not kidding. I mean, the guy's never had a one-on-one relationship with anyone that I know of."

And right then, it clicked. Her brain whirred like a tiny engine powered by a rubber band as it made connections.

"But he's obviously slept with women at the Salon."

Kate continued to stare straight into her eyes. "Of course. And you had to know that. He and Jared started the Salon."

"Not you."

Kate shook her head. "Not me."

Another rubber band snapped. "Annabelle."

Kate just stared.

"Of course." Talia felt like someone had taken her lungs in one hand and squeezed the living hell out of them. "I should've figured that out from the beginning. Well, damn. Wish I hadn't eaten that cupcake because I have a feeling I'll be shoving my face full of rocky road ice cream later today."

"Tal."

She held up one hand. "I'm fine. Really. And right now, we have work to do, don't we?"

Kate grimaced, shaking her head. "Damn it. I shouldn't have opened my fricking mouth but—Look, you need to talk to Dane about this. I'm such an idiot."

"No." Talia forced a smile, which she knew looked totally fake. "But maybe we should reschedule our meeting to another time. I've got a lot of stuff on my mind right now and another meeting later today that I need to focus on."

"*Shit.*" Kate looked sick to her stomach. "Damn it, Tal. Don't do this. Don't shut yourself down like this. You need to talk this out with Dane. Let him explain. Tell him I fucked up and this is all my fault. Jesus, I hate seeing you hurt."

Hurt? She wasn't hurt. Right now, she felt nothing. Except this huge hole in her gut.

She gave Kate another cool smile. "No worries. Weren't you listening earlier? It takes a hell of a lot more to make me cry than to find out the man I've been sleeping with had been screwing one of my best friends. And thanks again for the extra time to prepare for my meeting. I think I'm going to lock up and get a jump on traffic."

Kate looked heartsick and, though Talia really didn't blame her for spilling the beans, she wasn't in much of a mood to reassure Kate either.

"*Fuck.* I don't want to leave you like this."

Talia heard the frustration in Kate's voice but knew that nothing that had happened here was her fault. She just couldn't manage to think through that nice, numbing fog that had seeped through her body. She remembered it from her teen years, the hazy chill that shut down every painful feeling leaching through her system at the moment.

"I'm fine." Talia rose, walked over to the small closet by the door, and slipped on her coat, then gathered her tablet and a few folders and stuffed them all in her bag. Then she smiled at Kate as she waited for her by the door. "Thanks for the cupcake."

With a heavy sigh, Kate grabbed her stuff and walked over to Talia. When Kate hugged her, Talia managed to pat her friend on the back. It'd been a hell of a day, hadn't it? And no, it was in no way Kate's fault she felt like she'd been run over by a truck. But still... She couldn't return the hug. She felt nothing at the moment.

It was no one's fault, she kept telling herself as she drove down the maddeningly crowded Schuylkill Expressway. It just was.

Of course Dane had had a sex life before dating her. Once she'd known about the Salon, she should have realized there was more to Jed and Dane's relationship than they'd told her. And why should he have spilled his entire sexual history to her? She certainly hadn't. She'd just been another woman in his bed.

She couldn't allow herself to think she'd been more.

She had a business to run, which she'd built from nothing. She'd had two confirmed jobs in the past two days. Big jobs. An eightieth birthday party for the matriarch of a Main Line family and a second wedding for a Philadelphia circuit court judge.

Work. That's what she needed to focus on now.

Not Dane.

By the time she reached Philly, her headache had returned. Since she was too early for her meeting with Trudeau, she decided she'd find a quiet corner in a nearby coffee shop and do a little work. Greg's film offices weren't that far from Haven, so she decided to park at Haven and walk.

She took her time, trying to clear her mind. Or at least get it steered toward her meeting with Trudeau and away from Dane.

Since she hadn't gotten a phone call saying she'd been replaced for the Connelly Media board retreat, she figured she'd see him then. And by that time, she'd have gotten over this ridiculous crush. Because that's all it was. A crush. It couldn't be anything more.

As she walked along Chestnut Street, she caught a glimpse of greenery out of the corner of her eye. It wasn't quite freezing today and the bright sun made it feel warmer than it really was. And she needed a distraction.

Bronze gates enclosed a small park. Even in winter, the park beckoned her to come in and sit. No one else lingered there now, probably because it was too cold to spend more than a few minutes admiring the scenery.

Talia barely felt the cold. Her black wool slacks were more than warm enough, and beneath her down coat, she wore a cotton shirt and cashmere sweater.

Lowering herself onto one of the benches in a sunny spot, she felt the cold seep through her slacks for several seconds before she willed herself not to feel it.

Turning her face into the sun, she closed her eyes and breathed.

Every other thought was about Dane. Every second they'd spent together seemed to run through her head, a constant litany.

She didn't know how long she sat there, but when she finally roused herself enough to look at her watch, she realized she'd lost track of time and would be a few minutes late for her meeting. Not the impression she wanted to make on Greg's partner, damn it.

She only realized how cold she'd gotten when she tried to stand... and her legs protested.

Wow, okay, maybe she'd stayed outside a little long. Her legs didn't want to work right away, and she had to stand there for several seconds before she could get her knees to bend. Damn, they ached.

And even though she wore fur-lined gloves, her fingers felt

like they'd locked into fists. And they *hurt*.

She needed to be inside.

By the time she reached Greg's office, she couldn't stop shivering and she was cursing herself silently.

This is what happens when you let a man inside your head. You lose track of yourself.

"Talia, hey. Tru should be here in a— Are you okay?"

Talia forced a smile for Greg, who had been sitting at the reception desk. "Not enough to do, you need to be the receptionist, too?"

Greg didn't smile as she'd meant for him to do. "You don't look good."

"Nice to see you, too. I'm fine, thank you."

Greg shoved away from the desk and headed straight for Talia. His hands landed on her shoulders before he rubbed his palms to her elbows and back again.

"Damn, you're freezing. Where'd you walk from?"

"Haven. It's not that far."

"No, it's not, but it's freezing out there. Come with me. Let's get you warmed up and get a cup of coffee in you."

"Actually, do you have any hot chocolate?"

Greg wrapped an arm around her shoulders and guided her down a hall and into another room.

"Hot chocolate. Coming right up."

Even though she now shook uncontrollably, she still had enough sense to be suitably impressed by the room.

"Is this your office? You sure know how to live."

"No sense in renovating a building from the floor up if you don't make it into a space you want to spend time in. Let me get this fire going and then I'll have Tru find some blankets. Maybe we should get you to the hospital."

"No. Really. I'm not that bad." And totally belied that statement with a full-body shake. "I don't need a hospital. Seriously.

I feel stupid enough as it is. I'm just cold. As soon as I warm up a little, I'll be fine."

Greg didn't look convinced but he nodded and stood. "I'll go get Tru."

He disappeared and a second later she heard him call out for his partner somewhere inside the building while she sat there and felt so stupid. And so, so cold.

And miserable.

She wanted Dane. Wanted him to take her back to his place and tuck her into his bed and crawl in beside her—

No, that's exactly what she didn't want. Because she wasn't going to be seeing him like that again.

Sure, they'd meet professionally and she'd see him when her friends got together, but he'd move on and she...

Wouldn't.

She'd still be here in the cold. Alone.

A shiver ran through her and she berated herself for going there. Hell, she was twenty-six, not fifty-six. She still had a few years before she decided whether or not she'd ever be able to trust a man enough to tell him who she really was.

Then again, maybe you've already found him.

"Talia, here, wrap this around you," Trudeau said as something heavy and warm settled on her shoulders. "We sent an intern over to the coffee shop for hot chocolate. Are you sure you don't want us to call a doctor? You freaked out Greg and that's a tough thing to do."

Trudeau sat on the couch next to Talia and pulled the thick blanket she'd put on Talia's shoulders around her until it enclosed her completely. The younger girl looked worried, and Talia's cold lips curved in as much of a smile as she could form.

"I'm just cold."

"Did something happen? Did you get lost? Greg said you parked at Haven and walked, but it's not that far. I told him we need to get parking access somewhere in this building. I'll have to talk to the zoning authority—"

"I didn't get lost. I sat in that little park just off the street... and lost track of time."

Tru's eyebrows rose. "It's freezing out there. How—"

"Let's just say I have a lot on my mind right now."

Tru frowned. "Okay. But you're not leaving until we get you warmed up, and we'll get you a ride back to Haven. Do you want me to call Dane?"

"No." Talia grimaced at the sharp tone of her voice. "Sorry. No, there's no need to call Dane. We're not actually seeing each other anymore."

"Oh. Damn, I'm sorry. You guys looked—" Tru slapped her hands on her thighs and pasted on a smile. "You're looking better already. So, would you like to go over a few things while you continue to warm up?"

Grateful for the change of subject and the chance to get her head back into work, Talia nodded and reached for her bag.

She had to flex her fingers a few times before she could grasp her tablet and then Tru started to run down the agenda.

Talia saw a kindred spirit in Tru. They could become friends.

If you can thaw out enough to let anyone else close to you.

Wow. Now, she was taking potshots at herself. Fucked-up did not begin to describe her state of mind. Luckily she'd had enough practice to cover it all with work.

And who does that remind you of?

"HEY, it's Greg. Your girl's here and I think something is wrong. You might wanna get your ass to my office now."

The message was short but, coupled with the phone call

he'd had earlier from Kate, it made Dane run for the door.

He didn't stop to call Greg back or get a cab. With traffic in Center City, it'd take him longer to drive. Besides, if he walked, he'd expend some of this pent-up frustration and maybe be able to restrain himself from walking into Greg's office, throwing her over his shoulder, and heading back to his place.

Of course, she might send him packing once he got there, but he'd worry about that then.

Fuck. He should've known this was going to happen. Should've known she'd find out about his relationship with Jed and Belle. He should've fucking told her himself.

God damn it.

The walk normally would take a half hour. He made it in less than twenty minutes and, by the time he got there, his brain had cooled enough that he could think a little more clearly. Standing by the door to Greg's production offices, he knew he couldn't march in there and demand she let him take care of her.

She had every right to turn him away.

And if she did...

Taking a deep breath, he pushed through the doors.

No one sat at the reception desk, probably because Tru hadn't hired a receptionist yet. But somewhere, a bell rang. Down the hall to his left a door opened and Greg's head poked out. Motioning him forward, Greg disappeared again and Dane headed that way fast.

"No, that's not gonna happen. I already told you, we either get the permits or we don't film in the city. I'm not screwing ourselves on our production company's first film. Just get the fucking permits."

Greg threw his phone on his desk with a disgusted look on his face. "Kids today. I got a brilliant twenty-year-old first-time director who wants to be a fucking guerilla filmmaker. Jesus."

Greg headed back toward Dane and the door. "She doesn't know you're here, but I didn't figure it'd matter to you. I gotta warn you, though. She told me not to call you."

Dane followed Greg back through the door and through a maze of other rooms, most of them stacked with boxes or furniture. Only a couple looked occupied.

"Is she okay?"

"Yeah, she's fine. But when she walked in, she looked out of it and pretty damn near frozen solid. Said she lost track of time."

Dane's guts clenched. "What do you mean, 'out of it'?"

"I mean she looked like she wasn't thinking clearly. Like something happened and it fucked with her head."

Fuck. His fault. All his fucking fault.

First, he'd pushed her and then he'd lied to her, if not in words then by omission.

And now here he was, ready to steamroll her again.

Okay, he needed a plan. And he had no time to make one, because Greg had stopped and stuck his head into another room then motioned for someone.

Seconds later, Trudeau appeared, biting her lip.

Greg nodded toward the room. "How is she?"

"She's fine. Honestly. I think she just spent a little too much time outside. She can move her fingers and her toes and we were going over details for the premiere party and she's not confused or forgetful. I think you overreacted just a little."

Greg shrugged. "Sue me. She scared the crap out of me when she walked in. I like her. And she's one of Bree's best friends. No way can I let anything happen to her on my watch."

Tru rolled her eyes and shook her head, but Dane understood completely. "And you didn't tell her I was coming?"

Tru shook her head. "But I think she'll be happy to see you."

Yeah, probably not, but he wasn't leaving until he'd seen her.

Dane slipped into the room and found Talia standing by the fireplace in the wall, arms crossed over her chest as she stared at the flames. The second he stepped forward, she turned.

She sighed but showed no other sign of how she felt. "I should've realized he'd call. I'm sorry Greg dragged you away from work."

"He didn't drag me away. He called and I came."

Her cool smile made his hands clench. "I'm sorry you wasted your time. There's no reason for you to be here."

"If you think that, you're fooling yourself."

Talia stared at him, her expression a blank mask. "I may have been doing a lot—"

"Come to dinner with me tonight. We can talk then."

He was sure she was going to decline and braced himself for rejection.

She shook her head. "I'm not sure that's a good idea right now. I've got—"

"We need to talk, Tally."

Something flickered through her eyes but it was gone before he could decipher it. Probably nothing good. So he was shocked as all hell when she nodded.

"You're right. We should talk. Do you think we can do it closer to my home? I have an early app—"

"Of course. I'll pick you up at six thirty."

Again that cool, unemotional smile. "That's fine."

"Can I take you back to Haven? Are you ready to go now?"

She blinked and looked away and he thought he'd lost her.

"I'd appreciate the lift, thank you. If you don't mind waiting a few minutes. Tru and I have a few more items we need to discuss."

Yes. "That's fine. I need to talk to Greg. Just let me know when you're ready to head out."

He left before she could change her mind, though it took

everything he had not to hustle her out the door.

Greg waited for him in the hall and he cocked his head toward the office across the hall.

Dane followed and, once Greg closed the door behind them, Dane shoved a hand through his hair. "What the hell happened?"

"She said she sat down for a few minutes in the park down the street and lost track of time."

"She could've gotten frostbite, for Christ's sake."

"Hey man, she's fine. I'd be more worried about what sent her over the edge."

Dane grimaced. "I'm pretty sure I know the reason for that."

"Then fix it. For your sake and mine. I wasn't kidding about Bree. She'll eviscerate you if you hurt her."

Dane nodded, knowing he'd deserve whatever Sabrina handed out. "Hey, I got that information you wanted on Baz's lead singer. And it took a little work, but I tracked down the girl. I've got a file for you. I'll send it to you when I get back to the office."

"Great. Appreciate it. Just attach an invoice—"

"You know I'm not going to charge you. And you don't want to know where or how I got the information."

Greg raised an eyebrow at him. "One of these days, you and I are going to have a talk about exactly what you do at that magazine of yours."

"Exactly what's advertised."

"Bullshit." Greg laughed. "But now's not the time."

No, it wasn't. He wanted Talia to himself. Now. "Thanks again for calling me."

"Pretty easy to see how you feel about her. Kind of a no-brainer."

Grimacing, Dane shoved a hand through his hair. "Not easy for everyone."

Greg shrugged. "Sometimes, you just gotta work a little harder and a little longer for the good stuff."

Dane nodded, realizing he'd never really wanted anything in his life that he was willing to put so much time and effort into without a guarantee.

He'd been spoiled all his life. By his parents, his sister, his brother. He'd grown up believing it wasn't something to be ashamed of.

And he hadn't let it affect his career. He'd built his magazine from the ground up. He was ready to take on more challenges. And he was ready to take the next step in a relationship with Talia. His parents would love her. His brother and sister and brothers-in-law would think she was amazing.

They just needed to get beyond the fact that he'd had a sexual relationship with one of her best friends and that her father was a notorious embezzler.

Piece of cake.

Shit.

A knock at the door and Trudeau poked her head in. "We're done for now. She's getting her stuff together."

Dane was on his feet and headed for the door before Tru had finished. He squeezed the girl's shoulder in thanks but his mind was already on Talia.

She was stuffing things into her bag when he entered the room but she turned immediately. And for just a second, he caught a glimpse of hurt in her eyes.

Fucking hell.

"You ready?"

She nodded, flexing her fingers before reaching for the bag.

"Here—Can I carry that for you?"

He thought she'd refuse. Instead, she nodded. "Thanks. I... Thank you. I appreciate it."

That cool tone grated and he wanted to kiss her until she

melted against him.

Deep breath. Slow down.

They took a taxi back to Haven, the conversation quiet. He asked about the party she was planning for Greg's film premiere. She laid out her plans in the same quiet tone she'd been using since he'd asked her out.

She apologized again for him being pulled away from work for nothing. He told her it had been no problem.

He didn't say it wouldn't have mattered if he'd been in the middle of a board meeting. He would come whenever she called. Or whenever she needed him, even if she didn't call.

By the time they got back to the hotel, she looked like her normal self. So damn beautiful he wanted to undo the twist of her hair and let it fall around her shoulders so he could wrap his hands in it and hold her still for his kiss.

Instead, he slid out of the taxi then reached in to help her. She gave him her hand without hesitation and let him hold on to it as they walked into the hotel.

"Thank you for the company, but I'm sure you have to get back to work. And I'll see you tonight."

He had nowhere to be that couldn't wait, but that wouldn't score any points with a woman like Talia. So he nodded.

"I'll pick you up at six thirty." He didn't want to wait any longer to see her but he figured six was pushing it.

Her eyes narrowed, as if she were trying to figure out his angle.

Good luck with that, sweetheart.

This was no game, but he was going to win anyway. No other outcome was acceptable.

TALIA HAD ALMOST MADE it to the elevators when she

heard a familiar voice.

"Hey, I didn't know you were here."

Talia turned, plastering on a smile for Sabrina, dressed for work and emerging from an unmarked door near the registration desk.

"I'm not." She returned her friend's hug and, if she clung a little longer than normal, well, she'd had a tough day. "I had a meeting with Trudeau. I just parked here because it's easy. I didn't see you at the desk and I don't really have a lot of time. I have to get back to my office for a call."

Not completely a lie. She did have calls to make. Just not on a timetable.

"Bummer. I have a few minutes for a break. Do you have time for coffee?"

She didn't want coffee. She wanted to vent but she couldn't. Not now. Because if she started, she was afraid she wouldn't stop.

"I don't. I'm sorry. I can't—"

"Are you okay?" Sabrina's eyebrows drew down as she stared at Talia. "You look a little pale."

And she felt like she was about to hyperventilate. Which meant she had to get out of here. Now.

"I'm fine. Really. Just rushed." She gave Sabrina another hug then began to back away. "I'll call you later."

Now Sabrina looked worried, but Talia had to get away. She couldn't stand here any longer and spew small talk like everything was normal.

"Tal—"

"Talk to you soon." The elevator dinged behind her and relief poured through her in a rush. "Promise."

The elevator doors closed and she sucked in a deep breath as she hit the button for the parking garage.

Home. She just wanted to go home.

FOURTEEN

"What do you mean, you had a request for an interview?"

"Now, don't panic," Talia's mom soothed over the phone. "There's no need for it. I had a call earlier today from a reporter who wanted to interview someone at the farm about our work with rescued horses. I guess I should've led with that."

With a sigh of relief, Talia closed the oven door and leaned against it, the warmth soaking into her back. "Uh, yeah. That would've been the better way to start that conversation."

Her mom laughed and Talia's hands began to unclench from around the phone. "Sorry, sweetheart. I know how touchy you are about that stuff."

Touchy? You could say that, especially today. "So, are you going to do it?"

The horse farm her grandparents owned had saved Amelia's sanity after all the bullshit with Talia's dad. Working the horses with Amelia's father, who rehabilitated injured racehorses and ran a rescue for abused horses, had given her mom a sense of purpose, especially after Talia's brother had gone to college. Now that her father was getting older, Amelia did much more of the work with the horses.

Why shouldn't she want to talk about it to others?

"I think so, yes. And that's part of the reason I wanted to talk to you." A pause. "I'd like your permission to share our story, if the opportunity arises. I'm tired of living in fear. You should be, too."

Talia nearly choked at her visceral reaction to her mom's rational statement. Her lungs tightened as every muscle in her body tightened to the point of pain.

"But I hesitate to do anything," Talia's mom continued, "because I'm afraid it will adversely affect your business. And I absolutely don't want that. You're doing so well, and I don't want to be the cause of anything hindering that."

She didn't want to affect Talia's business? That was her first concern?

What about ruining their *lives* a second time?

The jackals would descend again. Reporters would be banging on their door demanding answers. Neighbors would give interviews about how they'd been spending cash like it was water. The people her father had ruined would threaten terrible retribution if they didn't come up with the money to repay everything her father had embezzled.

It'd start all over again.

Talia caught herself gnawing on the inside of her mouth, a nervous tic from her childhood, and forced herself to stop. To take a breath.

"Talia?"

She was no longer a child. She'd built her career on her own from nothing, with no help from her mother or grandparents. And certainly not from her father, who'd paid the ultimate price for his crimes.

No one had recognized her in years. No one had cornered her and badgered her, asking her how she felt about those people who'd lost their life savings while she wore designer clothes and took trips to tropical islands.

She was an adult who could take care of herself, today's foolish stunt notwithstanding.

She took a deep breath. "You do what you need to do, Mom, and I'll back you one hundred percent. Whatever happens, we'll deal with it."

Damn, that hadn't sounded convincing at all. Even though she meant what she'd said, with everything else going on right now, the thought of their secrets being told made her gut twist.

As if her mom had read her mind, Amelia said, "No. You know what? It's not the right time."

"Mom, wait—"

"No. No, sweetheart, I'd never forgive myself if I did something to screw up your business. I'll just call him back and decline."

"No, you will not." Now her voice sounded much stronger. "When's the interview?"

"Not for a couple weeks."

"Keep the interview, Mom."

Her mom sighed so loudly, Talia heard it through the phone. "I'll think on this some more—Oh, there's the door. Harry and I are going out tonight. I'll run it by him."

Her mom had been dating a neighboring landowner for the past several years. He'd been so good for her. "Wait, Harry knows?"

"Oh, yes. He's known for years."

Talia felt the floor beneath her shift. "You told him."

"I didn't have to. He recognized me."

Oh, my god. Her lungs constricted until she could barely breathe.

"Talia? Are you okay?"

No, she wasn't. "Yeah. I'm fine, Mom."

She needed to think, but she didn't have time. Dane would be here in minutes.

"You don't sound fine."

"Sorry. I'm just... waiting for someone to get here."

"Friends coming over?"

Her mom spoke like she hadn't just rocked Talia's world. "I have a date."

"Really?" Her mom sounded pleasantly surprised. "I didn't realize you were seeing anyone."

Talia hurried to explain. "We've only gone out a few times." Which was true but not the whole story.

"Are you serious about him?"

There was no way to answer that question. Not now.

"No. We're just..." What? "Dating."

But that wasn't right. They'd gone beyond dating. Especially after today, when he'd shown up at Greg's offices, hair windblown and cheeks ruddy. When she realized he'd dropped everything and walked blocks to be with her.

"Oh. Okay."

Talia knew that wasn't what her mom wanted to hear but she couldn't give her mom that type of resolution.

"Sorry to cut you short, Mom, I've got to finish getting ready. Have a good time to tonight."

Her mom paused. "You too, sweetheart. We'll talk more tomorrow."

"Sure, Mom. Tomorrow. Love you."

"Love you, too, sweetheart."

DANE KNOCKED on the door to Talia's apartment, anticipation a tight knot in his stomach.

He'd spent the few hours they'd been apart coming up with

a plan. They both had secrets. Hell, everyone had secrets. They just needed to talk them through and move forward.

Because he'd decided she was his. Now he just had to prove to her that she could trust him. He'd come clean, with everything. They'd talk and they'd move forward.

The door opened, finally, and she smiled at him. But something had happened.

"Come on in." She waved him through the door, closing it behind him. "It's bitter out there tonight."

Yeah, it was, but he wasn't here to discuss the weather.

Wrapping a hand around her neck, he bent to kiss her. No sense in pretending he was going to play nice. He wanted her, she wanted him, and they'd figure the rest out as they went.

Still, he had to admit he was relieved when she didn't pull away. She let him kiss her, opened her mouth and let him taste her.

Yes.

Wrapping his arm around her waist, he pulled her flush against him, groaning under his breath when she molded herself to his body.

He had enough self-control to keep from picking her up and carrying her to her bedroom, stripping her naked and licking his way down her body.

He didn't have enough not to pull her hips in tight against his so he could grind his swelling erection into her.

Christ, he wanted her naked and under him, but he needed to prove to her that he wasn't only here for sex.

He wanted to prove he was here for her, whatever she needed.

So with regret, he pulled away, opening his eyes to stare down at her. Her eyes were slower to open but when they did, he smiled to see the desire in them.

"Hi."

Her return smile looked a little hazy and he wanted to beat his chest like Tarzan. Until the worry began to seep back into her expression.

"Hey." She moved out of reach. "I hope you don't mind, I thought we could eat in tonight. I made lasagna, but if you'd rather—"

"Sounds great. Love lasagna and I'm ready to eat whenever you are."

Her wry smile faded fast. "You're way too easy to please tonight."

He had her all to himself for the whole night. Yeah, he was pleased. "If you want, I can make things harder for you."

She laughed, shaking her head as she turned and headed through the living room and dining area into the kitchen at the rear of her apartment.

But she didn't respond.

Patience.

The scent of red sauce caught his attention and his stomach growled, reminding him that he hadn't eaten in hours. And that she cared enough to cook for him.

Okay, yeah, he might be reading too much into a simple dinner but, damn it, he wanted her. And he was going to have her.

They kept conversation light over dinner, deliberately steering clear of any subject remotely controversial.

"Kate said she wants to get married on a beach," Talia said as they settled themselves on the couch with glasses of wine after storing the leftovers and loading the dishwasher together.

"I'm sure whatever Kate wants, Kate gets. Ty'll give her anything."

"They're good for each other. Like Annabelle and Jared."

The hammer dropped. He felt it like a kick in the gut as she stared straight into his eyes.

"I know you know about Belle and Jed and me. What do you want to ask? Anything at all."

She took a deep breath, as if screwing up her courage. "Were you ever going to tell me?"

"Yes." He hoped to hell she could tell that wasn't a lie. "I was looking for the right time, but there wasn't one. I know I should have told you."

"So tell me now."

"I'm not going to say it was just sex. It wasn't. I care for Belle. She's a friend I love. We had fun together, the three of us. But it was more about pleasure than emotion. She's not *mine*."

Not like Talia. She was his. Did she understand the distinction?

"Are you still—"

"No. I haven't been with them for a couple of months. And Jed was there every time. We were never together without him."

She blinked and her gaze fell, as if she were trying to process what he just said. It was hell, but he managed not to push her to respond.

"I'm sure you realize it was a shock for me."

"I do."

"I can't exactly hold it against you." She lifted her gaze and he breathed a sigh of relief. "I haven't exactly offered up my entire history to you."

Would she now? Christ, he wanted her to trust him. To tell him her secret so he could assure her he would never betray her.

She sighed and he braced himself for rejection. "I'm not ready to commit to a long-term relationship right now. I'm not sure I ever will be." She paused, biting her bottom lip before taking a sip of wine. "But I'm enjoying our sexual relationship and I'm willing to continue that."

Willing, huh? How about wanting?

Steady. Just... don't push.

"Okay. Sure." Fuck, that came out a little more bitter than he'd expected. "I'm willing and able."

TALIA REALIZED Dane was treating her with kid gloves as he settled back onto her couch. He looked relaxed, sated.

But she knew what lay beneath that calm exterior, and he wasn't fooling her. He was up to something. She just didn't have enough brain power tonight to figure out what.

All she wanted right now was for him to pick her up, settle her on his lap and use his body to take her out of her mind.

Even though she knew about his relationship with Annabelle.

That was a large part of the reason she didn't feel guilty for using him for sex. Sex was just a game to him. And she couldn't let it mean anything more to her.

"So when do you want to get naked?"

Dane's quietly amused statement refocused her attention on him and she found him watching her with a lazy intensity that revved her libido.

How did he manage it? How did he make her want him so much that she literally forgot about the fact he'd been sleeping with her friend?

"Can I finish my wine first?"

"Of course. I'm patient."

"That sounds like a warning."

His lips curved in that way that made her heart pound against her ribs. "I guess you can take it as one. It'll be more fun."

Yes. This is what she needed. This lazy, sexual back-and-forth. Nothing heavy. Or emotional.

Now, she just needed him to make her forget, to draw her out of her head. "What will?"

"When you finally give in."

"And what if I don't want to make it hard on you? What if I just want you to make me come?"

His smile became a wicked grin. "Then I'd have to tell you, you already made it hard."

The air in the room evaporated as her smile widened. "You've got a dirty mind."

"And lately it's all been focused on you, sweetheart. So it's all your fault."

She smiled back at him, shifting around on the couch until she sat on her knees facing him. She reached for his shirt, her hunger for him growing exponentially with every breath he took.

The flannel plaid felt so soft beneath her fingers but she didn't stop to stroke the material. She had another, more stroke-able goal in mind.

"Then I guess I might as well take the advantage while I've got it."

She popped his shirt buttons, anxious to get to the bare skin beneath. Touching him was like a fever in her blood. She wouldn't have been able to stop herself if she'd tried. And she would've warned anyone who got in her way to save themselves the heartache of defeat.

"Tally."

Her name came out close to a growl and she spared him a quick look. "You've told me often enough, I can have anything I want. Well, right now, I want you."

"And I'm not arguing—*Jesus*."

She had his shirt open and had leaned forward to bite him, sinking her teeth into one of his nipples. The warmth of his skin and the slightly salty taste made her moan. Her hands on his abs held him down as he jerked against her but he wove his fingers through her hair and held her tight.

While she licked and bit at him. She was deliberately rough with her teeth but she stroked her fingers lightly down his stomach. His abs contracted and she paused there for a few seconds to pet those beautiful ridges before continuing down to his jeans. She didn't take her time, too impatient for what she wanted.

And she almost had her prize.

Her fingers worked to release his belt and his buttons, baring the black boxer briefs and the hard ridge beneath those.

After she brushed the tip of her nose along against the line of hair disappearing into those briefs, she lifted her head and looked up into his eyes, currently slits of glittering black.

"Lift."

"Tal."

She raised her eyebrows. "Lift."

He did, shoving his hands in his waistband to help her drag it down and free his cock. But before she could move to take him in her mouth, he put his hands on her shoulders and held her away from her prize.

She looked up at him, a question in her raised brows.

Then he smiled. "I just needed to make sure. Just know, after you get me off, I'm going to make you come so hard, you won't be able to walk to bed."

Her breath caught in her throat and she choked out a shaky laugh. "I'm going to hold you to that."

"I really fucking hope you do."

With her lips curved in a smile, she let her gaze fall back to her prize.

Leaning forward, she rubbed her lips over the silky skin on the tip of his cock.

So soft. So hot.

Dane radiated so much heat, his big body a furnace that made her want to strip naked and rub every inch of her body against his.

She would. After.

Wrapping one hand around the base of his cock, she took her time tormenting him, moving her head back and forth, her lips brushing against the crown. His cock throbbed in her hand, seemingly trying to get her to take him inside.

But she wasn't going to be rushed in this. She wanted to torment him, make him squirm. Give her the sense that she was in control.

On her next pass, she let her tongue peek out and lick across the head. His guttural moan made her smile as he put his hands on her shoulders and exerted pressure.

He wanted to force her to take him in her mouth, but he stopped just short.

She needed to let him know she wanted his domination. Wanted him to own her.

At least in this.

With leisurely decadence, she parted her lips and took the head between her lips. She sucked in air through her nose as she swirled her tongue around the fat crown, sucking hard.

She felt his cock stiffen, his muscles tighten as he groaned again. She heard rather than saw his head fall back against the cushion, his fingers kneading her shoulders.

Giving herself over to instinct, she took him in deeper, her lips tight around the shaft, her tongue teasing as she sank lower, following her fingers to the base.

She moaned at the taste of him on her tongue. So good. She could lose herself with him and not worry about being found.

Drawing back to the tip, she started a slow, steady rhythm that finally coaxed Dane's hips into moving.

At first, his movements were gentle, hardly movement at all.

Not the wild, unrestrained motion she craved and was determined to draw out of him.

She increased her pace, fingers digging into his hips as if he was trying to get away. Her lips stretched to the max as she dove down.

It only took another couple of complete swallows before she got what she wanted.

His unleashed passion.

"Talia."

His voice held so much dominance, she shivered.

And he froze.

Moaning in protest, she ran a hand up his chest and clutched at his shoulder.

Please. Please.

As if he'd heard her, he began to thrust into her mouth.

Yes.

She took everything he had, let him sink deep into her throat and control the motion. Control her.

His hands cupped her head and held her steady. Even though he wasn't. He was losing control but trying not to.

So she bucked against his hold, forcing him to hold her tighter.

Losing herself in the motion, she let him take her.

When he groaned and clutched her tighter, she sucked him hard and took everything he pumped into her mouth.

FEELING like he'd just run a marathon, Dane gave himself a minute to catch his breath.

Tally rested her cheek on his thigh, eyes closed as she drew in deep breath after deep breath.

He still had one hand on her head, fingers woven through

her hair. He wasn't sure he could let her go if she tried to move away.

You really need to tell her.

The only questions were when and how.

She shifted, and his fingers automatically tightened but she wasn't going anywhere. She'd stretched her legs out along the couch. Still fully dressed.

He intended to fix that. Right now.

First, he pulled his pants back around his hips. Didn't want to be an idiot and stumble. Then he slid his arms around her and lifted her against his chest before he stood, heading for her bedroom at the top of the stairs.

She practically purred, wrapping her arms around his neck and holding on.

He was listing all the things he wanted to do to her in his head when she yawned halfway up the stairs.

"Wow, sorry," she said as she nuzzled her nose into his neck, making his cock stir. "It's definitely not the company, and don't get any ideas about leaving."

No way in hell was he leaving. He'd packed a bag. Just in case.

"I'm not. I've got payback in mind, sweetheart."

"I think I like the sound of that."

"Good, because I have plans." Long-term plans. Possibly lifetime plans.

"I like plans. Plans make everything better."

"True, but sometimes you have to be ready for the unexpected."

He felt her nod. "You were unexpected."

"I hope you mean that in a good way."

She flicked her tongue along his jaw and he shuddered at the light touch. "Absolutely. Sex like this is totally unexpected."

Yeah, this wasn't just sex and she knew it. But he wasn't going to push it. Not now.

A light shone in a room at the end of the hall and he headed for it, nudging open the door with his shoulder and carrying her to the queen bed.

Laying her out, he stripped her naked, slowly and carefully, making sure he stroked each bared inch of skin, until she squirmed. Then he tucked her under the sheets and took a step away.

Her eyes popped open. "I thought you were staying?"

Lips curving, he zipped his jeans though he took off the belt and let it fall to the floor. "Have to get my bag out of the car."

Her eyebrows lifted. "You packed a bag?"

"Didn't I tell you I was a boy scout?"

"You failed to mention that. And I don't believe you for a second."

"Maybe I just like to be prepared for all possibilities."

Her head cocked to the side before she nodded slowly. "Hurry back. Or I might start without you."

He bit back the words on the tip of his tongue. If she moved in with him, he wouldn't have to leave her.

Instead, he turned and headed down the stairs.

By the time he got back, she'd fallen into a dead sleep.

Disappointment warred with an overwhelming tenderness. Tossing off his clothes, he crawled into bed beside her, wrapped his body around hers and followed her into sleep.

FIFTEEN

"Talia Driscoll?"

"Yes?"

"I'm calling from Silvanwood Care Facility. You're listed as the contact for Frederick Van Dyke. I'm calling to let you know his health has taken a downward turn and he's not expected to continue more than a few days. Will you be coming to visit or would you like to be kept apprised of his situation as it develops?"

Talia felt like she'd been kicked in the chest.

Sucking in a short breath to combat the pain, she held the phone away from her mouth so the woman on the other end of the line didn't hear her.

"Ms. Driscoll? Are you there?"

"Yes." She forced in a breath through the tightness of her throat. "Yes, I'm here. I'm sorry, I'm just... I'm not sure... Can I call you back in a little while and let you know my plans?"

"Absolutely. Let us know if you plan to visit. If not, I'll be sure to call you as soon as he's passed. At this stage, it won't be long. Please call at any time."

Won't be long.

Talia set the phone on the bedside table and swung her legs over the side.

"Tally, you okay?"

Dane.

"Yes, I'm fine. Sorry to wake you. It's early. Go back to sleep."

"Hey." He put his hand on her arm. "You don't sound fine."

She froze, too many emotions battering at her. The strongest was the urge to spill her guts to Dane, let him hold her in his arms and comfort her. Which she couldn't do because she'd have to lie to him.

Now wasn't the time to spill her guts. She needed to get control first.

"Tally."

She moved off the bed and toward the bathroom. "I'll be right back." She tried a smile but knew it looked awful. "I just need..."

Hell, what did she need?

She left without finishing her sentence, barricading herself in the bathroom.

Taking deep breaths, she tried to calm her racing pulse and the urge to throw up. She was hyperventilating and she knew it.

She just couldn't seem to contain it.

She wanted Dane. But she couldn't tell him why.

After all this time, she still couldn't bring herself to come clean.

And it wasn't fair to Dane. She couldn't keep doing this. Couldn't keep letting him get close and then pushing him away.

It wasn't fair.

She'd already done it once.

And look how that'd turned out. He still ended up back in your bed.

Sitting on the toilet, she put her head between her legs and just breathed. Finally, she forced herself to her feet.

By the time she got back to the bedroom, he was dressed and sitting on the edge of the bed, elbows on his knees, hands clasped.

"Are you okay?"

The deep note of concern she heard in his voice nearly made her break down. She couldn't. Not now. She'd simply be prolonging the moment she'd have to let him go.

Because she couldn't keep stringing him along like this.

"I'm fine." She didn't smile or try to sell her lie in any way. "I need to take a trip out of town for a couple of days, but I'll be back in time for the retreat. I've got everything—"

"Tally, what—"

"—set and ready to go. I've already spoken to the catering manager at Haven and the menu and schedule are set, so there's nothing to worry about there."

He stood abruptly, curving his hands over her shoulders and staring down at her. In this position, he towered over her and she wanted nothing more than to wrap her arms around his waist and press her cheek against his chest.

"Talia. What the hell's going on?"

"I told you. I need to go out of town, maybe for a few days."

"Why?"

Because I need to see my father before he dies. "There's something I've got to do."

He stared down at her as if he could read her mind. "You're not going to tell me why, are you?"

She shook her head. "No. I— No."

A muscle in his jaw twitched, as if he had to try so damn hard to hold back his words.

Then his hands dropped. "I thought you'd realized you could tell me anything."

He took her breath away with those few words, and she was still trying to catch it when he turned to grab his bag off the bed.

"I guess I could say the same."

The words were out before she realized she'd said them. She wanted to take them back the instant his gaze narrowed at her.

"Tal—"

"I really need to leave. I'm sorry, but you have to go."

After a few seconds, he turned and headed for the door but stopped just before he left. "If you need me, you know how to find me."

"MOM, I need to make a short trip out of town. I just didn't want you to worry."

"Okay, sweetheart. Where are you off to?"

"Dad's dying."

The silence from the other end of the line made Talia question the reason for calling her mom. Amelia had moved on years ago. Talia realized she never had. She'd just shoved it into a deep hole where it'd festered all these years.

"I'm sorry, Mom, I didn't mean to—"

"Oh, sweetheart, I'm so sorry."

Her mother sounded sincere, and Talia felt tears well. She'd managed to hold them off since the phone call this morning.

"I've been expecting this for years. It's no surprise."

"But he's still your father. Have you told your brother?"

"Yeah. He's going to meet me at the hospital."

"Do you want me to go with you? I have to be honest and tell you I'd prefer not to see him again, but I'll go if you need me."

"No. Sammy and I will be fine. But thanks."

"I wish you didn't have to go through this."

"Me too."

"Did you tell your guy? Do you want him to go with you?"

Yes, she did. "No, I didn't. I don't... I'm not sure I'll be seeing him again."

Her mom sighed. "That's not really what you want, is it?"

She had no idea what she wanted. Only that she needed to get through this day without ending up a weeping mess in a corner somewhere.

"I'm not sure what I want. And it's not fair to him to lead him on."

"But if you told him..." Amelia sighed. "Honey, if you really like the guy, don't you think it's worth the risk?"

She wanted to say yes so badly. Instead, she said, "I'll call you when I get back. Love you."

"Love you, too, sweetheart. Safe trip. Call me if you need anything. For that matter, call me even if you don't."

DANE STOOD in his office in front of the window, one hand on the cold glass.

The burning sensation in his palm helped to ground him.

"Dane, just charter a damn plane and meet her there. This is a no-brainer."

"That's *so* not the way to handle this, Will. He does that and he can throw any trust she has in him out the window. No, he needs to let her handle this on her own..."

Listening with one ear to his brother and sister argue behind him, Dane only heard one thing... the absolute absence of emotion in Talia's voice when she'd told him she was leaving.

If she could so easily shut down her emotions when it came to him, maybe he was fooling himself. Maybe he'd fallen hard and fast. And maybe she hadn't.

Maybe he'd totally misread her.

"Dane."

Will's sharp tone drew him out of his thoughts and he turned with a frown. "What? Did you two finally stop arguing and figure out what I should do?"

Julia waved a hand in front of her, dismissing his bitchy question without a second thought. "Oh, please. The only thing Will and I agree on is that we hate seeing you so miserable. And I can't remember the last time you wanted something so badly that you seemed paralyzed. To me, that shows how much you care about this woman. We only want you to be happy, so if she makes you happy, then go get her. And if she breaks your heart, I will make her life a living hell."

Dane's eyes widened at the absolute sincerity in his sister's voice and in her eyes. "Julia, don't—"

"She's speaking metaphorically." Will shook his head. "She won't do anything stupid or illegal, like ruin the woman's life. We'll just make her pay."

Dane shook his head at his brother. "You're not helping."

"Yes, we are." Julia smiled at him. "You just don't appreciate us now that you're too old for us to order around."

Dane sighed. He loved his brother and sister, but they sometimes forgot he was an adult.

"Oh, I appreciate you. I just don't know what to do with you."

"Yes, you do. You can continue to ignore us like you usually do."

Dane grimaced at Julia. "I don't ignore you. I just don't always follow your every instruction to the letter."

"And there you go." Julia nodded as if that proved her point. "Your magazine wouldn't be half as good as it is if you'd listened to everything we'd said. You've got a good head on your shoulders, Dane. You just have to learn to listen to yourself sometimes."

"Apparently, we don't know everything." Will exchanged a glance with Julia. "She might think she does, but I'm not fooling myself."

Julia rolled her eyes at Will then sat forward in her chair, her expression completely serious now. "How well do you really know this woman, Dane? And think about your answer carefully. What are you willing to do to keep her? Are you willing to risk being wrecked? If you are, then that's the answer to all your questions."

He thought about that for several seconds then looked at Will, who nodded. "What she said."

Sucking in a deep breath, Dane sank into the chair behind his desk. "And if I totally screw this up and she wrecks me, what then?"

"Then," Julia held his gaze, "you have to decide just how far you're willing to go to make her change her mind."

TALIA SLID out of the taxi and stood in front of the hospital in Dallas.

Her feet felt rooted to the ground but her head felt disconnected.

She'd managed to catch a flight out of Philly with a connection in Atlanta. She knew her father was still alive because she'd called the hospital the moment she'd touched down.

Her brother hadn't been able to come at the last minute and, though she understood, she still felt abandoned.

You could've had company. You just didn't take him up on it.

She missed Dane. His absence was a grinding ache in her gut that had gotten worse the closer she'd gotten to the hospital.

And it's your own damn fault.

Tears welled but she blinked them away. She'd told herself she'd cry later.

After her father was gone and she went home to an empty house because she'd pushed Dane away for good.

After the press savaged her father once again when news of his death got out. And it would. She wasn't naïve enough to think it wouldn't.

He'd been hospitalized here under an assumed name since he'd been released from prison almost six years ago.

The stories then had been almost unbearable. So many people still wanted him dead, and even though he essentially was, that wasn't enough. Now, it seemed they'd finally get their wish.

The articles would start again. She wouldn't be able to hide her misery.

You were an idiot not to tell him last night.

Which didn't make a damn bit of difference now.

Shaking her head, she headed for the front door. The brick building didn't look at all like a hospital; the only way to tell it was a care facility was the sign next to the front door. There were no other markers that she'd seen.

You had to know what you were looking for to arrive here. Which was why this facility had been recommended.

At the door, she pressed the button and identified herself to the disembodied voice through the small white speaker on the wall. Above her head, a video camera's solid green light shone.

Once inside, the smell hit her first, antiseptic and cleanser overlaying the deeper scent of decay.

Her stomach rolled and she longed for Dane to be by her side, holding her hand.

I can't do this.

Looking around in a blind panic, she spotted a bench along the wall across from the reception desk.

The receptionist watched as she took a seat, not saying anything but nodding with a smile. As if this happened all the time.

And maybe it did. People died all the time here. Grieving family members probably sat on this bench at all hours of the day.

But it was her first time.

She had no idea how long she sat there, but it was long enough that the sixty-something receptionist with the motherly vibe finally asked her if she needed anything.

Talia forced a smile. "No, thank you. I just need a few more minutes."

"You take all the time you need."

Some time later, she heard a bell ring and the receptionist requested a name and a purpose for the visit.

The voice that came through the intercom brought her to her feet in a rush.

"I'm expecting him," she said to the receptionist. "I'm sorry, I didn't realize he would get here so soon. I should've—"

"That's quite all right." The receptionist reached over and patted her hand, clenched into a fist on the desktop. "Just sign him in with you."

She nodded, not trusting her voice. Oddly enough, she didn't feel like crying. Probably because she couldn't breathe deeply enough to do anything at all.

Another bell rang and she felt a rush of air. Turning toward it, she very nearly dissolved into a puddle of tears as Dane walked through the door.

He spotted her immediately and headed straight for her. She held herself in place as he made his way toward her.

She barely restrained herself from throwing her arms around him and begging him to handle... everything.

She wouldn't ask any questions, especially not how he'd found out where she was. Right now, she didn't want to know. She only wanted him to hold her.

Which he did as soon as he got close enough. Wrapped his arms around her and crushed her against his chest.

"Are you okay?"

She nodded. "Yes."

"Do you want to sit for a few minutes?"

"I've been sitting here for probably half an hour already." Pulling back just far enough to look at him, she didn't bother trying to smile. "I need to finish this now."

"Then let's do this."

He didn't release her hand for the next half hour, except to switch sides when they got to her father's bedside.

The man lying in that hospital bed wasn't the man she remembered from her childhood. From before he'd gone to prison. Before he'd been beaten and stabbed by another inmate and fallen into a vegetative state.

It'd been a year since she'd visited, and she no longer saw her father. Her dad had been gone for years and it was time get beyond it.

When the doctor arrived several minutes after they did and began to lay out options, Dane asked the questions. She couldn't get past the lump in her throat.

At the end, there was nothing more than silence. No more beeping machines, no more ventilator. Just quiet.

Dane stood by her side, she didn't know for how long. And when she finally took a deep breath and stood, he wrapped his arm around her shoulders and walked her to a small office down the hall, where a woman in a black dress had her sign several papers.

She understood why she needed to sign them, she just forgot what they were when the woman placed them back in the manila folder on her desk.

Later, in a taxi headed back to the airport, she turned to find Dane watching her.

And she got her brain to stop running in circles long enough to form a coherent question.

"How did you know?"

He didn't try to dodge the questions at all. "I've known for about a week. I was..." He paused. "The night after the wedding. I was hoping, if I knew a little more about you..."

"That you could figure me out?"

"That I'd understand why you were so determined to walk away from a good thing. And what we have is good, Tally. Don't doubt that."

She had no response for him. Probably because she didn't completely understand herself.

They spent the rest of the car ride back to the airport in silence, his arm tight around her shoulders. She had no idea how they were getting back to Philadelphia. She'd bought a one-way ticket because she hadn't been sure when she'd be leaving. She hadn't asked how he'd gotten here, but she wasn't surprised when he had the driver drop them off at the gate for private departures.

"I chartered a flight." He helped her out of the car. "I hope you don't have anything against small jets."

She shook her head. "I've been on a few, just not anytime recently."

When she'd been a kid, her father had never thought twice about chartering a plane to fly them to the Caribbean for a long weekend. Or to take them to Europe or Hawaii over school vacations.

Her father had done awful things, but he'd still been her

dad. He'd doted on her and her brother up until the moment he'd been indicted and he'd cut all ties with them.

Her brain wouldn't shut off now, pulling out sweet childhood memories she'd suppressed for so long and interspersing them with every horrible incident from those months between the first allegations of her father's guilt through the end of his trial.

While Dane made the arrangements to get them back to Philadelphia, he kept her by his side, either holding her hand or keeping her close with an arm around her shoulders.

They left an hour later and the second her head hit the backrest, she closed her eyes and darkness descended.

BY THE TIME they landed three and a half hours later, Dane had texted his sister, brother, and mom with updates and called Kate, who'd been trying to reach Talia all day and was about to call in search and rescue squads. He gave her the bare bones and, when it became clear she knew as much as he did about Talia's past, Dane promised to keep her up to date and to have Talia call her later.

By the time the plane landed, he'd had a car sent to pick them up and had attended his magazine's weekly editorial meeting by videoconference.

Talia woke as the plane landed, shaking her head as if trying to clear it.

Her eyes were bleary with exhaustion and Dane steered her toward the parking garage and her car. She didn't protest when he asked for the keys then drove them to his condo, barely saying a word as he ushered her in and steered her straight into his bedroom.

Handing her the overnight bag she'd taken with her to

Dallas, he pointed her toward the bathroom. He sat on the edge of the bed while he waited for her to come back out then watched as she climbed into bed and pulled the covers over her.

When he returned from the bathroom, he expected her to be asleep. Instead, she was waiting for him, watching him as he stripped, leaving only his underwear, and slipped into bed beside her. She immediately closed the gap between them and he rearranged her so they were both on their sides, her back to his front.

He wanted to completely surround her, let her know he wasn't going anywhere.

"Thank you."

Her voice sounded tired but steady.

"Of course." He pressed a kiss to the top of her head. "Get some sleep."

When he woke the next morning, she was still curled on her side in the curve of his body. And his phone was ringing quietly on the bedside table.

"What's up, Will?"

"The news on Talia's dad is breaking. Figured you'd want to warn her. How is she?"

"Sleeping. Seemed okay last night but I probably won't be in today."

"I guess we can do without you." Will paused. "And, Dane?"

"Yeah?"

"Try not to steamroll her."

After hanging up, he pulled on sweatpants and headed for the kitchen to make coffee.

All the major news stations had a piece on Talia's father. Some devoted more time than others. It was a slow day so some led with it, dredging up the entire scandal. Others skimmed it. A few mentioned it only in the crawl.

"He'll be forgotten in a few years, won't he?"

Dane turned to see Talia standing at the foot of the stairs. He couldn't believe he hadn't heard her come down. Her blue eyes dull with unshed tears, she looked lost and a little unsure. But she was dressed and had her bag in her hand.

Swallowing his immediate urge to order her back upstairs and into bed, he rose and walked over to her.

Instead of speaking, he cupped her face in his hands and kissed her. Hard, deep, and designed to make her respond. Which she did. She dropped the bag and wound her arms around his waist, tilting her head so he could kiss her even deeper.

When he finally released her, they were both breathing harder than they had been a few seconds ago.

But remembering his brother's warning, he forced himself to take a step away.

"How are you feeling?"

Her lips curved for a second. "Like I got hit by a truck." Then she shrugged. "I'm fine, just tired. And I do have a lot of work to do."

He wanted to insist she stay here and do her work, wanted to throw her back on his bed, strip her naked and make love to her until she fell back to sleep.

"Do you want me to drive you?"

"No, I'll be fine. But thank you. For everything."

"Would you please let me know when you get back to your place?"

"Of course."

He nodded, biting his tongue against everything else he wanted to say.

Staring up at him, she looked somewhat surprised that he didn't have anything else to say. Retrieving her keys from the breakfast bar, where he'd thrown them last night, he put them in her palm.

"If you need anything, call me."

She quickly masked the surprise that flitted through her expression with another smile as she nodded and headed for the door.

While he forced his hands to stay at his sides instead of grabbing her and pinning her to the sofa with his body.

By the time she finally walked out the door, his jaw hurt from gritting his teeth and he wanted to punch the wall.

If Jed had been home, he'd have thrown himself on his couch and talked this through with him. Will had already told him what he'd needed to hear.

Now, the only thing he could do was wait for her to come back. And make sure she had the support she needed.

———

"TAL, I just saw the news. Are you okay?"

"Kate, yeah, I'm fine. Thanks for calling."

Talia swore she could hear Kate frown over the phone. "You don't sound fine. What's wrong?"

"Other than the fact that my dad just died…"

"Oh, hon, I'm really sorry about your dad. I am. But from everything you told me, he's been gone from your life for the past six years. And as much as that sucks, and it does, it's time for you to let that part of your life go and move on to the next."

"I have."

"And does that next part include Dane?"

Did it? "I'm not sure I know what you mean."

"He called this morning. He's worried about you, wanted me to check in."

"Why didn't he call himself?"

But she knew the answer to that. Because he didn't want to push her.

"Hey, Kate, can I talk to Tyler a second?"

TY HAD LEFT Dane a message to meet him at the Salon Thursday night.

And because he had nothing else to do and he was climbing the walls of his condo waiting for Talia to call him, he figured what the hell.

He had no idea what Ty wanted but, whatever it was, Dane could use the distraction.

He didn't stop at the Haven reception desk to say hi to Sabrina, who gave him a bright smile and a wave. She reminded him too much of Talia.

Hell, right now, everything about Haven reminded Dane of Talia.

And it sucked, because he couldn't have her.

He didn't know what he was going to do tomorrow if she still hadn't called. A caveman routine wasn't in the cards. No, if he wanted to win her back into his bed, he had to be smarter.

By the time he got to the Salon, he wanted to have a few drinks to knock him out so he could wake up and it'd be tomorrow already.

Christ, now he sounded like a kid at Christmas.

And the only gift he wanted under his tree was Talia.

Opening the door, the first thing he noticed were the lights. They weren't on. And the fireplace was lit.

"Ty? Hey, did I get the wrong time? I don't want to see your naked ass right now."

"Whose would you like to see?"

The voice came out of the shadows of the corner where the bondage chairs sat.

He'd been hearing that voice in his sleep and he always woke up with a hard-on.

Now, his heart began to race and his damn palms actually got sweaty.

"Talia?"

He stalked toward the corner, narrowly avoiding a collision with the game table even though he knew the layout of the room like the back of his hand.

"I certainly hope that wasn't a question. I think I might have to be offended."

She sat on one of the chairs, legs crossed, hands on her knees. She looked prim and proper, in a belted purple dress that buttoned down the front. He wanted to rip every single button off with his teeth.

"It's not a question. It's relief."

Stopping in front of her, a couple of feet still separating them, he studied everything about her. She no longer looked exhausted. In fact, she looked... calm.

"How are you?"

Her lips curved. "I'm feeling much better. Now."

He didn't want to jump to any wrong conclusions, so he reined himself in. "I'm glad to hear it."

Nodding, she played with her skirt. "It's been a rough couple of days."

"I know. Tal—"

She held up one hand and he closed his mouth. "Just hear me out. Okay?"

He bit his tongue and nodded.

"I wasn't prepared for the feelings I have for you. They took me by surprise, and I've had enough surprises in my life. Most of them haven't been good ones. But you..."

His gaze narrowed as she paused.

"You've been one of the best surprises of my life. And I want to give us a chance."

Yes. He took a tiny step closer. "And you're the only woman I've ever wanted to get on my knees and beg for another chance."

She shook her head. "I don't want you on your knees."

He took another step closer, still not touching. "Then what do you want? Name it. Don't you know by now that I'll give it to you?"

Talia sighed. "I've never wanted anything from any other man. And here I am, willing to give you anything."

Dane crossed his arms over his chest, trying not to smile outright because he worried she still might bolt. "I don't want just anything, Tal. I want you. All of you."

"I'm not sure I can let myself give away that much."

He took another step and finally he was close enough to touch her. He cupped her face in his hands, letting his thumbs brush against her delicate jaw.

"Give me the chance to show you can."

He settled his mouth over hers and kissed, pouring every ounce of emotion he had into it. With a moan, she lifted her hands to his shoulders and pulled him even closer.

The feel of her lips against his was enough to make him groan but he resisted the urge to unwrap her like a present. Even when she slipped her tongue into his mouth to tangle with his, coaxing him back into her mouth and letting him control it.

The problem was, he wasn't in control.

He wanted her too much, and there was still so much left unsaid.

But he could fix part of that right now.

Pulling back, he waited until her eyelids fluttered and she stared up at him.

"What's wrong?" she asked.

"Nothing's wrong." He raked his finger through her hair and cupped the back of her head. "I love you, Tal. I just needed to say it."

Her bright smile lit an answering grin on his lips. "We've only known each other a couple of weeks."

"Time's not the issue here. I've never felt this way about anyone. I know I love you."

Shaking her head, her smile softened. "How do you always know the exact right thing to say?"

"I don't. Trust me, there are going to be days you're going to wish I hadn't opened my mouth. I'm demanding and, according to my brother and sister, I'm spoiled. But as long as I get what I want, I'm a pussycat. And I want you."

She reached for him, grabbing his forearms and pulling him toward the chair. When he was close enough, she reached for his pants.

"Then I guess you won't be upset that I want to tie you to this chair and stroke you. All over."

"Honey, you can do whatever you want to me. I'm not going to run."

Her smile made his heart pound harder, his blood boil a little hotter. For her.

"Then take a seat, and let me show you how much I love you back."

"Anything you want, Tal. Anything at all."

ABOUT THE AUTHOR

Stephanie Julian has been a daily news reporter, a freelance feature writer and a movie, theater and music critic but what she loves most is writing heat with heart. She's happily married to a Springsteen fanatic and is the mother of two sons.

Connect online through these sites:
www.stephaniejulian.com
Facebook
Twitter
Pinterest
Keep up with Stephanie's new releases and events
Newsletter
Contact her at
stephaniejulian@msn.com

THANK YOU FOR READING!
If you enjoyed this book, please consider leaving a review. It will help others find this story.

ALSO BY STEPHANIE JULIAN

REDTAILS HOCKEY
The Brick Wall

The Grinder

The Enforcer

The Instigator

The Playboy

The D-Man

The Machine

INDECENT
An Indecent Proposition

An Indecent Affair

An Indecent Arrangement

An Indecent Longing

An Indecent Desire

SALON GAMES
Invite Me In

Reserve My Nights

Expose My Desire

Keep My Secrets

Rock My Heart

LOVERS UNDERCOVER

Copyright © 2015, 2017 by Stephanie Julian

All rights reserved. No part of this publication may be reproduced, distributed, or transmitted in any form or by any means, including photocopying, recording, or other electronic or mechanical methods, without the prior written permission of the publisher, except in the case of brief quotations embodied in critical reviews and certain other noncommercial uses permitted by copyright law. For permission requests, write to the publisher at stephaniejulian@msn.com.

All characters in this book are fiction and figments of the author's imagination.

Made in the USA
Monee, IL
16 August 2020

38597423R00174